Smitten Image

Pam B. Morris

CRIMSON
ROMANCE
Avon, Massachusetts

This edition published by
Crimson Romance
an imprint of F+W Media, Inc.
10151 Carver Road, Suite 200
Blue Ash, Ohio 45242

www.crimsonromance.com

Dedication

TO BRETT, KATE, AND JACKSON FOR KEEPING THE GROUND SOLID
UNDER ME, AND RACHEL FOR HER UNSHAKABLE BELIEF.

Acknowledgments

A heartfelt thank you to my acquisitions editor, Jennifer Lawler, and everyone at Crimson Romance and F&W Media for making my lifelong dream come true. An extraordinary thank you to my editor, Jessica Verdi, for her patience, professionalism, and gifting *f* me with the realization that I needed an editor as much as I longed for a publisher.

Loving thanks to The Midnight Writers: Laura, Lolly, Robin, Martina, and Rachel. Special appreciation and love to Mary, Jackie, Wendy, Linda, Beverly, Pattee, Walker, Star, Jean, Nancy, Barbara, Cherry, my sister Holly, and my daughter Kate for the many years of reading my stuff and still saying "don't give up."

Thank you to the Montana Romance Writers Chapter of RWA. Finally and most especially, love and thanks to Rionna Morgan, Angela Briedenbach, Clare Wood, Danica Winters, and Casey Dawes, my writing sisters and the backbone in my spaghetti spine.

Chapter One

"Lily, you are pathologically incapable of getting a man." Ellen Reid took a long, appreciative sip of the double shot cappuccino.

Slouched in a chair in front of her boss's giant teak desk, Lily Barnett rolled her eyes.

Ellen glanced at her wall calendar with a digi-pic of New Chicago's techno glitz high-rises taken at night. It read: Thursday, October 14th, 2039. An appointment for Lily was penciled in.

"Don't get me wrong, Lil, you're a brilliant artist," Ellen said. "You can paint with the realism of a John Singer Sargent, then like magic switch to the drama of a Caravaggio. But face it, you'd rather watch leaves fall than ogle a gorgeous man."

"Whatever spin works for ya, boss." Lily slouched deeper. She'd heard her employer's affectionate litany so many times, the praise as well as the critique slid off her like hot wax from a candle. Not that she didn't appreciate Ellen's professional faith. Or accept the pathetic truth of her shortcomings.

Lily could get a date, sure. She'd agree to meet an interesting guy for drinks, even recall the time and place. But on her way to the meeting she'd get distracted by the light tickling a corner street musician's saxophone or the expressions of eager children playing ha'penny on the sidewalk. Out came her sketchbook, dragged from the ragged satchel she carried everywhere, and she would start drawing. And the guy waiting for drinks with her? He'd be forgotten before she even put pencil to paper.

Ellen eyed Lily over the top of her cup and seemed to come to a decision. Reaching into a drawer she pulled out a message slip and passed it across the desk.

"What is this?" Lily leaned forward to look but refused to take the paper.

"I made you an appointment at a service. Here are directions and the time."

She sent Ellen a withering glance and stood to gather her portfolio and satchel.

"Come on, Lil, what have you got to lose?" Ellen pleaded. "Carter and Bell's Dating Service is a fun, people-person place designed for non-people persons like yourself. And who knows, they may match you up with a guy who'd rather rake leaves than ogle a gorgeous girl!"

To avoid further argument, Lily snatched the note and started out the door.

"And, Lily, you have a sitting with Pete Bleeker in," Ellen checked her watch, "twenty-three minutes."

"You think I could forget my worst nightmare?" Lily tossed over her shoulder as she headed down the hall to her studio. Pete Bleeker, portly and arrogant, an unbearable bore. Or boar, she snickered, with his definite porcine features. Oops, she must act professional, she reminded herself, and slammed her portfolio down on a work table.

Not that she didn't love working at Ellen Reid's renowned portrait studio, Faces In Time. She'd never had a boss so caring or a job in such a creative environment where people actually enjoyed coming to work.

Faces In Time employed artists and photographers who offered all manner of portraits from typical to avant-garde, in any setting, with individuals, couples, families, and groups, fully clothed . . . or otherwise. Lily specialized in classic studio oils, often with clients dressed in period costumes or posing in dramatic stage settings of their choosing. Large "period portraits" done in the nineteenth-century style of Sargent and Mancini were the current rage with New Chicago's wealthy upper set. Lily was delighted with the steady work and as a bonus she got Ellen's sisterly advice on all matters of life, love, and general practicality.

*

Lily survived the two hours of sketching Pete Bleeker's sour face, his screaming anger, her fear that she would lose her temper and tell the bastard how big his ass really was and how well his fat head would fit up it. Somehow she held her tongue. When pudgy Pete finally stormed away, Lily tried to refocus and paint. But the portrait wouldn't mesh, and in the end she raced out of work, unwilling to face her boss.

Because she adored Ellen and tried to please her when possible, Lily walked to Carter and Bell's Dating Service that afternoon. The sidewalks swarmed with people pushy to get home, jostling crowds catching electric trolleys or the underground. Traffic sounds surged and eased like cresting waves on Lake Michigan. Lily looked up at the New Chicago skyline, so different now with every skyscraper and rooftop sprouting a forest of benevolent wind generators.

After the riots in 2032, the rebuilding of the city meant hundreds of new high-rise condos, corporate centers, and mega-malls sprawling like a jungle gym up into the sky instead of out across the land. The suburbs of the twentieth century were gone now, housing developments replaced by thousand-acre farms raising food and bio-fuel crops.

Lily's stomach fluttered with nerves as she tried to think positively about her upcoming "date" with destiny. Arriving at the address of Carter and Bell's, she stumbled to a stop. A heavy dread settled at the base of her spine. The service was housed in a very modern, very beautiful three-story stone building with a stunning rock archway. Elegant lettering etched into the window promised a clientele made of New Chicago's sophisticated and Nuevo wealthy. Lily could imagine Ellen breezing into this place, confident, swinging the world by the tail. But not herself, not in a million years . . .

Through the passing crowd she could see her reflection in the window, a short, attractive enough girl with thick hair impossibly tangled by the wind. A defeated sigh slumped her shoulders. Lily had no illusions about her looks; she was a portrait painter, for pity's sake. Her physical points of interest were few but striking: lovely blue eyes too large for her face and a full mouth. But unmanageable curls the color of straw, a pixie chin, and a height just topping five feet gave people the impression she was childlike and therefore negligible.

Her life did lack certain adult essentials. Hot, groping sex with beautiful men for one. And love . . . deep, satisfying, all-absorbing love. But could a woman like her-stockings saggy at the knees, cuffs smeared with paint, and carrying a stained canvas bag-waltz into this den of opulence and create a competent, compelling digi-interview of herself for prospective lovers to pick over? The very idea brought on the gag reflex.

Lily turned away from Carter and Bell's, closed her eyes, and thought back over the long day, hearing the raging voice of Pete Bleeker screaming inside her head that she couldn't paint a portrait by number! Heard, too, the woman in Spencer's Gallery who'd returned one of Lily's paintings. The woman's rant had gone on and on about Lily's insane color choices, how the painting was "highly agitating" and "would never fit a typical person's décor."

She felt the airy whoosh of e-cars passing by inches from where she teetered on the curb. Just breathe, she told herself. She'd survived worse days growing up a misfit on the Ohio farm. She'd heard worse criticisms, and in stronger language, from college professors. Just breathe! But standing solitary on the busy sidewalk, Lily knew she hadn't the chutzpah to stroll into a posh partnering palace looking for true love, and suddenly wished not for an attractive, exciting man, but a crack in the sidewalk to crawl into.

When she turned around and opened her eyes, she saw

a sign swinging in the breeze above her that read, "Madame Bagasha's Magicke Shoppe." The voices of Pete Bleeker and Mrs. Wind-Up-Her-Ass roaring inside her head began to warp into the sound of voices singing with symphonic rapture. The tightness in her throat eased. She took a hesitant step closer and realized the chimes hanging above the door to the nondescript shop were calling to her.

The window display refracted rainbows across the sidewalk from the dozens of crystals scattered amongst the candles, figurines, and spread of tarot cards. Lily pressed a hand to the glass, felt heat beneath her palm, and a halo of light shot out around her fingers. A burst of laughter broke loose in her chest.

Of course she knew who Madame Bagasha was. Who hadn't seen the psychic on late night digi-tube, dressed in a lush Romany costume with her head swathed in scarves, her wrists aglitter with gypsy spangles while she barked out a nine hundred phone number?

"Lost a loved one you wish to communicate with? Need stock tips? Want to know who thinks you're scorching hot at the office? Just call this number . . . "

*

That charlatan image vanished the moment Lily stepped inside the shop. Discreet and unobtrusive from the outside, Madame Bagasha's Magicke Shoppe seemed three times larger inside. Bright prisms floated above her head, warm light fell like rain through pyramid skylights. Luminous motes of dust hung expectant in the air . . . and sang to her! Lily didn't question how this was possible as they clustered in her hair, on her face and clothes until she glittered with their exuberant welcome. She felt a giddy warmth rush her limbs, her heart swelled to settle more firmly in her chest. In that moment Lily knew she was exactly where she belonged at precisely the right time.

All around her, rocks on shelves pulsed, orbs glowed, and a stuffed peacock's marble eyes seemed to follow her every move. Exotic scents drifted through the air; lavender, cloves, a tangy ginger soap bubbling somewhere vaguely reminded her of Daniel, the guy who lived next door to her. The room, organic and numinous, filled her head with strange images while shivery sensations played across her skin.

The shop was a place out of time where Mystical Vintage met New Age Wave. Every cabinet was crammed full with stone goblets, amulets, jars of powders, gemstones glinting in all sizes and colors. As she wandered the room, Lily fought a compulsive desire to touch everything. An ancient jukebox played haunting Celtic music in the background, and Lily began to feel the entire ugly day bleed away.

She jumped at the sound of a voice coming from behind a glass-fronted counter filled with jewelry and . . . wands, Lily decided, for the carved pieces of wood could be nothing else in a shop of magic. A young woman stood up.

"You must be Lily." The girl's eyes were a smiling, honey gold. She wore a peasant blouse and short skirt. Nut brown hair hung to her waist in a thick braid laced with ribbons. "I've been waiting for you."

At Lily's astonished look, the girl laughed. "My cousin Sarah works at Carter and Bell's. She called asking if I'd seen anyone wandering around. But you don't look lost to me. My name is Nila. And welcome to Madame Bagasha's Magicke Shoppe."

"Magic as in pulling a rabbit out a hat?" Lily's voice sounded her skepticism.

"No." Nila grinned. "Magic as in turning the hat into a rabbit!"

The girl plucked a pair of hexagonal dice marked with hieroglyphs out of a glass bowl and casually tossed them across the counter top. "They had to cancel your appointment next door, but not to worry. The dice tell me you won't find what you're looking for at Carter and Bell's Dating Service."

Lily looked askance at her and Nila said, "I worked a spell."

"A spell? How?"

"Using numerology and a few conjuring words."

"So you can do magic?"

"Yes. As can most people, including you. Your magic is in your art."

Lily's mouth dropped open. "Don't tell me you've seen my paintings . . . ?"

"No, but I've seen you, here in the prisms over the last few days. Ephemeral projections. I truly have been expecting you. It shocks people to know that the universe is teeming with mystical forces. More accessible now since the magnetic pole switched, of course. Everything and everyone possesses magic of one sort or another; a particular attribute, a special skill, an extra sensitivity. Like an intuitive extension of who and what you are."

"I think I know what you mean." Excitement edged Lily's voice. "When I'm painting I feel this kind of unconditional giving of core energy to my work."

"Exactly." Nila reached out her hand and without hesitation, Lily took it. A spark of magenta flared when they touched.

"See?" The girl said. "The magic in your hand just greeted the magic in mine. Most people don't believe in mystic power so they never recognize or acknowledge it. Those people don't find Madame's shop." She dropped the hexagonal dice in Lily's hand. "Your turn. All you have to do is unzip your heart, focus your energy, and throw."

Lily closed her eyes, felt the room's effervescent light stir like fingers in her hair, saw in her mind's eye every object emitting a color uniquely its own . . . and tossed the dice. The overhead lights flickered.

"Wow." Nila stepped back. "You have some power, girl! I felt it coalesce and then shoot into the dice." She bent to read the symbols. "They say you're on the rise professionally. That you're lonely, afraid you'll never know real love. And you want the perfect mate. Well," the girl winked, "here at Madame's all you have to do is ask."

"I thought all I had to do was try a few dozen men on like sweaters and hope one fits," Lily said.

Nila laughed again and Lily heard the voices in the air giggle along with her. "The dice indicate you are surrounded by love, Lily. Every day. From friends who are more family than your own flesh. And yes, you do deserve the very best of love from a wonderful guy. So if you can spare thirteen dollars, I'll get to work."

"Thirteen?" Lily's face fell but she found herself digging in the satchel for her purse.

"Thirteen gets a bad rap but it's actually a very auspicious number. Signifies resurrection and rebirth. Are you ready to be reborn?" Nila thrust her hands into the air, flinging her fingers wide. Lily felt, more than saw, an orangeish light spring from the girl's fingertips and watched, awe-struck, as jars lifted off shelves around the shop to drift through the air towards where the two women stood. Nila pulled a mid-sized, fat-bellied pot from a shelf behind her and placed it on the counter.

She flashed a sheepish grin at Lily. "Cliché, I know, but potions must be mixed in a cast-iron cauldron. And I'm showing off, of course."

From the jars Nila measured out bits of one preserved something after another, bending to sniff each before dribbling it into the cauldron. Adding a fair amount of what looked to Lily like red wine, the girl murmured a chant as the concoction began swirling as if stirred by an invisible wind.

"One alone, heart is young, spirit sprung, soul unstrung.
Two conjoined, blessed in kind, souls entwined, knot and bind."

At Lily's dubious look, Nila smiled. "Don't worry, I am a trained witch. A bona-fide, certified, card-carrying member of the New Chicago Cohort."

"New Chicago Cohort?" Lily was beyond amazed. She felt a

combination of bewilderment, disbelief, hope, and more than a little fear. "And are you making what I think you're making?"

Sudden laughter bubbled up at the absurd miracle of this place, at how comfortable she felt standing here watching a seemingly regular girl stir a love potion without lifting a finger!

Nila poured the mixture from the cauldron into a crystal goblet and hesitated before handing it over. "This isn't your run-of the mill, 'vanilla' Love Potion Number Nine, Lily. Best be careful what you wish for."

The potion was a lovely plum color and Lily guzzled it without hesitation, felt it settle, cool and pleasant, in her stomach. And then she felt . . . nothing. No change. No metamorphosis into a shiny new woman ready to take on the maddening world of men. With an enigmatic little smile, Nila ushered Lily out of the shop. And that was that. Except as Lily plopped her tired body into an e-bus seat for the ride home, she found herself wishing she'd spent the thirteen dollars on a couple of lovely, limb-loosening margaritas at O'Connor's Pub instead of a silly love potion.

Chapter Two

Lily waited to feel different, waited for the love potion to fill her with ecstasy or giddy happiness or to feel as glamorous as a vid star. But as she climbed the stairs to her third floor apartment, she felt only exhaustion. Tripping on the last step, she fell flat on her face. The clasp in her hair popped free to skid across the carpet. At the same time, the three pencils lodged in her curls flipped down the stairs.

Too weary to move, she lay sprawled in the middle of the hallway looking up at the light fracturing through the chandelier high above her head. She wished she could just stay here, unmoving, until this endless, horrid day passed into tomorrow . . . except someone was sure to step out of the ancient elevator, trip over her, and sue. Probably poor Eleanor McCready in number 312 down the hall, half-blind behind her Coke bottle lenses.

Lily pushed to her feet and, ignoring her scattered sketchbooks, satchel, and portfolio, moved to open the door of her corner apartment. And then she discovered she'd forgotten her keys. Again. Cursing a stream of creative gutter language, she went to the apartment next door.

"Daniel?" She knocked on the door. "Please be home . . . I'm locked out. Again."

A long moment passed before Daniel Harris swept open his door, a grin wide on his face. The grin died when he saw Lily's strained eyes and tangled hair.

"Doesn't it get old, laughing every time I forget my key?" she snapped.

"I don't laugh every time," Daniel ducked inside to grab a clipboard hanging on the wall and consulted it. "Just the fourth time this week." He showed her the tally sheet for the month of October.

"Nine times already?" Her voice broke over this tiny but final straw.

"And, Lil, it's only the fourteenth."

"Don't lecture me, Daniel. Not today."

"A day of days, was it?"

"Without mercy, fortune, or kindness," Lily sighed.

*

The fatigue in Lily's voice cut Daniel to the quick. "Want to talk?" he asked. "I've got a box of cheap wine with our names on it."

"All I want is bed and sweet dreams."

I could give you that in a heartbeat, Daniel thought, then chided himself and grabbed her spare key off the hook hanging just inside his door. Draping an arm across her shoulders, he turned her towards her apartment and saw the mess at the top of the stairs. His arm tightened.

"I tripped." She leaned into his ribs.

"No mercy at all . . . " Daniel murmured against her hair smelling of apple blossoms and autumn mist. He knew he should step away now, before his emotions fully engaged and tore through the mental shield he kept rigid between them. Already he felt the irresistible pull of her distress and fought against a need to sweep her up and carry her off to bed. His bed.

He let his arm fall away and bent to help her stuff pencils, brushes, charcoal sticks, crumpled sketches, and a scruffy coin purse back inside the canvas satchel.

"Thanks for always being there, Daniel. I appreciate you going beyond the call of duty for me. Do I tell you that enough?"

"Yes, you tell me everyday." Arms full of books, he followed the girl inside her apartment and paused as he always did to breathe in her living scent: a hint of summer, tangy linseed oil, and the pungent odor of oil paint drying on canvas. Of all the apartments in the building Daniel managed for his aging aunt, Lily's was his favorite. He found it energizing. Every molecule in the air vibrated to her pulsating, restless spirit. Light poured in through a row of tall, wide windows.

Half the floor was covered by a paint-spattered ground cloth and held a hodge-podge of work tables cluttered with the tools of her trade: paint, brushes, rags, cans of thinners, and cleaning solutions. An old sideboard stood against the back wall, filled with more paint supplies tucked among books on anatomy, art history, and famous artists. A large easel, collapsed flat, leaned in one corner. Another easel stood front and center hidden under a draping sheet. Canvases of all sizes stood propped against the wall.

An overstuffed couch and matching chair divided the room from the small kitchen along the opposite wall. Mismatched dishes filled a dry rack and two fat goldfish swam around a castle in a fishbowl beside the refrigerator. An antique cabinet housed her computer deck and VPEG player, the satellite transceiver, and a mid-sized digi-console. Strings of pink flamingo lights hid among sprawling houseplants large enough to eat someone. Lily's home, like her heart, radiated a wild energy. Most days.

But not today. Her distress dragged at Daniel as he set her books on the overcrowded kitchen table and briefly touched the forgotten key ring lying there. He found himself wishing, not for the first time, that her absent-mindedness betrayed a subconscious need for him. He tortured himself with the wanting of her, the wretched, fierce need for her . . . even though he knew better.

Lily needed nothing this turbulent corporate world of 2039 offered except its kaleidoscope of colors and textures. As for himself, a clairvoyant Reader, he needed to maintain the strictest of mental and emotional shielding. Otherwise every thought, every feeling that humans projected would overwhelm his senses and drive him insane. Literally.

At the sharp squeal of springs, he glanced up to see Lily flopped, arms and legs askew, on the couch.

"I'm not going to cry," she promised the ceiling.

"Of course you aren't," Daniel said. "You never cry."

He watched a single tear track the side of her face and gritted his teeth. Gods afire, how he wished she'd let him love her. But he was just the guy next door, her best friend, there to help her navigate the everyday life she found so befuddling. Even as he watched, her beautiful eyes, large and blue as his Gran's Wedgwood china, misted over and she was gone, disappearing into yet another idea zinging around inside her imaginative brain. Lily had so much vision . . . she just didn't have eyes for him. He turned away to fill the tea kettle, setting it at low to give her time before the whistle raged and pulled her reluctantly back to earth. Then he slipped unnoticed out the door.

Chapter Three

For a long moment, Lily lay dissolved in the idea of golden light shining through a cadmium red glaze. The long, trying day faded away as she worked out in her mind how she'd layer the paint, which colors she'd brush on first, and how thick. Then she bounced up from the couch, peeling off her coat.

Restless now and weariness forgotten, she stripped out of her dress and stockings, tossing them in a careless pile on her bed as she pulled on a faded shirt and ragged jeans before donning her paint-crusted smock.

Her blood sang with the jazzy impatience she always experienced near the end of a project, this one a painting of a male nude she'd begun the day before. She wanted him in shadow and light, and had chosen a palette of warm yellows and soft reds to highlight his outstretched hand, his upturned face, and surging chest. As she whipped the cover sheet off the easel, she could see her naked man reaching out of a dark, broiling background.

The whistling tea kettle made her jump. At the same time, a knock sounded on the door. She tried to ignore both and then, resigned, tossed the sheet back over the painting and went to answer the door.

Ellen Reid stood in the hallway, tall, sleek, confident. Lily should have known, after ditching work earlier, that there'd be no escape from her boss.

Ellen breezed into Lily's apartment, tossing her leather coat over the back of the couch. The tea kettle still screamed. Lily swept it off the burner as her boss kicked her pricey, spike-heeled boots across the floor before flopping down into the easy chair.

"Heard you had a day." Ellen leaned back and closed her eyes.

"I'm getting over it." Lily shrugged. "Tea?"

"Please. I'm going nowhere until I've heard every gruesome detail." Ellen eased out a long sigh and, stretching her legs across the top of the coffee table, wriggled her manicured toes. She looked as out of place in Lily's untidy, eclectic apartment as the Charlie Russell of two cowboys hanging on the wall above the computer console. Ellen's hair, expensively streaked, fell in perfect waves to her shoulders.

The plucked eyebrows accented the beauty of her long eyes, and Lily wondered again why Ellen refused to have her portrait painted. She'd make a kick-ass mythological goddess, maybe a wise Athena or conquering Diana with her strong chin, sculpted cheekbones and long limbs. But no, Ellen hated the thought of herself captured forever in a moment of time. Claimed it would mess with her *chi*.

Lily picked two mugs from the dry rack and dropped a tea ball into each. There was a time when Ellen's sophisticated suits and European hair had made her feel like a bumbling idiot. But no longer. Now Lily took great pleasure in the fact that her home was the only place Ellen Reid ever really relaxed and let her hair down. In reciprocation, Ellen bestowed Lily with all the warmth and humor she rarely showed to anyone.

Over the past two years, the women had developed a deep affection and appreciation for each other. Complete opposites, their personalities jelled as compatibly as berries and honey. Ellen knew the true value of Lily's talent and paid her accordingly. Lily depended on Ellen to help her manage money, her career, and, on occasion, her social life.

"I brought another comic strip, Lil," Ellen said. "This one is so you it's scary."

Lily groaned. "Not another *Lost and Found*! I hate that blasted strip, and you know it. It's not even funny."

"It is to those of us who delight in the absurdities of human nature in a world gone mad."

"I'd like to slap whoever writes it upside the head," Lily said. "G.I.L.! What kind of name is that and why does he pick on artists, squints, and musicians?"

"He picks on all of us, lovingly exposing our soft underbellies. I'll bet G.I.L. is the computer geek character hiding behind those big glasses while life passes him by." Ellen reached for the mug Lily held out and stuck her nose in the rising steam. Lily set a plate of cookies, compliments of the McCready sisters down the hall, on the coffee table and curled herself into a corner of the couch.

"I appreciate humor as much as the next guy but not when it's personal."

Ellen pulled the comic vid-print from her purse and passed it over. "See the girl? She's out on a date, which you never are so you can't take that personally. And she can't decide what to order. At a hot dog stand!"

"What's so funny about that?"

"Lily, a hot dog stand only sells hot dogs! I love this comic because I've watched you do this exact same thing. Believe me, it's hilarious." Ellen nudged Lily's foot. Lily grudgingly admitted it might be a little funny. They sat in companionable silence for a moment before Ellen shifted tone.

"I'm sorry about your troubles with Pete today. I smoothed it over with him, you don't need to sweat it."

Lily sat up with relief. "So no beheading in my future? No crows pecking my carcass? Thank the Powers! Did you know the man dressed himself as Henry the VIII for his portrait? How creepifying is that? I've repainted his face a dozen times and it is, without a doubt, the stuff of nightmares. Nothing I do makes him happy, and then he goes all snarly and mean. I'd rather paint his backside than endure one more sitting with him."

Ellen shuddered at the horror. "Some people just can't live with the way they look. He didn't like Sam's photographs either. Poor pig-headed Pete."

"Look around the room," Lily gestured. "I took down my piglet lights-couldn't stand the sight of them."

Ellen laughed. "Never mind. I refunded the man's down payment and suggested the name of another studio."

"Thank you, and I am sorry I couldn't please him. But now I can start with the two sisters. They're adorable. I can't wait for the first sitting."

"You're the strangest portrait artist I know. No one likes children's sittings."

"I do. I love all that fidgety energy. Children's souls shine like the sun through their skin, have you noticed?"

"Mmm. And I don't know another painter who can capture that as well as you do." At Lily's uncomfortable blush, Ellen laughed. "Just say 'Thank you, Ellen.' You must learn to accept accolades with grace, Lil, especially if your work is carried by Gradyn Spencer."

Lily's face fell as she told Ellen about the woman who'd bought her painting at one of the prestigious Spencer Galleries and then returned it. With plenty to say about why. "Gradyn called to tell me this morning."

"Oh my, you did have a day. But you can't please everyone, Lil. Her opinion isn't shared by others who know your work. And certainly not by the illustrious Mr. Spencer. I hear he's over the moon at signing you. Thinks you're a genius with color."

"Only because he's Daniel's friend."

"Not true. And Gradyn shouldn't have told you what the woman said."

"I asked him for her number so I could call and apologize. This is business and I have to be professional. I have to know what people think."

"Believe me, you don't!" Ellen said. "So, enough dancing around the subject of why I really came by . . . did you or did you not go to Carter and Bell's Dating Service? And did they match you up with someone delicious?"

Lily stood to whisk Ellen's empty mug away and load it in the dishwasher.

"You wimped out!" Ellen accused over her shoulder.

"No, I went," Lily answered. "How could I not when you defied the natural order of the universe by making me an appointment?"

Ellen ignored her. "What did you think of the place? Pretty posh, huh? Like only the beautiful and intelligent would list there."

Lily plopped back on the couch. "Get real, Ellen. I am so *not* their kind of client. But I made myself go. I stood in a cold sweat outside their perfect arch and tried to force myself to step through those elegant glass doors. Truly, I did. But I panicked. And then I saw Madame Bagasha's Magicke Shoppe next door."

"What shop next door?" Ellen frowned. "Madame Bagasha? As in the 'psychic fortune teller' who advertises on late night television?"

"Yes." Lily told Ellen how the shop sang to her, how the sights and smells of the shop sank into her skin, left her swimming in sensation. Told her, too, about the hexagonal dice that revealed her heart's wish and the tall, willowy witch whose fingers called ingredients from shelves across the room. Finally, reluctantly, Lily told her about the love potion.

Ellen's feet hit the floor. "A love potion? Are you insane? Carter and Bell's might have been a wish of whimsy on my part, but Holy Gods . . . tell me you didn't drink it, Lily!"

"Of course I drank it." Lily shrugged. "I paid a whopping thirteen dollars for it."

Ellen leaped up to pace the room. "Are you out of your fricking mind? The potion could be . . . toxic! Or cause warts. Make your teeth fall out, your head spin 'round on your neck or . . . or turn your hair into snakes!"

"No." Lily shook her head. "The shop felt right, perfect, in fact. And the potion tasted good, like licorice. I am so going back, maybe to buy wizard mini-lights. You should come with me, you'd love it."

"I wouldn't!" Ellen declared with a shudder. "And it terrifies me that you'd drink some concoction of God knows what made by a God knows what! Did you feel sick? Or . . . are you suddenly slobbering over every guy wearing jeans . . . or wearing nothing?"

The delight faded from Lily's face. "No. In fact, nothing's happened. I don't feel any different."

"What's supposed to happen? Did you even ask?"

"No."

"Gods afire, Lily!" Ellen reached out as if to throttle her before dropping back into the chair with a ferocious scowl. "You are dangerously dumb sometimes, know that? Promise to call me if you begin levitating or sprouting beans from your ears. Or speaking in tongues! Even better, call your cute neighbor, what's his name."

"Daniel. 'Daniel-on-call' I call him."

Ellen glanced at her watch, made a sour face and began forcing her feet back into her tight boots. "Well 'Daniel-on-call' is yummy, Lil, and right under your nose. What'd the little witch say, that you're surrounded by love? I'd let him 'surround' me anytime."

Lily rolled her eyes. "Daniel's my best friend. I'd never mess with that. You know how hopeless I am with guys. I couldn't get mouth to mouth if I was dying in a ditch."

"Only because you'd rather stare at cloud bunnies than a cute guy." Ellen gave Lily a quick hug before dashing out of the apartment, pulling her coat on as she ran down the stairs.

Lily leaned for a moment in her open doorway breathing in the smell of dinners cooking in the apartments around her. So yeah, Ellen mostly had it right. Lily did live her days in dreamy distraction. But her boss didn't know everything. The two socialized together sometimes, but Lily'd never felt at ease around Ellen's fast, urbane crowd. The "eat, drink and be merry" scene was not her preferred smorgasbord of fun. Still, Ellen would be shocked at the fierce attachment Lily felt for this old apartment building and how much strength she drew from the hallowed walls no longer square after more than a century of settling deeper into the earth.

Lily often cruised the winding hallways of an evening, sometimes chatting, sometimes just brushing her hands along the burnished wood. These walls didn't contain, but supported. The wood pulsed with the heartbeats of those who dwelled within as well as those who whispered from the past.

She'd moved two years ago into this quiet, overlooked hamlet of New Chicago called Little Belfast, one of the few neighborhoods to quietly and quickly rebuild after the Great Surge of 2024 and the resulting stock market crash, government chaos, and street riots. The Surge was named when, out of the blue and in a matter of hours, the earth's magnetic pole switched from north to south, frying all things electrical from utility grids to mega-computers. Earthquakes toppled thousands of cities and towns around the world. Tsunamis left devastation on every coastline. Millions died. Governments collapsed, famine and disease swept the globe.

The United States recovered the quickest. Once small, insignificant companies morphed into super-corporations as a second industrial age sprang up, creating alternative energy products that were bigger, faster, and more technically efficient. But a worldwide economic depression caused stark divisions in wealth. Unemployment skyrocketed. Riots broke out in every major city across the country.

In a desperate attempt to control the seething populace without declaring martial law, the interim government enacted a disastrous mandate under the Patriot Act that forced neighborhoods to segregate according to race and religion. Citizens rebelled. The violence escalated. What was left of major cities were burned, skyscrapers razed to the ground, buildings bombed. Once again people died in their streets. It took an agonizing two years of socialist reforms and welfare programs before new financial infrastructures created jobs and began to stabilize the economy.

Little Belfast, a predominantly Irish Catholic neighborhood barely a mile and a half from downtown Chicago, survived the upheaval because people living here refused to follow the law and evict their non-Irish Catholic neighbors. That amazing grace saved the borough.

During that time, called Liberty's Reconstruction by politicians and historians, Lily was an unhappy teenager on her uncle's safflower farm in Ohio. Finally graduating from high school, she left Springfield behind and arrived in New Chicago a hopeful, optimistic stranger.

Now she lived as a member of the Lennox Apartments patchwork family. Down the hall she could hear the McCready sisters playing piano, their front door always open. Children's voices sang out; the Forman twins were "visiting" the two elder ladies until their mother got home from work.

Mr. Newton, a retired guard officer living across the hall from Daniel, would be down at O'Connor's Pub with his buddies. Thirty-two apartments cradled thirty-two families in the ancient Lennox, with Daniel Harris keeping watch over everyone from the deaf woman on the second floor to the intolerable Lonnie Ranchero, sleazy writer of pulp thrillers living on the first.

Lily knew them all, and avoided Lonnie, who invariably hit on her like a dirty bomb but often shared an afternoon with eight-year-olds Georgia and Chris Forman or a glass of wine with Ruby, the teenage bride suffering newlywed jitters in the apartment below hers. Yes, Ellen would be shocked indeed that Lily took such profound comfort in this building, her surrogate family, and Daniel.

But Lily did admit to one thing. She shouldn't have guzzled the love potion. What an impulsive, irrational thing to do . . . except, when she'd walked into Madame Bagasha's shop she'd breathed in magic, felt it seep as natural as rain into her psyche and fill the hollows of her heart with a confidence that the potion would lead her to love. Crazy? Oh, yeah. But Lily refused to give up hope that her soul mate roamed the world out there, somewhere.

She picked up the *Lost and Found* comic strip Ellen had left on the coffee table and frowned. This G.I.L. person hit too close to home sometimes with his four-frame vignettes. Still, the cartoon revealed an affectionate insight into his characters and their goofy antics at work, on dates, shopping. Despite Ellen's opinion, Lily didn't think she resembled the girl in the strip at all. She was small and dopey, the cartoon girl tall and broody.

But like the character, Lily's hair resembled a snarled mass of string and she did stick it full of pencils, paintbrushes, the television remote. The two did share a sense of worldly confusion, the cartoon girl forever losing herself in big words like Lily lost herself inside color. Picking up the vid-strip, Lily taped it to the refrigerator door with her other *Lost and Found* mementos. They were a reminder to laugh at herself, especially on days like this one where mayhem wreaked havoc in her already discombobulated life.

Suddenly starving, Lily forgot *Lost and Found* and rummaged up a meal of cold pizza and breadsticks dipped in peanut butter. Flipping on her VPEG player, she donned her paint smock, snatched up her pallet and brushes, and disappeared into alizarin crimson, the perfect color to bring the sensuality of her male nude to life. Such a brazen red would highlight the man's strength, the masculine line of his jaw and chin, his confident brow. Oh yes, his vigorous, male features definitely needed more attention . . .

Hours passed while songs shuffled in her comp-deck and Lily lost herself inside her work, brushing paint in long, sensual strokes across the curve of a manly shoulder, over the shadow of his collarbone, emphasizing an arched cheekbone or the sweet curve of his mouth. She breathed in linseed oil, tasted licorice, and worked her magic. The nude took on a vitality of his own, arm stretched upward towards the light, face lifted in anticipation. His face looked nothing like the model she'd sketched in her drawing class Monday night but that always happened, her own inner vision replacing a less substantial reality.

When at last she stepped back and stretched to relieve cramped muscles, Lily felt a jolt of pleasure at her creation. The painting worked, composition-wise, the greens and purples an ambiguous dark behind his skin of crimson and gold glowing with virility. She dropped her brush in a jar of waiting paint thinner, tugged free other paintbrushes she'd absently stuck in her hair, and realized a hot bath would ease her aching bones and perhaps cool the tingling excitement she felt after stroking paint over male muscles.

She had pulled her paint smock off over her head, skimmed out of her T-shirt and unzipped her jeans when she heard a loud sucking sound behind her. Turning, Lily watched in horror as the figure in the painting moved. Just a twitch of a hand at first, a stretch of an arm. Then in one violent lunge, the man tore himself free of the canvas and stepped onto the floor, real, animated, looking around her apartment with every naked inch of his skin gleaming in fresh oil.

Chapter Four

Lily stared, paralyzed. The man in front of her glistened with beauty, his face shaped by a strong, curved jaw, full lips, straight nose, and eyes a long lashed, deep chocolate brown she wanted to melt into. Those eyes, awkwardly familiar, looked back at her with an intensity that sizzled down to her toes. His body, oh Lord . . . his sleek body made her knees wobble. His shoulders rippled with power as he turned in effortless grace to survey the room. His chest heaved as he sucked in air like a newborn. Her own breath puffed in panicked gasps. She could feel her heart bashing hard enough to break her ribs.

He was perfect, standing full fleshed and real. And she'd created him from oil paint, sensuous brush strokes . . . and magic! Lily drew a tight breath and backed away from this heated dream born out of her lonely desperation. Oh God, how could this be real? But when his eyes locked on hers, Lily felt herself tumbling into possibilities and couldn't keep her hands from reaching to touch him. Her gaze skipped down his chest, over his flat belly and below, and darted back to his face as blood rushed to her cheeks. She certainly hadn't painted that *not* insignificant detail!

At her blush, a delighted grin split the man's face. He took a step towards her. Her hand fluttered to her throat as she realized she wore nothing but a bra and unzipped jeans. She stood like a party gift already half unwrapped for him!

"Stay!" She thrust her hand out to ward him off as he took a step towards her. With her other hand, she fumbled for the paint smock and spread it to cover her chest. He took another step. She knew he wanted to touch her, wanted to feel sensation with his brand new fingers, and so she scrambled on hands and knees over the couch, placing it between them. Grabbing a dish towel from the kitchen counter, she tossed it at him. "Cover up, for pity's sake."

He laughed at the skimpy cloth he caught one handed.

"Can you speak?" Lily stammered. "Is there a working brain behind all that . . . all that brawn? And paint? Gods afire, this isn't happening!"

"Am I not what you wished?" he asked, voice soft as he stretched the skimpy towel across his hips, slanting her a look to melt the staunchest of hearts. "Did you not ask for me?"

Lily closed her eyes and sucked in an unsteady breath. "Yes, I did ask. But—"

"I can be anything you want. Do anything you want. Yes?"

"No! Well, yes, eventually maybe . . . oh, hell! You need clothes, something." She backed towards the bedroom, her stare never leaving him as he turned to look at the room, the draped flamingo lights, the cluttered splashes of furniture. Grabbing her tattered robe off a bathroom hook, she returned and, halting just out of reach, stretched to hand it to him.

In truth, she was afraid to touch him, afraid if he touched her she'd become a mindless puddle of lust. Did she want those lips on hers? God, yes. Could she already feel his long fingers moving across her skin? Sweet mercy, yes! She shivered inside her paint smock and turned her head away as he dropped the towel to pull on the robe, and caught sight of the canvas where she'd painted him. Only a blur of smudged paint marked the place he'd once been. Lily remembered the taste of licorice on her tongue while she painted, remembered how she'd downed the love potion like a milk shake. So . . . she truly was responsible for this man. In every way. She'd swallowed an unknown concoction and allowed her loneliness and longing to bring her imagination to life!

She studied him, dressed in her green striped bathrobe stretched too tight across his shoulders and barely covering his thighs. Curiosity shone on his attractive face as he stroked the leaves of an ivy plant, fingered the plastic flamingos, and spread his palm across the rough fabric of her overstuffed chair.

What now, she wondered? Did she leave him accessible in only a robe and just use him for sex? Lily shuddered at the thought. She wanted so much more in a man; friendship and understanding, deep conversations, and plenty of laughter to help make the world a place she no longer wished to escape. She wanted real love wrapped around her like afternoon sun, cozy blankets, and sweet summer winds. She wanted security and warmth and excitement filling her heart, opening her up to love unrestrained in return. That's what she wanted.

Instead she'd asked for the perfect man . . . and got this painted "thing" come to life through magic. Oh, he was gorgeous. His full mouth invited kisses, his hands seemed more than eager to explore. But was he capable of love? And could he inspire it? What does one do with an image, even a vision as wondrous as he?

"Are . . . are you hungry?" Lily asked and his gaze shifted back to her.

"For you," he said.

Lily laughed. She couldn't help it. This had gone past absurd into the ridiculous. She'd created a sex slave! One who looked like he'd stepped straight off the cover of one of the lurid romances her aunt used to devour on hot beach days.

"Sit down. Please. Here." Lily pointed to the chair and backed away as he moved forward and sat. Good Lord, he was hers to command! She felt moisture steaming off her breasts, her belly. Backing into the kitchen, Lily snatched a plate from the dry rack and opening the refrigerator, began filling it with slices of pizza, crackers, lunch meat, cheese. She poured a glass of milk and, carrying both to the coffee table, set them in front of him before scuttling away.

He didn't even glance at the food. "Are you afraid of me?"

Yes, she wanted to scream, but forced herself to sit on the couch and try to explain. "What I feel is . . . is more complicated than that. I'm not quite sure what to do with you."

He stood, shrugging out of the robe. "I know exactly what to do." Grinning, he lunged for her. A frightened squeak escaped her as she jerked out of his reach and fell backwards over the couch.

Scrambling to her feet, she felt his hand grab the paint smock and tug her towards him. Popping the buttons, she slipped free.

He chased her around the table, around the couch, cut her off when she tried a dodge towards the bedroom to put a locked door between them. Wherever she ran, he pursued, a mounting excitement curving his lips. He'd backed her into the studio and she felt the hard edge of a work table slam into her as she tried to spin past. His hand snagged her wrist and held on, hard.

"Please," she said, struggling to twist free. "I don't do sex on a first date! We need time to—"

But he was already pulling her against his chest and suddenly Lily was angry. Her fists slammed into him, catching him by surprise. He let go. Off balance, she fell back against the table. An open jar of turpentine flew into the air, spraying paint thinner across her, the canvas beside her and the painted man. For a brief second, shocked astonishment flooded his face. Then he began to melt, eyes, mouth, limbs smearing, caving inwards, falling, dripping in rivers of reds and greens and purples until what was once a body lay in thick pools of paint on the ground cloth.

Bile rose in Lily's throat, her stomach heaved, and still she could not tear her gaze away until he was completely gone. She barely made it to the bathroom before throwing up.

"I killed him . . . " Lily sobbed into the sat-phone. After emptying her stomach, vigorously brushing her teeth and gargling for ten minutes, she'd dialed the only person she could think off.

"Then call 911, for Christ's sake," Ellen snarled sleepily. "It's one thirty in the morning!"

"But he wasn't alive," Lily rushed on. "Not really. Except he was. At least enough. But did I have sex with this hot, hungry man? No, I made him put on my bloody bathrobe! Then I accidentally splashed him with paint thinner, and he dissolved all over the floor. Oh God, I'll never paint again. I'll never *sleep* again!"

"Lily." Ellen's voice firmed as she woke more fully. "Calm down, you're making no sense. Are you sick? Was it that damn potion?"

"Yes! And yes. I can't stop shaking. Ellen, I've never . . . I've never melted anyone before!"

"Lily, will you snap out of it? Take a deep breath. Calm yourself. Now, tell me in small sentences what you think you did."

"What I did was melt him before I could get laid! My perfect man," Lily cried and in garbled, hysterical words the story poured out. When she finished, she burst into fresh tears. "Now he's in puddles, and I have to . . . I have to clean him up!"

"Can you wake Daniel, get him to help?"

"No!" Lily yelped. "How in hell's name do I tell him I'm a love-starved lunatic who drank a magic potion? He already knows I'm silly as flying pigs. I mean, could you explain painting a picture of a man, your perfect man, who then came to life and melted before your eyes? Ellen, how would I tell him that? Jeez, Ellen, I was dripping with lust!"

"It was the love potion, okay? Call Daniel. He'll understand—"

"No! You don't understand. I can't possibly call Daniel."

"Why not?"

"Because this guy, this perfect man I painted?" Lily drew a quaking breath. "He was the spitting image of Daniel."

Silence stretched over the wireless. "Are you telling me that your perfect man is the guy next door? Gods above, Lily, get yourself committed somewhere and soon!"

Lily darted a miserable glance over her shoulder at the drying canvas. Which was more insane, that a man that she'd painted had come to life? Or that in her possible heart of hearts and in some warped alternative universe, she was in love with her best friend?

"Lily?"

A sudden, echoing stillness filled Lily's mind and in that silent breath of space, she could think again. "I'm sorry, Ellen, sorry I woke you. I . . . I freaked out. But now I know what I have to do. Thanks for listening, for being there. See you tomorrow."

"Wait! You're now suddenly, inexplicably okay? Lily, are you sucking down that bottle of brandy I gave you last Christmas?"

Lily barked a laugh. "No, I'm totally, horrifically sober. Feet planted firmly on the ground. I . . . was responsible for creating this guy, I have to be the one who mops him up." Her voice cracked, she had to get off the phone while this small spark of fortitude held her together.

"Okay," Ellen said, "now I'm freaked. You sound far too rational to be trusted. Can't you please just get Daniel?"

"No," Lily whispered and disconnected. She knew if she went to Daniel now with her blood pumped full of hungry need, she'd jump him the second he opened the door, all sleep rumpled and sexy. And it would be the biggest mistake of her life. Her pathetic, lonely life full of a thousand mistakes.

She wasn't in love with Daniel. He just happened to be the most convenient guy, in fact pretty much the only guy, in her very small world. Of course, she could fall in love with him. Who couldn't? He had it all: good looks, a contagious grin, and a generous, easy nature. Plus big-time smarts. He read anything and everything. And loved movies, was passionate about art . . . and he laughed at her jokes.

Oh, yeah, she could so fall for him. But he could never love her. Who would? Not that she didn't have attributes. Some men couldn't resist a blue-eyed blonde petite enough to tuck like a football under his beefy arm. And she was intelligent, at least enough for creative ambition, imaginative concepts, and a sense of humor. But two facts were absolute and indisputable in her muddled, untidy life: Daniel Harris's friendship was the unshakeable cornerstone of her world. And she'd rather die than lose him.

Lily realized then, with uncharacteristic clarity, that the hushed stillness she'd felt on the phone with Ellen wasn't an acceptance of responsibility for a cocked-up job, but the echo of her solitary existence. She'd been lonely all her life, losing her parents in a car accident when she was seven years old. After that her life turned into a series of lessons in coping with abandonment and heart-wrenching loss. Survival meant dissociating as often and as thoroughly as possible from whatever happened around her.

At the time of the accident her brothers, ten and twelve years older than she, were already in college. So Lily was shuffled off to her mother's sister in the Ohio corn belt. Aunt Dora, Uncle Ned, and her three cousins had done their best to accept her, a silent, dreamy child who didn't fit in. And she'd been well loved. But also browbeat over her maddening habit of disappearing into books, her wild ideas, and her drawing. Despite knowing she'd never win their approval, Lily grew into an affectionate, cheerful girl. She still went home to Springfield at Christmas, loaded with gifts she'd learned over the years would please them.

Now as Lily gathered rags and a bucket to clean up her unholy mess, she confronted the echoing silence inside her head and vowed to remake herself. It was high time she grew up, became a sensible, down-to-earth person who could stand on her own two feet. The kind of woman who remembered to match her socks before putting them on, someone who never forgot her keys, or when she'd last eaten, or run a comb through her hair. If she stayed Daniel's hapless, incompetent neighbor, Lily knew he'd lose patience with her, and she would lose him. Especially if he guessed at this sudden physical awareness of him as not just best friend, but male. And, Gods help her, a very attractive, currently unattached male!

Oh yeah, she would have to tread lightly around him from now on, maintain a casual distance, stay nonchalant. Because Daniel was one perceptive guy. Lily loved that about him . . . but now she had reason to fear his uncanny insight.

Feeling stronger, perhaps even mature with a specific goal laid out in front of her flashing like a road sign, Lily grabbed the giant can of thinner from under the sink. On hands and knees she mopped up drying puddles of paint, all that remained of her perfect man.

Chapter Five

Lily slept restlessly, legs tangled in clammy sheets and her mind tormented by images of her painted man, the memory of his silky eyes, his lips parted with excitement . . . and the horror of his melting face. Finally, she got up to gulp down a sleeping pill. Within moments she was out cold.

She woke with a heart-pounding gasp, her feet freezing and daylight streaming in through her bedroom window. Every muscle in her body ached from her struggle to keep out of the man's grasp the night before. She longed to lose herself under a hot shower. Until she looked at the clock. Almost ten o'clock. Holy crows, Ellen was going to kill her! Even as the thought hit her, the phone rang.

"Lily, tell me you're all right!" Ellen's shout was shrill enough to wake the building.

"Sorry, yes. I overslept. I'm coming in right now. Sorry." Lily snapped her sat-phone shut, crammed her sketchbook in the portfolio already bulging with loose drawings, grabbed up her satchel and raced out of the apartment. Halfway down the stairs, she slammed into a body coming up.

"Whoa there, Lil. Where's the fire?" Daniel grabbed her to keep her from falling.

At his touch all breath left her. She stared into his eyes, only inches from her own . . . large, long-lashed eyes a melting chocolate brown. Keen, observant eyes disguised behind his glasses and now amused, she realized, at having her in his arms. A blush stained her cheeks, her skin quivered to warm life where he touched her. Her gaze slid to his mouth, full lipped with dimpled corners prone to smile. She found herself leaning into him, wondering what he tasted like-

"Lily," he said, his palm cupping her cheek. "Are you okay? Let me help you back up—"

"No," she snapped alert, tried to wriggle from his grasp. "I overslept, I'm late for work."

"You're going dressed like that?" He glanced down her body and grinned. "I like it, informal yet somehow commanding."

Lily looked down at herself and saw she was still wearing her nightgown. "Oh, Gods! I'm losing it, Daniel. That little grasp I have on reality? It is so circling the drain!"

Daniel brushed tangled curls off her face and smiled. "Not true, Lily. You're brilliant. A walking, talking work of art."

*

Gently taking Lily's elbow, Daniel steered her back upstairs, unlocked her door with his spare key, and led her inside. She stood in the middle of her apartment blinking in a kind of weary stupefaction. He watched her eyes fill with tears. She needed his arms around her, he could sense it, and wanted her breath mingled with his while he kissed this confusing present away. But instead of reaching for her, Daniel jammed his hands in his pockets. "Talk to me, Lil. Tell me what's wrong."

She shook her head and backed away to dash into her bedroom, slamming the door shut between them. Snarling his frustration, Daniel paced the apartment. He wasn't leaving until he saw her again, until he knew she wouldn't fall apart under whatever emotional storm was tearing at her this time.

The covered easel caught his eye. He never looked at her work unless she offered, never pried into anything she took pains to hide. Maybe it was time he did. As he stepped forward, the sole of his shoe lifted off something sticky on the ground cloth. Glancing down, he saw where she'd cleaned up spilled paint . . . a lot of spilled paint. Dropping to a crouch, he touched a finger to the smear, felt a taut chill creep up his arm and become a stirring fire in his blood.

Jerking his hand back, he cursed under his breath. The paint felt as tacky as drying blood. A cold fear swept over him. Pressing his open palm down on the smear, he opened his senses and felt a quick rush of heat. Lust tightened his belly with a mindless hunger, his mind filled with an alien curiosity and fierce excitement. Then he was tumbling into Lily's panic, a growing fear, explosive anger, and, at the last, a sense of deep terror. Daniel cursed again. What the hell had happened here?

Behind him, he heard her bedroom door opening and quickly stepped away from the easel. A defensive fury rose inside him. He rarely allowed himself to Read when he touched objects or people. Absorbing the thoughts and emotions of others had always been disorienting and painful. Not a power he particularly treasured. His grandmother, a strong Reader as well, had discovered his magic when he was a child. She taught him how to survive it by building mental barriers that allowed him a protective emotional distance.

He'd been living behind those barriers ever since, ignoring, for the most part, his magical gifts. When he'd caught Lily barreling down the stairs, the careful wall he kept erected between them fell apart. Never in his life had he let another's feelings rush him with such ferocity.

Standing near the couch, he watched Lily cross the room. His heart quickened. He flexed hands that ached to touch her and fought down a longing he didn't dare let her see. His feelings would only confuse her. Get a grip, he commanded himself and forced a smile. Not difficult when he realized he was seeing Lily at her rarest, her hair brushed and gleaming like sun-touched silk, her dark stockings straight, skirt and lavender sweater tidy with each button in its proper hole.

She looked composed, quietly sensible . . . and achingly fragile. Gods, he wanted her now. On the couch, on the floor, his hands sliding under that flirty skirt to drag off her stockings, his fingers skimming her naked thigh-

Lily stepped close, snapping his attention back to her as she looked up. Her chin barely reached his chest. In the depths of her china-blue eyes he saw defiance. And determination.

"Daniel," she spoke in a voice rough and unsteady. "Last night I made a promise to myself, a promise to change, to pull my head out of the clouds. Plant myself solidly in reality. I . . . I've become way too dependent on you. And rather than wreck our friendship, I'm going to stop."

Daniel found he couldn't breathe. "Stop what?"

"Stop needing you."

"Lily," he swallowed the cry in his throat. "Don't change. Please. You're amazing and—"

Lily shook her head, "It's high time I grew out of my childish ways." She looked down at their feet and rocked forward until the toes of her shoes rested on top of his. "I'll be thirty in ten months, do you realize that? Thirty years old. And I want so many things that aren't possible if I stay this unreliable, muddleheaded person living helter-skelter." She darted a glance at the covered easel across the room.

Daniel grabbed her shoulders, purposely brushing a finger over the bare skin at her neck and braced himself against the spill of her emotions into him: confusion, loneliness, fear . . . and guilt. Never in the two years he'd known her had he ever sensed guilt in her. Confusion, yes, and sadness, boundless joy, eager awareness. But never guilt. His hands on her shoulders tightened. "What happened here last night? Did someone hurt you?"

"No." She shook her head, met his fierce gaze with reluctance. "I hurt myself, Daniel, like I always do. I believed in something stupid and then watched it melt into nothing. One day I'll follow some bizarre impulse that ends up hurting you. It's what I do. I'll presume or forget something important and . . . let's be realistic, shall we? I know you won't be around forever to let me in when I forget my key, or remind me to feed the fish, or stop me running off to work in my nightgown. You're the most generous, considerate man I've ever known, and you've got better things to do than douse every little fire in my life."

Beneath his palms, her body burned an icy cold. He found himself rubbing warmth down her arms, felt her tremble. "Don't do this to yourself, Lily. We're a team, you and me. I'm here for you, always."

She straightened and stepped away, suddenly all business. "Well, you deserve better than me. And someone really special out there deserves you. Now, I'm so late Ellen will fire me. I already lost her a good client yesterday . . . see what I do to my friends?"

She bent to pick up the satchel and portfolio where she'd dropped them on the floor.

"Something happened here last night." Frustrated, Daniel reached for her again. "Something that scared you. Tell me what it was."

She rose on tiptoe, her breath warm on his cheek before she kissed him. "My bad karma."

"I'm not giving up on you, you know." He followed her out the door. "You need to talk, I'm your guy. You hear me?"

"Right-o!" She waved back at him as she bumbled down the stairs, the portfolio banging at her knees, satchel already sliding off her shoulder. Daniel crossed the hall to lean over the railing. Lily could try on adulthood like some women try on sexy underwear . . . but dressing up a package rarely changes the essentials. Or so he hoped. She was a rare one, didn't she know? Couldn't she see how her irrepressible spirit enchanted those around her?

Watching her from above, Daniel waited. Sure enough, she walked smack into the glass security door as always, forgetting it was there and had been for the last three months. The heavy portfolio fell to the floor, he heard her swear like a sailor as she bundled it back together. And he smiled, reassured. Stubborn will aside, her whimsical mind stayed true to form, already drifting off towards Never Never Land and her very own "second star on the right."

Before closing the door to her apartment, Daniel ducked inside to dribble food to the two goldfish. Miss Elizabeth and Mr. Darcy were Lily's Christmas gift from the McCready sisters down the hall. She'd named them after the infamous lovers in Jane Austen's *Pride and Prejudice*. The two fat fish rose to suck in flakes, lacy tails sweeping the fairy tale castle inside the glass bowl.

Daniel would never forget the day shortly after Christmas when Lily had run to him with a dead Elizabeth in her hands.

"She needs mouth to mouth and I must be doing it wrong!" she'd cried, placing the tiny fish face near her lips to blow tender puffs into the gaping mouth. In that moment Daniel's well constructed world fell to pieces as he tumbled ass over tea kettle in love.

He remembered her face streaked with tears, how outraged she'd been at herself. "I forgot to feed them. Yesterday, and probably the day before!"

He'd taken the dead fish gently in his hands. "Miss Elizabeth wouldn't die of starvation in that amount of time, Lil. She must have been sick. We'll get another one."

"I'll just kill her, too," she'd wailed. "I'm horribly irresponsible, Daniel, you know that!"

"So you'd condemn poor Mr. Darcy to a life without his Elizabeth?" he'd teased and they'd gone that afternoon to buy a new goldfish.

Lily buried the first Elizabeth Bennett under a giant hastatum plant. Since that day, she never forgot to feed the fish and religiously cleaned their bowl every Saturday. Still for safety's sake, and Lily's, Daniel sometimes snuck them food.

*

Walking away from Daniel felt like ripping chewing gum from her hair. As Lily jumped an e-trolley heading downtown, she fought against a strange compulsion to run back to him. The sensation left her uneasy, as if she'd missed seeing a flitting but important image at the edge of her vision.

The urgency faded the farther she got from home but the need still lingered, a teasing presence at the back of her mind. Leaving the e-trolley six blocks from work, Lily headed towards Madame Bagasha's Magicke Shoppe.

Questions for Nila, the witch girl, ran circles in her head. Questions like what the hell had gone wrong with her "bona-fide, certified" love potion? As Lily approached the pretty stone building that housed Carter and Bell's, she slowed, stopped, and stared. No magic shop stood beside the dating service today. No arcane sign swung in the wind, no joyous voices sang. Madame Bagasha's Magicke Shoppe had disappeared! In its place stood a dull gray building with a door that said Keenan Tax Accountants.

Lily unfroze long enough to open the door into an office with a secretary at the front desk who looked up with a pleasant smile. Lily ducked back outside. She stared up the street and down. Her pulse began pounding in her ears. The magic shop stood here yesterday, she'd swear it! Or, and this seemed the more likely probability, she'd finally well and truly cracked. Her overly imaginative brain conjured up a shop to grant her deepest wish. And a shop full of witches to make it come true! Lily felt ill. Had her painted man been a delusion? No. She'd cleaned up paint for over an hour, for pity's sake!

Shocked and dizzy, Lily lowered her head between her knees. Hyperventilating in the middle of the sidewalk was not an option, she told herself, breathing in slow drafts of morning air. She remembered Nila saying people who didn't believe in magic never found the shop. Straightening, she turned to shout at the gray door, "But I do believe, damn it!"

Two nearby pedestrians swiveled to stare. A few others cast her a wary glance and crossed the street away from her. And still the little shop did not materialize. Chilled now, Lily wrapped her coat tighter against the wind. She'd wait, she decided. But after ten long minutes, she gave up and stormed away. In her gut she knew the shop had been real. And she wasn't nuts.

She was, however, more than a little stupid. Guzzling a love potion knowing something as unpredictable as magic existed in the universe? Idiotic! Lily knew she'd stumbled into more than a little cauldron bubbling with trouble. Messing in magic powerful enough to vanish an entire building, or bring a painting to life, meant the number of disasters still out there waiting to happen were, well, inconceivable!

Chapter Six

Daniel spent the morning doing odd jobs around the apartment building, angry at Lily for pushing him away and even more angry at himself for stepping back. Like he always did. Lack of action in personal matters was his stock in trade. As long as he didn't Read what other people felt, he didn't have to get involved. He could stay aloof, a casual observer with no obligation to respond to them, their emotions, their wants, their needs. Or take much responsibility for his own. In the whole of his life, he'd never committed himself to another human being beyond the act of friendship. Until Lily. And now she'd sidestepped him, determined to stand on her own.

She was wise to retreat, he told himself as he replaced Lectro-bulbs in the Lennox stairwells. She deserved better than a man who possessed an extra-sensory perception and refused to use it for altruistic purposes. As the morning progressed, Daniel's mood darkened until the moment came, as it always did, when his thinking wandered full circle and he found himself laughing at how skewed and self-important he could make his so-called "gifts."

After all, he had no more control over other people and what they felt than he did over the weather! His only real power lay in the truth of his own heart and the common sense to accept what he was-a Witch, a Sensitive, a Telepath, a Reader . . . a man who could know all, but for the sake of his own sanity and morals, did little more than tend to his own business.

Take his parents, for example. If he had the power to affect change by using his magic he'd have made marriage to his dictatorial father easier on his mother. Almeida Harris's magic was in her cooking. She could, by simply preparing a meal, fill any heart with a sense of homey support, soothe, encourage, bolster hope, provide protection, and help enhance anything her husband, two sons, and daughter wished for in their daily lives. Daniel's father, a fireman in Little Belfast all of his adult life and now district fire chief, ate his wife's meals every day and so escaped hundreds of close calls on the job.

She'd used her simple kitchen magic to keep him safe. She was the reason he'd risen so fast to the position of Battalion Chief. Yet in more than thirty years of marriage, his father never once acknowledged her magical skill. In fact, the man refused to acknowledge magic of any kind. He'd never believed in his youngest son either.

No, Daniel felt his Gift as more curse than blessing and, defying his own grandmother, had vowed never to become a member of the New Chicago Cohort. Opening himself to Read Lily that morning hadn't been the smartest of moves if he wanted to keep their relationship companionable and casual.

Lily remained a preoccupation throughout the morning. While he repaired a lamp cord for the McCready sisters he remembered her body, naked under the thin nightgown, pressed against his on the stairs. Could still feel the silky warmth of her tangled hair around his fingers. Driving the week's accumulation of paper, glass, and plastic to the recycling center, his heart raced as he thought of her trembling sweetly beneath his hands as if his touch had flipped some switch on inside her. By the time he tackled soldering a leaky pipe in the basement, he was so distracted he had to stop and grip the ladder when a tremor shook him remembering the way she'd stared into his eyes like she wanted to dive in. He should have kissed her. He'd wanted to . . . Gods on fire, he'd wanted to! Instead he'd stepped back. Like a good friend, he told himself. And laughed at his own delusions.

He tried *not* to think of Lily as he listened to Lonnie Ranchero down in apartment six ranting about the Forman twins running their race-boards down the first floor halls again. As he was leaving, with Lonnie still fuming over only a promise to talk to the twins, Daniel paused to give the man a hard look. "And stop hitting on Lily."

A leering grin replaced Lonnie's heavy scowl. "You taking care of her then, Danny boy? 'Cause if there was ever a hot tomato needin' ripening, she's it."

"Save that tripe for your fiction, Lon."

"Or what?"

"I'll let her tell you what she really thinks of you." Daniel grinned at the man's startled face.

While nodding absent-minded over coffee and his Aunt Lorraine's rambling conversation in apartment twelve, Daniel listed in his head the pros and cons of actively pursuing Lily. His aunt had inherited Lennox Apartments when her husband died, and Daniel leaped at the job of manager when she, overwhelmed by grief and the sudden responsibility, asked him if he wanted to take it on. Now his daily visits kept her up to date on the business, kept her company, and kept her involved. When at last he climbed the stairs to his own apartment, her grief clung to him like a sad perfume.

Sitting down at his comp-console at last, Daniel tried to tackle the real work in his life, the creative work that kept him alive and inspired. But a nagging ache for Lily sent him spinning off in an arousing fantasy of her wearing nothing but thigh-high lace stockings. He ended up so consumed he found himself pulling paper from a drawer and began sketching her. Mostly clothed, of course, but as he relaxed into his old graphic hero style of drawing, she became a lean-legged warrior clad in very tight, very skimpy leather . . .

He ended up slamming the sketches in a drawer and soaking his head under a cold shower, and afterwards felt more like himself. Back at his console, he opened Photoshop, selected the six vid-pages he still had to colorize for the next issue of the comic book *Grave Gladiators*, put on classic Rolling Stones, and for the first time that day, disciplined himself to focus. The completed pages were due the following day at Graffic Blues, one of the comic book publishers he worked for freelance.

Daniel had never considered himself artistic while growing up part nerd, part jock, and obsessed with comic books and graphic novels. His middle school art teacher turned him on to Japanese manga, got him interested in action figure drawing. Drawing lit the fire of creativity in Daniel's young soul and became his passion. It was an occupation completely opposite the scholastic and athletic achievements his parents were so proud of in their other two children.

Graduating from high school, Daniel left home to attend art school. Two frustrating years later, he quit to take any job he could find in the comic book industry. His first steady job for Graffic Blues was sketching storyboard ideas. Moving rapidly up the creative chain, he eventually co-wrote and designed the graphic novel *Ragged Edge*, which had a brilliant four-year success before Graffic Blues spun it off into two separate series based on the more popular characters. At first Daniel enjoyed drawing for *Hellketcher*, but when the storyline veered towards horror, he lost interest. Graffic Blues asked him to try colorizing, and Daniel at last found his niche. A colorist is the superman of the comic book industry. Many artists find it tedious, diddling with software by the hour, exploring color variables that best fit mood, drama, danger, or romance and then filling the space between the lines on the black-and-white pages of action and story. Daniel loved it. What's more, he could work from home, which allowed him the freedom to explore other creative and personal interests.

He'd first discovered Lily's paintings in a small gallery on the west side of New Chicago almost six years ago. Being a colorist, he was immediately charmed by her unique intimacy with color hues and tones, a gift he recognized, admired, and knew he would never possess. He'd bought that painting, a landscape of Lake Michigan at dawn, alive with light, the city a faint shimmering warmth in the distance. It hung on the wall above his work station. For years he kept an eye out for more of her work without knowing the slightest thing about her. He'd discovered two more paintings three years ago and could only afford to buy one. Not six months later, she'd walked into his life looking for an apartment, a tiny waif of a woman full of astonishing naiveté and joyful vision.

She'd given him a painting this past Christmas, a true masterpiece that hung in his living room. It was a large landscape in a style that danced between impressionism and realism, of a stone bridge stretching across water pulsing streams of light and color. The painting's eloquent and vivid beauty took his breath away every time he looked at it.

When she'd lugged it into his apartment and he'd torn away the paper wrapping, he'd stared speechless for a long moment. Then he'd exploded. "You can't give me this, Lily! Gradyn Spencer could sell it for a fortune in his gallery. You could buy yourself a house, for Christ's sake."

"I don't want a house," she'd replied. "Sometimes a painting claims a person while I'm working on it. This one belonged to you almost from the start, Daniel."

That's when he'd taken her back to his office, showed her what he'd found so many years before. Her mouth had dropped open, she'd stared at the painting of Lake Michigan as if at a long-lost friend. "I painted this when I was in college. I can't believe it's here!"

"I've been a Lily Barnett fan for a long time."

She'd laughed then, leaping into his arms and wrapping her legs around his waist to plant a wet kiss on his mouth. The kiss, recklessly innocent, had kindled instant arousal in him. He'd dropped her and stepped back in trembling shock. Being Lily, she'd seemed unaware of his discomfort, just danced around his apartment like a runaway come home at last. And Daniel immediately fortified a more resolute force-field between them.

*

Daniel made himself work for three frustrating hours before deciding he needed brisk air and a dose of Gradyn humor. Gradyn Spencer, Daniel's comrade in trouble and triumph since childhood, was rarely an accommodating listener, but his stories about the frivolous wealthy rivaled the best celebrity gossips and could distract one for hours.

Walking towards downtown where Spencer's latest gallery had just opened, Daniel felt the tension slowly slide off his shoulders. Patches of blue sky peeped from between a dirty gray overcast gathering for yet another autumn rain shower. Ah, fall in New Chicago . . . bitter with a wind that bit to the bone and a sun gone cold whenever it managed to break through the clouds. Tonight the stormy murk looked pinned like a banner to the sky by the thousands of rooftop wind towers with their rotating blades. Daniel kicked his feet through piles of fallen red and gold leaves littering the sidewalk. He tasted their dusty tang on his tongue. The crisp crunch underfoot satisfied his mood.

Winter would be early this year, he realized with a glance at the darkening sky. Pausing at an intersection for an e-trolley to pass, he glanced up and saw a face in the window so like his own it might have been his reflection. Startled, he stared up into dark, brooding eyes staring out at him. The hair on the back of his neck rose. Then the e-trolly swept past, leaving Daniel shivering with unexpected foreboding.

This late in the business day, the gallery was empty and Gradyn worked alone at a large desk set behind a curved sales counter. His round glasses had slipped down his nose, so absorbed was he in his books. He glanced up when Daniel walked in carrying two cups of steaming coffee.

"Ah, I recognize an angel of mercy!" Grinning, Gradyn unfolded his long frame from the chair and tugged loose his tie to unbutton the neck of his shirt. Reaching beneath the counter, he pulled out a bottle of scotch. "Thanks for the rescue, Danny boy.

I forget how much I despise paperwork until I trash a perfectly good day doing it."

"I never did understand your waste of a degree." Daniel declined an offer from the bottle and watched his friend tip a generous shot into his coffee.

Gradyn said, "If I'd known back in college how business really worked, I'd have majored in P. E."

"So you always say, Coach," Daniel answered, voice thick with sarcasm. The two had played basketball and run track together in high school. Aside from height under the net and some speed over hurtles, Gradyn's loose jointed, gawky frame hadn't offered much to athletics. His head for math, on the other hand, had him recruited into a brokerage firm right out of college. But it didn't take long for Grady Spencer to realize there wasn't a job in the world that beat working for himself.

"When's the grand opening?" Daniel asked, glancing with interest through the half opened door leading into a back room where an untidy clutter of crates stood, some partially opened.

"Week and a half. Lily's agreed to bring in four pieces."

"She's really good, isn't she? I mean—"

"She's genius, and as her work matures it will only increase in value. You, my lucky friend, have one of her best pieces hanging in your living room. Golly gee, she must like you a lot."

"Shut up."

"Have you made your move on her yet, big guy?"

"None of your damn business." Daniel stepped away from the counter, already regretting his impulse to come.

"Ask her to the opening," Grady suggested, taking a gulp of the doctored coffee. "You know how she hates them. All those moneyed people start crowding close, and she goes into that 'deer-pinned-by-headlights' shock. Even you couldn't make the night worse."

Daniel shot him an unfriendly look. "I'm afraid she's sworn off me."

Gradyn's eyebrows rose. "But you're her best friend. One doesn't dump a—"

"She's decided to stop counting on me. Thinks she needs to become more independent and act like a grown-up."

"Why?" Gradyn's wide-eyed horror was comical.

Daniel tossed back the last of his coffee and leaned over the counter to bank the empty cup into the recycle bin before turning to survey the impeccably arranged showroom. "She's got some misguided concept of what adulthood is supposed to mean. But if space is what she wants, space she'll get."

"Christ's Apostles, Daniel, what a statement! Shows an insipid lack of backbone on your part, if you ask me." Gradyn sloshed more scotch into his cup.

"I didn't ask you." Daniel wandered out onto the marble floor, paused to study a watercolor landscape and an abstract oil of . . . a cow's reproductive organs, maybe? He stopped in front of a beautifully rendered bronze of two entwined figures. "What choice do I have, Gradyn? She's so damn stubborn with no clue how amazing she is."

"Or how you feel about her. I've known other artists like her. They can't separate who they are from what they do. People will compliment them, and they assume the praise is only for their work. Lily doesn't understand praise on a personal level. You need to give her more than pretty words."

Daniel rolled his eyes.

"Offer up yourself, man. The whole package: mystical mind reader, artist, comic genius hiding behind a—"

"No. Adding that much information to our relationship would only confuse the issue." Daniel turned to face his friend. "Look, she asked me to back off, to let her make mistakes, and learn how to deal with them herself. She wants to stand on her own. I respect that. Didn't I have to fight for the same thing? Gods afire, between my domineering grandmother and my tyrant father, it's a miracle I don't spend my days drooling in a padded cell. Pop's never forgiven me for choosing art school over an engineering degree. And Gran won't stop nagging me to join the Cohort."

"I know. Sorry for oversimplifying." Gradyn joined Daniel out on the floor. "But Lily's coming into her own now, realizing her true professional potential. She's gaining more confidence and deserves a healthy social life to go with it. Don't you think? As for her personal life . . . well, both of you are infested with a cornucopia of social phobias. Are you thinking that if she starts seeing herself in a different light, she'll finally take a closer look at you?"

Daniel's shoulders shifted restlessly. "I don't know. Maybe. It's just . . . I hate that she's been so unhappy lately."

"It's positively unnatural for her to be unhappy!" Gradyn exclaimed. "Which is why you two have to resolve this. Tell her how you feel, for God's sake. Tell her *what* you are—"

"No! One day, yes, but not yet. She's got huge trust issues."

"Wouldn't you if your best friend kept the biggest part of himself locked away? Damn your stubborn hide, Daniel. She's not the only one who sells herself short."

*

Gradyn's words echoed in Daniel's head as he walked home through the dimly lit streets. He wished unlocking his life was that simple, wished he could lay himself and his heart at Lily's feet. But he'd already waited too long, kept too much from her. He pretended to the world that he was just an apartment manager, just a simple graphic artist turned colorist.

How would she react when she found out he was a powerful telepath? Some secrets turn exponentially darker the longer they stay hidden. He hadn't a clue how to tell her all that he was . . . and still keep her in his life. Shivering under a blast of frigid wind, Daniel shoved his hands deeper into his jacket pockets. If only he could make her fall in love with him. She'd forgive him anything if she truly loved him, wouldn't she? But he'd lived long enough to know you can't force someone to love you.

Daniel stopped for an e-trolley and as the brightly colored car rattled past, he knew he had the power to do it. He, Daniel Harris, could make Lily fall for him simply by using his Gift. In his head he saw clearly how he could work her, first with sweet psychic whispers followed by seemingly casual touches, a brushing of bodies here, an impulsive clasping of hands there before he moved on to actually maneuvering her thoughts towards-

Daniel swore aloud. What the hell was he thinking? Love, the tender, hot, wondrous kind of love that he ached for and Lily deserved, couldn't be manipulated. That he possessed the power to force someone . . . it was a fact beyond frightening! That he would consider it-even in fantasy-terrified him! Yeah, Gradyn had way oversimplified the situation. They were better off apart, he and Lily. At least for now. She needed space, he needed to cool the obsessing. But hearing his footsteps hollow in the night, Daniel knew he was making excuses, pulling away, letting time pass without grabbing for opportunities yet again. And that wasn't living, not really.

And it was certainly no way to win the heart of a lady.

Chapter Seven

More than a little frightened and, yes, angry as hell at not finding Madame Bagasha's shop where it was supposed to be, Lily arrived at Faces In Time that morning all out of sorts. Cramming the last of a breakfast muffin in her mouth, she sneaked up the back stairs to slip into her studio. The last thing she needed was the third degree from Ellen over how well she'd coped with painting a man to life that looked exactly like Daniel. Or the fact that she'd dissolved him.

Eager to start on her portrait of the Wilson girls, Lily spent the morning sorting through studio drops the artists at Faces used for settings and background. Heavy, awkward, and nearly impossible to detach, the backdrops hung on an electronic rack sporting swinging arms, similar to what held area rugs at a carpet store. Sandwiched between a musty, mottled brown drop and one of flamboyant blues almost too bright for the eye, Lily jumped at the sound of her boss's voice. "So?"

Struggling out from between them, Lily gave Ellen a warning scowl. "So, what? Go ahead and fire me for being late."

"Not today, my dear." Ellen grinned at Lily's show of temper and held up a clothing bag. "Lindsay and Carmen Wilson will be here at three thirty this afternoon for their first sitting, and Mrs. Wilson just dropped off the outfits she wants them to wear."

Lily growled, her temper increasing. "What do you bet the girls had no say in the choosing? It takes so little to make children happy, obliging. Cooperative!"

"You look very pale," Ellen observed. "Should you even be here today?"

"Yes." Lily unzipped the bag, tugged the hangers free, and swore profoundly. "White dresses! Why am I not surprised? The girls are blond, they need color."

"Then pick a bold, dramatic backdrop, Lily. And stop whining. This isn't like you."

"I'm trying to act more adult. I've noticed adults tend to whine."

"How unexpectedly perceptive of you. You must have a fever. Adults do whine. And vent. Let me know when the venting urge comes on, I'll alert the others. Should be quite a show."

"Nope, I'm over it." Lily shook out the two lace-encrusted dresses and hung them on a clothes rack.

"So," Ellen began again. "Did you call on 'Daniel on call' last night?"

"No. I was perfectly capable of cleaning up a melted man on my own, thank you very much."

"Thought you were over it," Ellen sniped and breezed from the room.

Lily stayed cranky and distracted all morning. She kept remembering the sensual way her paintbrush slid over her nude's face . . . Daniel's face. And how intimate it felt dropping cadmium gold light into his chocolate brown eyes, stroking indigo shadows over the lush curves of his mouth. Her palms began to sweat.

She stood staring blankly at backdrops while fixating on the handsome sweep of his cheekbones and how appealing he looked in glasses, how amazingly hot he would look without them. Had she ever seen Daniel without his glasses? His eyes were magnificent, rich, warm, fringed with thick lashes that had no business hiding behind poly frames. They were eyes that dominated his expressive face, lively and captivating. Most women went ga-ga for a guy with a well shaped ass. Not Lily. Beautiful eyes got her every time. More than her palms began to sweat.

His mouth had looked so . . . kissable. Why hadn't she ever noticed that about him? She was famously unable to keep her fingers off things, so of course she'd touched him before, shoving about, friendly hand clasps, casual hugs. Why couldn't she remember what his skin felt like under her fingertips? Gods, what an oblivious dolt she was!

She should have followed her impulse the night before and knocked on his door, all worked up and horny, straddling him then and there in the middle of his living room floor. Would he have shoved her aside offended or eagerly slipped his hands inside her shirt and-

Sam, the photographer, popped his head through the door to ask if she wanted coffee, jerking Lily out of her fantasy. "I'm perfectly capable of getting my own coffee," she snapped.

Sam's face fell.

Lily dropped an armful of velveteen throws. "Oh, Sam, I'm sorry. It's just . . . I'm horribly cranky today. Let me get my coat, I'll walk along, help you carry."

While Sam moved room to room collecting orders from the other artists, Lily stood back to scrutinize the backdrop of forest green she'd chosen. Even with the white dresses stark and shining against the bold color, she felt the contrast held no dramatic appeal. Pulling on her coat, she closed her door on the problem, the only thing to do under crabby circumstances.

*

As she and Sam walked the six blocks to Jolt of Java, he pointed out how the trees were already dropping leaves and it was only mid-October. When Lily didn't respond, he bumped her with his shoulder. "What's wrong, Lil? Got an itch you can't scratch?"

Lily turned on him in astonishment. "I do, yes. And an unbearable itch it is too, with scratching not an option."

"Why not?"

"Because he's my closest, very best friend! That ever happen to you? Falling for a friend, but afraid dipping a toe in to test deeper water might drown a perfect relationship?"

Sam laughed. "Not with a woman, no. With my career, yes."

"Really?" Lily stopped, intrigued, and Sam hooked her elbow to propel her inside the coffee shop.

"A couple different times, actually," he spoke above the noisy afternoon crowd. "I studied photography in school, but got a degree in accounting. After graduating, I set up a small studio, did weddings, graduation portraits, sports team photos mostly. And failed miserably. So I gave up, grew up, and made the hard choice. Abandoned the dream."

"But—"

They reached the head of the line and Sam read out the order to the barista before moving to the end of the counter to wait. Jolt of Java seemed especially busy today and Lily got sidetracked studying the variety of footwear on the people around them. Watching her, Sam grinned.

"So what happened?" Lily picked up the conversation as, each carrying a tray loaded with cups, they headed back to the studio.

"I went to work at a bank, became a loan officer, got married, had a kid, then another. Got a mortgage, two cars, you know. Anteed up. Made myself get serious about life." He stopped talking as leaves swirled around them in wind dervishes. Flocks of raucous gulls swarmed to the north. Pigeons, sparrows, and an occasional black crow swooped to earth seeking tidbits before flying back to roost on ridgepoles and trolley cables.

The new high-rises of downtown scraped the sky, connected to each other by a criss-crossing mesh of glass-enclosed bridges hundreds of feet off the ground like some Escheresque space station. The walkways were lined with shops and apartments, every space efficiently used. Older buildings that had somehow survived the destructive riots looked as out of place as covered wagons. These historic remnants of a by-gone era wore their granite and brick facades like aging soldiers in proud uniform.

Sam inhaled, as if the breeze from the lake smelled like a blooming garden instead of barge sludge and moldering fish. He looked at Lily. "But the itch never went away, you know? In fact, it got worse. I became short tempered, depressed, my wife threatened divorce. She's ballsy, my wife, and finally confronted me, said the wisest words I've ever heard."

"Please tell them to me," Lily cried. "Save me from my wretched self!"

Sam laughed. "She said, 'Life is like a Twinkie. If you only nibble the outside, you never get to the creamy filling inside.'"

"Ah . . ."

"So I quit as a loan officer, went to work for Ellen. I want as much filling as I can stuff myself with, Lily. You know what I'm talking about. My God, you live knee deep in the stuff, and it didn't take a mid-life crisis for you to get there. So scratch your itch, for pity's sake. With my blessing!" Sam swung open the door to Faces In Time and climbed the stairs.

Lily followed. "But you only see me at work, Sam, where I have at least a modicum of professionalism. The rest of my life is a disaster. I'm spacey, forgetful, get distracted by the oddest things—"

"Like people's shoes?"

She blushed.

"As I said, Lily, you live knee deep in delicious, creamy filling. Every minute." He flashed her a beatific grin and headed down the hall with the coffees.

*

The first sitting with the Wilson girls did *not* go well. Both girls picked unhappily at their scratchy, frilled dresses while Lily snapped digi-pics of them standing and sitting in various poses against the forest green background and draped maroon velveteen. Then she let them change into their own clothes for the headshots. Asking them to sit quietly while she sketched today was out of the question. Instead, she took them to the costume room.

Lindsay, nine years old, and Carmen, seven, stared in open-mouthed delight at the room full of exotic clothing of every size, shape, and color from all periods in history.

"Who wears these?" Lindsay asked reverently.

Lily smiled. "You will, during our next sitting. So get busy picking out your favorite. The children's sizes are back here, but if you absolutely fall in love with an adult costume, I can make adjustments. Your mom will be here soon, but not to worry. If you don't find something today, we'll take time later. And during our next session, we'll spend half the time in the white dresses—"

Both girl's groaned and rolled their eyes.

"-and half in the glam-goody of your choice. I always work up several rough oil sketches so people can get an idea of how a final painting will look. With a bit of luck, your parents will decide on the composition with you wearing what you love."

"Right," Lindsay grumped, "and how often does that happen?"

"Almost always." Lily dropped an arm around each shoulder and strolled them down aisles of sensational dresses done up in brocades, velvets and satins. "In a portrait, what you feel shows on your face and in the way you hold your body. I paint what I see in you. If you're sad and miserable that's what shows, big time. When you're happy and having fun, a painting glows with vitality and beauty."

"Why don't grownups get that?" Lindsay asked.

Lily bent to whisper, "They've forgotten about Twinkies."

Carmen nodded. "Yeah, the creamy filling."

*

Working late, Lily missed the e-trolley and decided to walk the two miles home. She didn't mind. Inhaling, she smelled yet another storm in the air and looked up to see that clouds had once again slunk in low and thick over the city. Cold rain by nightfall and, with the rain, a wind to strip the last glorious color from the trees. Another fall passing, she thought glumly, with yet another depressing, damp winter to follow.

She hated the way time spun its unyielding passage on and on and yet here she stayed, forever single, forever yearning and alone. Leaving the business district of downtown behind for the clustered neighborhoods, Lily walked down tree lined sidewalks littered with children's bicycles, wagons, a broken doll stroller. Maneuvering around a scooter, she looked up and saw a familiar sign swinging above her head.

Madame Bagasha's Magicke Shoppe! It was the same building, the same roof line, same sky lights but nesting now on a strange new corner beside a neighborhood grocery. Only half believing her eyes, Lily darted up the walk to grab the dragonhead door handle and step inside.

"Lily!" Nila called from behind the counter where she was unpacking a box of books. "I'm glad you got here, I was just about to close. Tell me, have you got a gaggle of guys following you everywhere yet?"

Lily glowered at her. "Very funny. Except I'm not laughing. Don't tell me you haven't seen my disaster in your magic crystals?"

Nila looked up, startled. "Disaster? The potion didn't make you sick, did it? Hasn't your guy found you yet?"

"Depends on how you define 'my guy.'"

Nila lost all interest in her unpacking. "I mean your perfect man, as you well know. Something went wrong?"

Lily told her story, choking against guilt as she finished with, "And then he just dribbled into nothing! I didn't mean to melt him, but I'm not sorry I did. How psychotic is that?"

"Holy saints!" Nila sat down on the stool, stunned. "I don't understand. The potion was simply a *glamour*. I've never heard of one reshaping reality before. Your own magic might have interfered . . . which means your power is more complex than I thought. Gosh, what fun you and I will have experimenting, huh?"

Lily gave the girl a seriously pained look. "Painting that man was delicious fun, but his aggression and the fact that he'd become a distortion of my pitiful emotional state was terrifying. I mean, I am lonely and desperate, but all I want is love and companionship."

"And sex," Nila waggled an eyebrow, "obviously."

"Yeah, well. So what went wrong? Will every person I paint now come to sudden life? Because at the moment I'm working on a portrait of two little girls who are adorable, but heaven forbid duplicates of them stepping off the canvas!"

Nila ducked down behind the counter and came up with a fat book so heavy she half dropped it on the countertop, raising a cloud of dust. Placing her palm flat on the thick, ancient tome, the young witch closed her eyes and whispered a string of unintelligible words. Carefully opening the cover she began flipping through pages, a frown of deep concentration on her face.

Lily took the opportunity to wander, the day's frustrations already dissipating in the hushed, aromatic quiet. She bent to sniff a pine-scented candle, toyed with an oddly shaped dream catcher. Her fingers, hungry to feel everything, splayed across a beautiful geode with its cavern heart sprouting tiny purple and rose colored crystals. At her touch the stone blazed to life with sudden, hot light. The crystals inside began to pulse.

Nila snapped upright. "Gods afire, you do have power! And that particular geode now belongs to you."

At Lily's mortified look, Nila elaborated. "You *woke* it, Lily. It'll never work for anyone else."

Gingerly, Lily hefted the good-sized rock to check the price and flinched.

"I'll give you a discount," Nila said. "I owe you, after all. I mean, one can't guarantee magic obviously, but the potion I gave you should have summoned potential lovers. That's all. I think Madame Bagasha would agree that your own magic, not insignificant as you've just proven, somehow changed the philter's properties."

"And what does your big book say?"

"Not much. Without knowing the true nature of your power, whether you are a Sensitive or an Elemental, I'm pretty much guessing. I do know I underestimated you, to put it mildly. And there will be hell to pay when Madame hears about it. But yesterday when you threw the dice, I didn't get a pre-cog vibe that you possessed magic strong enough to wake a geode. They don't come to life for just anyone. Oh, yeah, the Madame will be all over my ass." Nila's grin was more excited than worried. "Yours too, Lily Barnett. Because right now you have enough magic, and enough ignorance, to be very dangerous."

The young witch reached to take Lily's hands, then hesitated. "Before I touch you, I'd like you to try holding your magic inside, keep it from spouting outward. Can you do that?"

Lily nodded, thought of the energy she possessed when she painted, and focused that energy in towards her gut before she reached for Nila's grasp. No lights flared, no lamps flickered.

Nila let out a whoop. "Not just a powerful magic but a powerful will, as well. Good for you. I'm beginning to feel sorry for this perfect man of yours." She saw the pleasure fade from Lily's face and gave her hands a squeeze. "I'm teasing, of course. Whoever is lucky enough to fall in love with you will be strong enough to handle you, believe me."

"And why should I believe a girl who can turn me into a toad?"

"I would never!" Nila flashed her wicked grin. "Besides, a witch's most sacred creed is *do no harm*." She was suddenly serious. "Lily, it's imperative that you learn to understand and control your magic. Soon. Madame Bagasha and I will help. That's one reason we have the shop, I suss out new magic potentials so Madame Bagasha can teach them."

"Why couldn't I find you this morning?"

Nila shrugged. "I can't tell you how or why the shop shifts from place to place like it does. It's part of Madame Bagasha's magic and, like her, is eccentric. I do know that when the time is right, you will always find us."

"But that's not necessarily when I need you?"

"It isn't and I'm sorry. Like life, magic will force certain discoveries, confrontations, choices, and actions. Finding answers through adversity is part of the process. Now bring me that geode and I'll wrap it up for you to take home."

Holding the rock's hefty weight against her chest, Lily felt a rush of comfort knowing it would sit inside her apartment where she could see it, touch it, every day. As the witch wrapped it in newsprint, Lily asked, "What does one do with a magic geode, anyway?"

"See the hollow inside full of crystals? Very womblike, wouldn't you say?"

Lily snorted.

Nila hefted the geode to let light refract off each angular facet. "Pretty, too. Geodes are very personal. You'll need to experiment, see what this one does for you. Most people use them as a focusing tool, a way to center energies. I've heard they can trap negative magic as well but that seems a waste of beautiful space to me. Here, I'll throw in this booklet on the mystical properties of rocks and minerals to get you started. You wanted wizard lights, too, didn't you?"

Lily looked disconcerted. "I didn't say . . . but, yes. You are scary, despite that sweet-as-apple-pie face."

"Scary works for me. Much better than sweet ever has." Nila handed Lily her parcel and the receipt. "See you soon, Lil."

"You'd know that better than I."

Nila laughed. "Oh, one more thing, Lily. When dealing with magic it's wise to keep in mind the saying, 'There is lightning . . . and there is a lightning bug.'"

"And 'hindsight's worth a bird in the hand?'" Lily misquoted glibly.

Then the bell above the purple door jingled and Daniel Harris strolled into Madame Bagasha's Magicke Shoppe.

Chapter Eight

"It's you!" Daniel's face lit up at the sight of her. Lily's mouth gaped open. Gods, but he looked good with his easy, long-legged grace and big grin, and dark hair tumbling above eyes warm with laughter. A sudden heat filled her chest and her heart momentarily stopped beating.

"You're here . . ." she stammered and then, ridiculously, blushed. How much of their conversation had he heard? A quick glance at Nila's shrug and blank face only increased her embarrassment.

"So you found Madame Bagasha's shop," Daniel was saying. "Amazing, isn't it? I never pass up a chance to stop in."

For some reason Lily seemed rooted to the floor. "You . . . you believe in magic?"

Daniel looked around the astonishing room. "Why not? I am surprised to find you here, though."

"Oh," Lily waved a vague hand, "sometimes a girl needs a bit of this, a bit of that."

Nila laughed from where she leaned on the counter. "Nice to see your face again, Daniel. It's been ages. But I'm about to close up."

"Did those books I ordered come in?" he asked.

Nila turned to pull two faded, dog-eared books off a shelf behind her. As Daniel stepped around Lily, she unfroze with a gasp, spun toward the door, and was gone before he could blink.

*

"Way to go, handsome," Nila snipped. "You know what she's thinking, don't you? But, of course you do . . . better hurry up and catch her, she's embarrassed as hell."

"Why?" Daniel asked in surprise.

"So you don't know? Glad to see you respect some privacies."

"Give it a rest, Nila. You were, what, eight years old? And if I hadn't learned you were a witch, you'd never have studied with Gran. I did you a favor."

"So you keep telling me. Then it's you, is it?"

"Me, what?" Distracted, Daniel tossed two twenties on the counter and hurriedly crammed the books in his jacket pockets. "Keep the change, Nila-crocodila."

She stuck her tongue out at him as if she were still eight and he laughed. "Give my love to Noreen and Gilly when you see them, will you?" Then he, too, raced out the door.

Daniel saw Lily already two blocks ahead and moving fast. His resolve to keep away from her vanished as he sprinted to catch up. She still wore the dark schoolgirl stockings he'd spent the day fantasizing about. Watching her skirt twitch madly about her legs, Daniel had no trouble guessing her embarrassment was about more than getting caught in a magic shop.

"Hold up, would you?" he called. "I'm not invading your space, I promise—"

She stopped and spun on him. "How do you know about the shop? How do you know Nila?"

Daniel skidded to a halt, nearly toppling into her. "She's like a second cousin three times removed or something. Her mother and my mother were—"

"Do you have powers?" Lily demanded. "Are you a witch or warlock or whatever they call men who possess magic?"

"Labels mean nothing . . . Lily?" He snagged her arm before she could run from him again. "Are you crying? Jeez, Lil—" She surprised him by throwing herself at him. When his arms came around her, the unhappy blast of her confusion, and a panicked mortification he didn't understand, hit him.

Night closed down suddenly over them. Streetlights flickered to life, traffic sounds faded, window lamps cast golden spears across sidewalks and grass. They'd become one more muted shadow beneath trees shedding leaves like eiderdown. Daniel's heart raced over the fact that Lily was in his arms for the second time in one day. Soon she would push him away. But for this singular moment she belonged to him and he couldn't resist pressing a kiss to her feather soft hair.

Her arms tightened briefly then dropped away. He forced himself to step back, jamming his hands into his jacket pockets to keep from grabbing her again.

"Why won't you talk to me, Lil? I don't have a clue what's going on with you."

Face averted, she dragged the sleeve of her coat across her face smeared with tears. "I'm just, it's just . . . never mind. I can't tell you what's wrong, Daniel. Suffice it to say I've done something utterly stupid."

"It's not the first time." He smiled tenderly. "And won't be the last, thank the Gods."

"Yeah, well, thank them for nothing," she sniffed.

Throwing caution to the wind, he trapped her cold hand in his and turned them towards home. He could tell she wanted to unburden her heart, and knowing she'd hate herself afterwards, he amiably changed the subject. "No cumbersome portfolio tonight? No heavy sketchbooks?" And then, "Lily, where's your satchel? You never go anywhere without that thing."

But she didn't seem to hear him.

*

Lily had gone blank at the shivery feel of Daniel's fingers twining warm around hers. She imagined them trailing fire down the skin of her naked back.

"Lily? Your bag?"

Snapping back to earth, she blinked and glanced down at herself. "My what? Oh blast, I left it in the shop! And God knows when I'll get it back the way that place shifts in and out of existence." She turned around to go back but Daniel stopped her.

"The shop's long gone by now. And you needn't worry. My guess is you'll find the satchel waiting for you at home."

"Nila's that good?"

"Yes. Why? Did she work a charm or something for you, and it didn't work?"

Lily's cheeks, already pink from the wind, deepened to red. "That's none of your business." She tried to pull her hand from his.

Daniel held tight with an indifferent shrug. "I learned at my granny's knee how to respect a woman's magic. And her privacy."

A quick glance at his face told her nothing and Lily settled down to walk beside him. "I only learned yesterday that magic is real. So your grandmother is a witch, too?"

Daniel hesitated before answering. "Yes."

Lily knew from his abrupt tone she'd crossed into forbidden territory and was about to get told to mind her own business. But he surprised her. "My gran is a gifted healer, knows all about plants, herbs, the mystical properties of organics. She's also a Reader."

"A Reader?"

"A psychic. Someone with telepathic powers who senses other people's thoughts and emotions."

"Gods, please tell me she isn't Madame Bagasha!" Lily exclaimed.

"No." Daniel smiled. "The Madame is . . . well, Gran has an intimidating magic but Madame Bagasha is a force unparalleled. Madame has what we call Gypsy Magic. Mysterious, unique, versatile, and extremely powerful . . . like the shop. I imagine you'll meet her soon. Was it Nila who told you about magic? Did she tell you your magic shines in your paintings?"

"You knew?"

"Ever since I first saw your oil of Lake Michigan all those years ago."

Lily settled her hand deeper in his. "What's your magic, Daniel? None of my business?"

"Can't you guess?" He grinned down at her.

"Charm? Male magnetism?"

He laughed, let go of her hand to hook his arm around her shoulders and steer her through an intersection. Without thinking, Lily slipped her hand inside his jacket and pressed it flat against his back.

Under her palm, she felt his heart skip faster. "Daniel . . . "

He drew an uneven breath. "I feel it too, Lily."

"Then how do we *unfeel* it?" Her voice held a resentful panic. "Our friendship is sacred to me. It can't change. I can't lose you!"

"What makes you think you'd lose me?" His eyes looking down at her were darkly serious behind his glasses.

"Because people who start out friends and then become lovers . . . " Lily stopped, flustered, and finished angrily. "They always break up horribly. Words slicing hearts to bits like bloody road kill. Every precious thing they shared dies hatefully, forever."

He drew her closer against his side. "Don't you ever want to be more than friends?"

"No!"

"Then if I were to do this . . . " he bent and kissed her mouth, "our friendship would change?"

"Yes, damn you!" Lily pushed him away even though his lips were soft and warm. She swiped the back of her hand across her lips. "Stop playing around, I'm serious."

A light danced in his chocolate eyes. "You taste like . . . mmm, I'm not sure what. Let me have another go."

She held him off, trying not to laugh. "No, and stop acting so junior high."

"I was too shy to kiss girls in junior high."

"Really? Not even cousins? You know, goofing around?"

He looked shocked. "You kissed your cousins in junior high?"

"Not for real," Lily said huffily. "Growing up in the same house, my cousins were almost like brothers. They tormented me like brothers, too. Toby's a year older than me and he would get me in these head locks and lick my face all slobbery and gross. I hated it and knew he'd never stop until I got him back and good. So one day I just planted a big kiss on him. He totally freaked, then decided he liked that a lot better than the licking."

Daniel backed from her in mock disgust. "I'm not sure I can be friends with someone who kisses her cousin. That's just plain creepy."

Laughing, Lily gave him a playful slug. "It happened maybe twice before he discovered making out with Marta Brown was much more fun. I understand she was quite the expert."

"And you weren't?"

"Not then." She slanted him a look. "I'm way better now after practicing on guys not related to me."

"How many guys?"

"Like I kiss and tell." She flashed him a flirty grin and let him pull her back under his arm again. Her hand found its way back inside his jacket.

*

Daniel's blood heated. The press of her fingers between his shoulder blades sent a shivering sweetness through his veins. He could Read her excitement. She was aware, and a little afraid, of her effect on him . . . and the heady, playful game she played, but couldn't seem to stop. Something else sang in her blood, he realized suddenly, a thing of magic, feral and out of control. If he kissed her again, he would taste it, know it.

Instead, he forced a nonchalance. "So, what'd you buy at Madame Bagasha's shop?"

"What did you buy?" Lily countered, still brazen and still half afraid.

"Books," Daniel answered noncommittally. He needed to stay the gentleman here, not force her hand. His words to Gradyn earlier that evening rang hollow in his ears. He did owe Lily the respect and restraint she'd asked for. Yet here, walking side by side beneath trees closed in and concealing, her every glance, her provocative scent, even her touch begged him to take her.

A strained silence grew between them before Lily spoke in a nervous rush, "I'm sorry, Daniel. How nosy of me. I bought strings of wizard lights and a beautiful geode with purple crystals. Nila said that since I touched it, the geode wouldn't work for anyone else."

Daniel stopped in his tracks to stare at her. "You *woke* a geode? Good God, Lily! Only very strong Elemental magic can do that. Magic as in powerful, highly trained witches. This is . . . well, highly unusual, actually. What else can you do?"

"I don't know. I guess I have more power than Nila suspected since my own magic messed with a potion she—" Lily bit off her words and color flooded her cheeks again.

Daniel laughed in sudden understanding. Grabbing her face between his hands, he kissed her a second time, this time deliberate and slow. He knew now what raced hot in Lily's veins. A love philter! Gods on high, why she thought she needed one blew his mind. Lily had beauty, wit, talent, and passion . . . and was already loved beyond reason. If she only knew! A thought sliced through the giddy haze in his mind. Oh, he could so tweak this potion thing to his advantage, pretend it filled him with an uncontrollable desire for her. And maybe if she thought the potion was responsible for his attentions, she'd find him less emotionally threatening . . .

He let his hands slide around her neck and into her hair, plucking free the clip to release the thick curls down her back. "Did it ever cross your mind, Lily, that maybe I can't help kissing you? That you've enchanted me, and I'm now completely under your power?"

Lily's eyes flew wide and her face paled to a ghastly white. She broke away from him.

"I'm teasing, Lil—" He reached for her again.

But she was gone, bolting down the street and calling over her shoulder, "I'm so sorry, Daniel. It'll wear off soon, I know it will!"

Cursing, he saw her dart down a dark alley and raced to cut

her off before she reached the locked sanctuary of her apartment. Ordinarily, Lily was quick to see through his teasing, sticking around long enough to give him back a bit of his own medicine and with interest. Jeez, how stupid could he get? The moment he'd seen her tonight in Madame Bagasha's shop, so chummy with Nila, he should have guessed she'd asked the little witch for some idiotic magic that would . . . what, have every random male on the street sniffing after her? The very idea chilled him to the bone.

Why was she so bloody naïve? How did she not know that her delicate little body and big, china blue eyes were enough to have men slobbering all over her? Christ, he wanted his mark on her now! She was his, damn it. He'd stood back long enough, respecting her autonomy, waiting for her to come to him.

Now she roamed the night streets with Gods knew what magically enhanced pheromone wafting behind her, enticing every lecherous beast she passed. Nila was a gifted witch; a charm from her would be strong indeed. If Lily, too, had power . . . Daniel shuddered to think of what could happen. Taking the Lennox stairs two at a time, he reached her door and pounded hard enough to rattle the chimes she'd fixed overhead.

*

"Lily, open up! We should talk about this. I'm not under any spell . . . you didn't do anything to me, I swear! Lily?"

But she didn't answer and pressing his ear to the door, Daniel heard only the quiet hum of her refrigerator.

"Shit!" He unlocked his own door, stormed inside to kick it shut behind him. Which didn't satisfy his temper in the slightest. Where was she? The corner deli? No, she knew he'd look for her there first. Grabbing a beer from the fridge, Daniel popped the cap with a savage twist and downed half in one gulp. Where was her favorite place, her solace when he wasn't available? A sudden grin split his face. He found a bottle of red wine in the cupboard, snatched two more beers from the fridge.

Trying to jam a corkscrew into his coat pocket, he found it already bulging. The books. Tugging them free, he glanced at the titles. One said *The Science of Empathic Awareness: a Magical Approach*. The other, smaller and newer, was titled simply *Emotional Courage*. Daniel's mouth twitched at the irony as he pulled them from his pockets and jammed them into the nearest drawer. Too bad he wasn't a speed reader, he could use whatever advice the second book offered immediately. Speed Reader . . . he snorted at the pun, plucked a wrought iron key off a hook and with the wine bottle tucked under his arm, left the apartment.

Chapter Nine

Lily sat curled in a sun-bleached wicker chair at the darkest end of the rooftop solarium. A chilly draft blew across her legs. Shivering, and not just from the cold, she tucked up her knees under the baggy coat. She was being hunted and knew it, but would run no further. Staring through the clear panels of the long, narrow greenhouse Lily could see, silhouetted against the city lights, the Lennox's half dozen wind generators rising a monstrous twenty feet above the highest trees.

The perpetual hum of their rotating blades made a sound like a quiet lullaby. Lily did not find the song soothing tonight with the dark sky choking on clouds. On nights like this she missed the farm country of Ohio and the clear milky streak of stars, the air full of scents; dried hay, rain after a storm, the smell of freshly turned earth. The solarium smelled of rich loamy earth tonight, too. Daniel's aunt Lorraine must have potted plants in here today while the weak autumn sun heated the glass house to tolerable warmth.

The solarium was Lily's favorite thing about the Lennox Apartments, next to Daniel. A few weeks after she'd moved in, he'd brought her up to the roof. Seeing her starry-eyed enchantment, he had offered her a key. She'd already settled contentedly into her corner apartment by then, had met and liked most of the other tenants. But hefting that ancient, cast-iron key in her hand, she knew she'd finally found home.

Lily didn't remember her real home. In fact, she had few memories of her parents at all. Bullied at her new home at her aunt and uncle's farm and barely tolerated at school, she grew up impatient for the day her oldest brother Vernon would graduate from college and come for her. Except he never did. He moved to San Francisco, became an architect, married, and started his own family.

Lily once again felt the agony of loss and abandonment and withdrew even further inside her eleven-year-old brain. She'd seen Vernon once in all the years since her parents' deaths. He showed up for her high school graduation, young family in tow, shook her hand like a stranger, and left again. Occasionally Lily received checks from him, which confused and annoyed her. She deposited the money in what she called The Superfluous account and never touched it.

When her other brother Kent finished graduate school and got a job at an engineering firm in New Chicago, the first thing he did was take her in. The two spent three contented years living together while Lily attended art school. Kent traveled a lot, which worked for Lily, who enjoyed being alone to study and paint. Then Kent fell in love and Lily knew it was time to move out on her own. For years, she roomed with various artist and musician friends before finally saving money enough to afford an apartment of her own.

Curling deeper in the wicker chair, Lily closed her eyes and plucked the scents of individual plants from the air, a pungent oregano nearby and closer, a tangy lemon basil. She wished she could slow the thunderous pound of her heart and relax in this quiet, aromatic jungle. But her lips burned with Daniel's kiss, and she liked it. A lot . . .

Not many buildings in the city had rooftop solariums anymore; the cost was prohibitive. They'd become popular in the last century, glass-enclosed buildings filled with trees and flowering bushes, birds, planting benches, and beautifully tiled mosaic floors. When Daniel's uncle died and his aunt asked him to manage the Lennox for her, he spent months restoring the lofty greenhouse. Lorraine, devastated by her husband's death, needed a place of solace and peace. Never one for gardening while her husband lived, she took to it with an avid appreciation. Now she practically lived up here, especially during the winter, thinning, planting, grafting, and generally dirtying hands she no longer took to weekly manicures.

Tonight the solarium, still warm from the day, wrapped Lily close but did not comfort. She knew Daniel would find her here soon. She was locked out of her apartment, her key in the errant satchel, of course. At least in here she didn't feel the biting north wind. When she first arrived tonight after grabbing the emergency key from behind its rotting brick, she'd wandered around the flat rooftop, following the flagstone paths laid out between long, wooden troughs of dirt where, in summer, she grew vegetables.

The solarium belonged to Lorraine, but the rooftop garden was hers. And Daniel's. It was Lily who nurtured the tubs of junipers, miniature pines, and cinquefoil that created sheltered alcoves for the benches scavenged from second hand shops. Her hands worked the tidy vegetable beds and cultivated the large urns overflowing with scented flowers, now withered and gone to seed. It was time to spend a Sunday up here culling dead plants and turning the soil before it hardened. She'd get Daniel to help her haul the planters into the little gazebo where the perennial trees and bushes hibernated for the winter.

Fingering her dead tomato plants, Lily wondered how she could charitably explain to Daniel that his attraction for her was the result of a love potion. She'd sound like a witless fool . . . again. Not to mention cruel and manipulative, trying to trick someone into feeling emotions that weren't real. Would he forgive her this latest stupidity spawned of loneliness? She had considered hiding in the gazebo but refused to cower like a timid mouse waiting for a fox. Because Daniel was her friend, the very best kind of friend. And the best part of him had always accepted her, the good along with the bad.

She'd only wanted him to see her as a woman, a capable adult for once . . .

At the far end of the solarium a grow lamp emitted an orange glow casting warm shadows over the sensitive orchids and other exotics basking under the protective hood. Lily drew another long breath and strained her ears for the sound of Daniel's footsteps. Would he come to her angry? Daniel never held onto his anger, it always faded as quickly as it flared. She loved him for that. Growing up strange, Lily had been an easy target for people's resentment. She'd learned to use it herself with a lightning viciousness she despised.

Or would he come with teasing eyes that would tighten her stomach into knots of sexual hunger? As friends, she and Daniel had spent hundreds of evenings here on the roof together, sharing a beer in summer at the end of a sweltering day, drinking wine over impromptu dinners or a game of chess, building planters in the spring.

In the fall they cleared away dead leaves and plants, bagging them to drop from the roof, leaning out like children to wager on whether the bag would burst or not when it hit the ground. Talking, sharing, laughing . . . always laughing. Often Lorraine joined them. Sometimes the Forman family and the awkward newlyweds, Ruby and Brian, came up for a barbecue. These few were the only tenants who treasured this unique sanctuary where the stifling noises and hectic pace of city life faded to insignificance.

Oh, why did Daniel have to ruin it all by kissing her? And now rising inside her like a horrific monster from the deep was this freaky, run-amok power that made a painting come to life! Magic . . . the exhilarating, inspired energy she always so unconsciously and joyously put into her work had suddenly transformed into a frightening, alien thing. Magic, Nila had warned, volatile and dangerous unless she learned where it came from and how to control it. What inside her created supernatural power? And why had it sprung to sudden life now? Lily pressed her face against her knees trying to quiet the questions hammering at her brain.

The shriek of a door opening made her jump, and Daniel stepped down into the light. She watched him pause to gently brush an orchid, leaning to sniff the delicate scent. Straightening, he saw her down the length of the greenhouse. For a moment he just looked at her, then held up the bottle of wine in a gesture of truce.

"Wine or beer?" he asked in a neutral tone. She couldn't tell his mood and her pulse beat faster in her throat.

He wove his way between benches of ripening tomatoes, begonias and mint to set the bottles on a nearby worktable before flopping down in the chair beside her. Lily pointed at the wine, which he uncorked.

"I don't need a glass." She snatched the bottle and tipped a mouthful down her throat. Her eyes on his were defiant and wary. "I'm primed for a night of oblivious debauchery."

Daniel raised a quizzical eyebrow and twisting the cap off a beer, clinked it to her bottle. "Then here's to a night of dissipation. And other utterly stupid things—"

"You always do this, Daniel, pick up a conversation where we left off. Even if it's days later. I'm not keen on continuing this one."

"How can I turn a blind eye on you, Nila, and-let me guess-a love potion?"

"So what? I need a lecture from you since now I attract men like dogs to a training whistle? I'll just say it. You are not responsible for destroying what was a perfect friendship."

"I should hope not," he responded. "And let me just say that I've wanted to kiss you since the day you knocked on my door asking for an apartment." His gaze was confrontational.

Lily sat forward. "Then the potion isn't affecting you?"

"Nope."

"Good." Lily took another swig of wine. "So forget the kiss and stay friends?"

He hooked an ankle around her chair to drag it closer to his. "I don't happen to think kissing ruins a friendship. And I'm pretty sure someone who snogs her cousin hasn't the right to judge—"

"Like you've never humiliated yourself."

He grinned, "I kissed you, didn't I? It was all right but might have been more inspiring if you'd participated."

She laughed, gave his chair a kick. "You're wacked."

They sat in silence for a while, Daniel sipping his beer and plucking at the label while Lily slogged back wine like it was flavored water. His face, caught in the mellow light of the grow lamp, was a captivating blend of mauve and indigo shadows. She wished she could paint him just this way, all softened angles and sweet curves . . .

"So, Lil. Tell me what happened in your apartment last night?"

"Last night?" She frowned. "This day has been endless, I don't remember last night."

"You cleaned up a hell of a lot of paint."

She sent him an apologetic glance louder than words that said she wished she could tell him everything.

Draining his beer, Daniel set the bottle on the floor and reached over to grab hold of her legs and pull them up on his lap. Her eyes went drowsy as he slipped off her shoes and began to rub his thumbs over the arches of her feet. Discovering her toes cold to the touch, he tucked them inside his shirt against his warm belly.

"Can you remember the last time you ate, Lily? Because you're knocking that wine back pretty fast on what I'm guessing is an empty stomach."

"Have you forgotten I'm headed for drunk? And I think I had lunch. Maybe."

"Will you stay put if I run to the deli for sandwiches?"

"Will you get me a Reuben?"

He frowned. "You only eat a Reuben when you're depressed."

She dug her toes into his stomach so hard he flinched. "It doesn't take a psychic to see I'm depressed, Daniel. Just like it doesn't take a genius to figure out you inherited your grandmother's gift. You're a Reader too, aren't you? I've seen how you carefully and oh-so-casually keep your distance from people."

Anger flitted across his face and was gone. "I don't *casually* do anything. And you aren't one to talk about keeping your distance."

She leaned forward, outraged. "How can you justify never

sharing something this big with me? A telepath . . . Christ, Daniel, you must know all there is to know about me."

"I don't snoop—"

"Or maybe our friendship is about keeping you safe?" she sneered. "I mean, who better to hide behind than a friend whose thoughts and emotions flit about like soap bubbles? And being a woman," she smiled and skimmed her heel up the inside of his thigh, "I can offer much more in the way of friendship than Gradyn Spencer can."

Brows thunderous, he flung her feet off his lap. "Yeah, but you won't. You're afraid to offer anything that's real, Lily."

"What's that supposed to mean?" Her eyes shot hostile sparks at him.

Daniel leaned back in his chair. "That our friendship has always been defined in your terms, not mine. And don't think I won't kiss you again to up the stakes, Lily."

"Well," she pretended a yawn. "I'd rather be asleep than kiss you."

In one quick move, Daniel's had his hands on her waist, lifting her out of the chair and onto the bench. Fire blazed in his eyes. "Is that so?"

Fire in her belly, she glared up at him. "Absolutely."

His mouth hit hers with lusty, bruising force, and she rose to meet him. Their arms tangled around each other. Lily buried her hands in his hair, pasted her body against him, soft breasts to solid chest, belly to belly. Her legs slid around his waist to lock him close. She knew he'd wanted this, had goaded her into it, but the moment his mouth touched hers all anger melted into steaming flame.

Sweet Jesus, she wanted this, too . . . this fusing of lips, deep, eager kisses sliding into devouring, open-mouthed hunger. He tasted of beer and an exhilarating, raw power kept carefully contained. She arched closer, needy sighs escaping her throat. His fingers cupped her chin, stroked her cheek while his hot mouth pressed wet kisses on her throat. Breath ragged, Lily felt sanity shred under the fierce exchange of caresses. Tugging his shirt tails free, she ran her hands up the skin of his back, felt his muscles shudder beneath her palms. His hands, frenzied now, poured over her hips to curve under her bottom and lift her roughly, precisely, against him. And still he kissed her, tortured her with nips of his teeth and flicks of his tongue until she felt herself dissolve in a mindless delirium that excluded breathing, thinking, everything but a fevered need for him inside her.

Lily knew the moment his careful control slipped. His fingers cradled the back of her neck, flesh to flesh, and she felt a sudden, exploding awareness of his every thought as if she swam inside his blood. She sensed his power straining to break free, felt his elation, his ready passion wrapped up in sweet longing and a loneliness as penetrating as her own. She half sobbed his name and pressed her mouth to the unsteady throb of his pulse. And tasted, like brandy, the velvety dark of his magic.

*

Daniel knew he should slow down and couldn't. To have her like this, her skin blazing under his hands, her body begging. His heart swelled to bursting with an unimaginable joy. Her fingers plucked away his glasses, smoothed the line of his brow, the hard bone of his cheek before settling tender and trembling at the back of his neck. Her every touch fired his nerves with the desperate wanting of her. And so he took, locking his mouth hard on hers until their teeth clashed then backing away to tease and bite, tempting, torturing. Gods afire . . . the taste of her soared through his veins like golden wine and innocent sins.

He was shaking. His fingers tore open the buttons of her coat, then her blouse until at last he held her small and perfect breast in his palm. His other hand slipped up under her skirt, found the naked warmth where her thigh-high stocking ended and soft flesh began. She groaned at the bold stroke of his thumb over her pulsing femoral artery and thrust closer. His fingers edged inside her panties. She froze, pushed away from him with a gasping cry. They stared at each other in shock.

Panting for breath, she whispered, "You want this instead of a friendship? Be sure, Daniel. Please be sure. Before we go too far. Can you promise me that this . . . this desire is real? That what we feel has nothing to do with the potion?"

He lifted his hands, tremulous and reluctant, off her body. "I swear it's not the potion, Lily. I've wanted you this way since the day we met." His grin was unsteady. "That's what passion is. And love."

"Love?" Her eyes widened, a deep and vulnerable blue.

"God, yes, Lily. How can you not know I love you?"

"Like a friend. Like I love you."

"Right," he laughed bitterly and stepped away from her.

"Daniel, please . . . I can't deny I want to strip you naked right here and do it in the dirt, but is sex worth losing our friendship?"

Pain flashed across his dark face. "Being with me would just be sex to you?"

"I don't know!" She slid off the table to snatch his hands in hers. "It's been, well, more than a year since I've had sex, and not even good sex . . . isn't it obvious I'm horny as hell? Aren't you? You haven't dated since last summer!" Panic showed in her eyes. "Daniel, how do you know we'll work?"

"I just know."

"And you're willing to risk what we already have?"

He moved in to quiet her quivering body with gentle strokes of his hands. "I don't see it as a risk, Lil. I know you love me, you kiss me like you're on fire, for God's sake. Is it lustful? Yeah, so what? I'm not afraid to want you in bed, not just my life." He stopped her protest with a finger pressed to her lips. "Will you at least think about it? About an 'us'?"

"How can I think? All I want is your hands on me, your mouth on me." She reached for the wine bottle and took a long, gasping drink. "Damn you, Daniel."

He grinned then, a wicked quirk of his lips. "We could not think, get really drunk, and just have monkey sex."

"Then what? What if I'm the lousiest lay you've ever had?"

He laughed. "I already know that's impossible. Gods and Saints, Lily, I practically tore your clothes off." He flicked at her opened blouse, which she snatched hastily closed. "Let me love you, Lil. We need each other, haven't you figured that out yet? And not just as friends it seems. So take me for a test drive, see how my chassis hums."

Lily laughingly slapped away his hand edging towards her breast. "I think it's my chassis that hums. Your piston fires."

"Let's hope so." He swooped in for a long kiss. "Okay, we'll play it cool. Take it slow. I promise. Now, as much as I'm dying to shag you 'til dawn's early light, I need food."

"But I'm not nearly drunk yet!"

"There's time." He smiled down at her face cupped between his hands. "We've got time, Lily. But I'm telling you right now, our 'friendship' has run its course."

Chapter Ten

The next morning Lily woke to a silky tickle on her cheek. She smiled, eyes closed, and breathed in humid air, the rich scent of growing plants. Her groggy brain wondered how she could still be in the solarium when she lay cocooned in her warm bed. The tickle became a glide over her throat, and her eyes snapped open. She sat up to discover the hanging ivy plant had, overnight, overgrown her room, and now twined in loving tendrils around her body!

Through her bedroom door Lily could see fat philodendron leaves, three times their normal size, spreading thick and lush across the ceiling of her apartment. Plucking free of the vines wrapping around her, she eased out of bed and down the hall. Gods and Saints, she'd woken up to domestic plants on steroids!

Even as she watched, strands of andreanum and cordatum tangled around lamps and easels, computer deck, and couch, swarming the room like the thickets around Sleeping Beauty's castle. Lily tugged them clear in distaste. Well, it took no great leap of imagination to see that this sudden green house explosion came from magic. Her own damned magic! Somehow her lovely houseplants were feeding off her powers as if she'd offered up bloody fingers like the clerk in *Little Shop of Horrors*!

She gulped down half a cup of scalding coffee and got to work, hacking and tearing the run-amok greenery away from every window to let daylight back into her home. Then she pruned the stems back from the lamps, overhead lights and ceiling, pausing once to wonder if perhaps they would grow like this at Christmas so she could deck them with bulbs and tinsel. And mistletoe . . .

She'd hauled a ladder up from the basement and was cutting free the ceiling when she heard a tinny voice near her ear. "*Half a league, half a league, half a league onward!"*

On the string of lights dangling amongst the leaves, a pink flamingo grinned at her.

Lily's jaw dropped, and so did the shears, and she hugged the ladder in sudden, disconcerted vertigo.

Another voice spoke, *"Shall I compare thee to a summer's day?"*

Christ's Apostles, the plastic flamingos were quoting poetry! Shakespeare and Tennyson, no less.

Lily closed her eyes, rested her forehead against the ladder and drew a long breath. How she wished she'd never seen Madame Bagasha's shop, never felt that incredible sense of rightness there! She wished Nila was a girl she hadn't met, and the potion a thing she'd never guzzled. What in the hell was she to do about this latest insane magical hiccup? If Daniel heard the flamingos' blather or the McCready sisters came to investigate-

"Take thy beak from out my heart, and take thy form from off my door! Quothe the Raven, 'Nevermore.'" A flamingo hanging eye to eye with her winked. Edgar Allen Poe? Ye Gods!

"Shut up!" Lily shouted. "Just stop. I'm a blink away from the nuthouse already. You guys can't do this to me, okay? It's my magic, damn it! So you, hungry plants, stop growing like you're on replacement hormones. And you, babbling flamingos, stop spouting like someone crowned you poet laureates. Please!"

All the flamingos along the string giggled and bounced, and not quietly either. In the end, to drown them out, she fired up classical music on her comp-deck. When she left for work, the flamingos were arguing over whether this sonata was Beethoven or that symphony was Schubert.

And so, going slowly mad with ravenous plants she cut back daily and plastic flamingos who never ran out of poetic ditties, Lily lived through three desolate, Daniel-less days before she realized he was avoiding her, too. She seemed to see him everywhere, blurred glimpses of his face as he rounded a corner blocks away or through the window of a coffee shop when she sped by on the e-bus.

Walking home from work one night, she caught him crossing to the other side of the street when he saw her coming. Granted, his truck stood parked there, but still he barely waved. She pretended a careless nonchalance, acted busily absorbed in her paintings for Gradyn Spencer's grand opening less than two weeks away. Pretended too, to forget the way Daniel's kisses made her feel both cherished and possessed. How, held close against his body, she'd felt his lonely need . . . as he'd felt hers. What was left in her world that rivaled his generous mouth, his sensitive touch? Oil and canvas? Gods afire . . . she missed him with a grief that at times dropped her shaking to her knees.

She'd always lived in the abstract; floating among the textures, patterns, and colors she found so inspiring. Now filled with new and undeniably disturbing emotions, Lily felt helpless, in thrall, like a rabbit cornered by a coyote. She possessed neither the skill nor experience to navigate back to accustomed ground.

Her life made no sense without Daniel's steadfast presence. He'd said their friendship had run its course, but he'd also said there was time. He just hadn't specified how much time. Damn it, he knew her, knew she didn't do well with either/or ultimatums . . . and that's all he'd left her!

Every day Lily found a new *Lost and Found* cartoon Ellen left lying about like housekeeping tips; sitting beside the coffee machine, on top her drawing table, taped to her work stool. It seemed these days G.I.L. was picking on the techno-nerd character. In one strip, the guy wrote an email to his grandmother in unintelligible geek-speak and she answered back in Hungarian. In another he was online gaming and missed a date with his dream girl, unaware she'd blown off her date with him because she was his anonymous on-line opponent. And a third cartoon showed him going to job interviews wearing a tie that said "Byte me."

Lily marched into Ellen's office waving the strips in her hand.

"So I'm clueless, is that what you're trying to tell me? Because I'm already acutely aware of that fact."

Ellen looked shocked. "I wasn't suggesting anything, Lil. The cartoons are a hoot, I want to hear you laugh again."

At home Lily pared her houseplants and quoted poetry along with the flamingos while she carried her geode everywhere, tucked to her chest like a football, waiting for the impossible moment when the purple crystals would flare to magic life again. The rock sat on her worktable while she painted, nested beside her pillow where she tossed in twitchy sleep.

When she bothered to cook a hasty meal she rarely ate, the geode resided inside the goldfish bowl where Miss Elizabeth and Mr. Darcy dipped to kiss it again and again. But despite her ministering attentions, the geode remained mute and unresponsive.

On Monday night, she dashed to her life drawing class where she hoped to disappear into sketching what was real by making it her own. Arriving late, she found a chair and moved it closer to the model, groaning when she saw that, once again, he was male. And nude. So be it, she sighed in resignation.

Half afraid a complete body sketch might jump to life out of her sketchbook, she focused on drawing only the model's hands in different positions, the angle of his arm meeting the shoulder, or a foot curving into an ankle. Usually Lily fell easily into a meditative state where transforming with pencil what her mind's eye envisioned came as naturally as breathing. Not tonight.

Tonight she felt wound tight as a hair trigger, waiting . . . waiting for the articulated body parts to animate themselves like zombie limbs in a B horror flick! Long before the session ended, she'd slapped her sketchbook closed and splurged on a taxi cab ride home. That night she dreamed of headless torsos walking the streets and woke screaming, clutching the geode to her chest like a talisman.

The idea that an incomprehensible power she couldn't control lived like a freakish thing inside of her became a kind of suspended panic in her mind. She painted like a mad fiend, slapping tumultuous emotions onto every canvas along with the paint. Her loneliness consumed her. She hid in her apartment, ignored voice mail, refused to check vid-mail and generally side-stepped all obligations, including a meeting with a new client Ellen had specifically asked her to attend. This particular client could generate a lot of business for Faces in Time.

The next day Ellen dragged Lily into her office and yelled at her. Gradyn Spencer, usually so patient, left daily messages asking about the paintings she'd agreed to do for his upcoming show. She never called him back.

Her only light during those dark days came from Lindsay and Carmen Wilson. She adored the two girls and their bubbly conversation during the portrait sittings. They had collaborated, odd for siblings, and chosen complimentary costumes of the same historical period. Both were determined their portrait in costume would be the one their parents chose . . . and not the one of them in what they called the "baby doll" dresses.

Lily admired them for taking such personal pride in their portrait, pride that tripled after they saw themselves dressed like princesses in the preliminary photos. The three of them became "bosom" friends (Lindsay was reading *Anne of Green Gables*) and spent their sittings laughing and sharing stories.

Both girls turned into eager artists themselves after realizing if they stayed still and kept composed during a sitting, they could finish early and spend the rest of the time painting with Lily until their mom or dad came for them. Ellen got a kick out of glancing into the studio and seeing the three straight backs, side by side like stepping stones, in front of their easels, brush and palette in hand, intent on their work.

Lily took a *What Guys Want In Their Woman* survey in Ellen's latest *Cosmo* magazine and discovered guys did *not* want their women blond, petite, energetic (except in bed), or creative (except in bed). She snorted a bitter laugh. It seemed all she had going for her these days was a love potion working on her more than any guy in her vicinity!

And so the madness closed in. On the fourth Daniel-less day, Lily forgot her key. She knocked tentatively on his door and wondered if she'd forgotten it on purpose just to see his face. She knocked again, louder. He wasn't home, wasn't waiting in his apartment pining for her.

"I'm such a moron," Lily muttered, slumping to sit in a corner of the hall near her door. After ten restless minutes, she pulled a white charcoal pencil from her satchel and began drawing on the wall, very lightly so she could rub it out when she heard him on the stairs. A quaint village wandered off the end of her pencil, squat, tiny huts that meandered around knotholes and cracks in the wood. The chalk sighed almost plaintively against the grainy surface and she hummed nonsensical tunes under her breath.

So absorbed was she, she missed hearing the voices on the stairs until they were just below her. Daniel was finally home. And he wasn't alone! Lily rubbed her sleeve fiercely over the chalk. It smeared but didn't disappear. Just as he and his companion reached the turn, Lily spun around to plant her back against the wall, hiding her crime like a naughty child. Daniel, arms full of boxes, looked up, saw her sitting there, and grinned. "Forgot your key, did you?"

But Lily's gaze was on the woman beside him, a tall, pretty brunette . . . everything the *Cosmo* survey said men most wanted in a woman.

"Lil, meet Megan. Megan, this is Lily Barnett."

The brunette's face lit up. "The oil painter! Oh, wow, it is so great to meet you. I love your work!"

"Thank you." Lily flashed her an over bright smile.

"Megan works at Spencer's Gallery," Daniel explained. "I was just there and—"

"I need a key," Lily broke in rudely.

Daniel looked abashed. Lily looked at the floor, the railing, everywhere but at the lovely Megan while he unlocked the door to his apartment. Setting the boxes inside, he reached for a bag Megan had over her shoulder. "Thanks for helping me carry this stuff," he said with a smile.

"Anytime." The girl smiled back. "See you next Tuesday?"

"Yeah, Tuesday," Daniel responded absently, eyeing Lily who still sat on the floor, her back pressed to the wall. He grabbed her spare key, unlocked the door to her apartment, and stood waiting.

"Thanks." Lily refused to move.

Frowning, Daniel slid to a sit beside her, studying her ragged face. "More merciless days, Lily?"

"No. I'm fine. Doing the grown up thing, you know. Surviving in real time and space. Feet firmly planted."

"I wish you'd stop all this nonsense."

"You're talking to me like I'm a child, Daniel. Please go away."

"Not 'til you say you miss me."

Lily couldn't help a grin. "I miss you, okay? Megan seems nice."

He shrugged. "I guess. What's going on, Lil? Why are you still sitting here? Why were you rude to her?"

"Was I rude? Sorry. I just don't happen to like tall, pretty brunettes these days."

"Are you doing a portrait of a particularly nasty one at the moment?"

"No. Actually I'm—" She half turned, eager to tell him about the Wilson girls.

Daniel saw the chalk marks and tugged her away from the wall. "Damn it, Lily, not again!" But he was laughing as his gaze roamed the sketch of the tiny village. "It's very Tolkienish. I like it. But not on my wall."

Half splayed across his warm chest, Lily breathed in his windblown scent. His hair brushed her face . . . Gods, she had missed him. Pressing her face to his neck, she felt his arms close around her. With her weight full against him, he toppled onto his back. Then his hands were cupping her head, and he dragged her mouth to meet his. Excitement leaped in her veins as he pulled the length of her body tight, answering the fever of her lips with a frenzy of his own. Time stood still as they fed eagerly on one another.

Finally Lily broke away, gasping. Daniel seemed to realize they lay in the middle of the third floor hallway and started to laugh. Lily, blushing fiercely, rolled off of him.

"Maybe we should take this inside." He kept his arm around her waist.

"No." Lily moved away, reaching for her pile of books. "I can't. It's too—"

"Out of control?" Daniel danced his fingers up her spine. "What's wrong with that?"

She stood quickly and backed against the wall. "This plays like a fantasy, Daniel."

"Doesn't everything with you?" He stood too, raking frustrated hands through his hair. "If you're looking for excuses, Lily, let's make a list—"

"I want this, us, to be real. To feel true and right and perfect. And it doesn't. It feels . . . desperate."

Daniel lifted his hands in defense. "What you're saying is I'm rushing you. Except this time you went after me, Lily."

"I'm sorry—"

"I'm not. And you aren't, either. Be honest. I think we're both grown up enough to handle that." He grinned suddenly. "At the very least."

"Okay." She gave him a long look. "You said the potion isn't affecting you. But it is affecting me. I think that's why I'm so, well, rabid when I get near you."

"Hear me complaining?" Daniel took a step closer but stopped when she held up a hand.

"It's the magic, Daniel. It frightens me. I don't understand it, and I don't want its influence, to be explicitly honest. I'd like to know my heart is behind my feelings and not some ambiguous power."

Daniel's eyes turned serious. He leaned a shoulder against the wall. "I can understand that, Lily. More than you know. So you'll get no pressure from me, okay? You can relax, I promise to behave."

"Until?"

"Until you're ready to tear my clothes off. Then all deals are null and void." He shoved his hands in the pockets of his jeans to reassure her but a wicked gleam lit his eyes.

"So, friends?" Lily asked tentatively.

"Friends . . . with prospects," Daniel agreed with a dopey smile. Changing the subject, he bobbed his head at her chalk village. "Just so we're clear, I understand compulsions, Lil. At least yours are innocent."

She scowled. "Think it's time for therapy again?"

"We both know you're incurable. Thank the Gods."

"I'll get soap and water right away," Lily promised, "before the Forman twins see this."

Daniel gave a mock shudder and they stood looking at each other for a moment before Lily escaped inside her apartment. Collapsing against the door, she heard the voice in her head urging her to forget her fears, forget everything but the feel of his hands on her, the thrust of his body molding to hers. He wants you, the voice said. And you want him, you've always wanted him . . .

But she wasn't ready for him. And she didn't completely believe he was as immune to the potion as he claimed. When a touch from her had him fumbling at her clothes in the middle of the hall . . .

And now there was this Megan person. They'd acted very chummy on the stairs, she and Daniel. Maybe he would lose patience with Lily, a midget blond without a sexy bone in her body, and go for a slinky brunette. Why wouldn't he? She'd behaved like a silly child, drawing on the wall, for bloody sake!

Lily filled a bucket with soapy water, grabbed a handful of rags, and scrubbed every mark off the wall with a ruthless energy she didn't quite understand. She finished as the sobs she'd been holding at bay bubbled over.

*

Snatching the roof key, she slipped across the hall and up the narrow stairs. Pushing through the heavy door to the rooftop, the night air hit her like a bucket of ice water in the face. Which she needed. With arms hugged about her against the cold, she stalked out into garden, cursing herself for the chaos she'd created in her once simple life. Guzzling a magic potion, painting a man that popped to life, and losing herself in wild moments of hot and heavy grappling with Daniel? Was she insane?

Tuesday. The brunette had said she'd see him Tuesday. Daniel had a date with a Megan? Lily sat down hard on a wooden bench. Hell and damnation! Their friendship having run its course, he'd moved on to someone who would love him back. Glancing into the solarium, Lily stared at the table where she and Daniel had kissed like lovers. It only took a small mental nudge for her to imagine their bodies tangled naked together, arms and legs entwined . . . she turned away with a groan.

God, how she wished she could love him back, braving the unfathomable depths of that complex personality he never showed anybody. She longed to meet his magic. She ached to disappear inside the storm of emotions she'd so briefly touched while locked in his embrace that night. She wanted to swim inside his blood again, wanted him inside her, knowing and loving the whole of her. Not because she was lonely or horny or desperate but because she wanted more than just nibbles of the damn Twinkie. Didn't she?

Lily had never given much thought to loving; in fact, she had trouble wrapping her head around the idea of giving such consuming energy to a person instead of a project. Was love like the breath-catching wonder she felt at her first glimpse of green every spring? Or the feel of cool lake water sliding over her body on a hot day? Could love be as simple as sitting in a hall laughing over a full grown person unable to resist scribbling on the wall? Lily hoped it was all these things and more. She wanted to know love like she knew the nuances of a Prussian blue or a viridian green.

Shivering with cold, she lifted her face and felt the first drops of icy rain. Who was she kidding, anyway? She might slap herself into the resemblance of a woman who could love Daniel. Might even paint herself as someone he deserved. But she couldn't escape the facts. Lily Barnett rarely stayed long in the real world. And she could side-step a relationship as nimbly as a figure skater. Which, if she was honest with herself, made the idea of being in love with Daniel simply another avenue of escape. So here she stood under the softly whirring wind generators, sleet soaking her clothes until her teeth chattered, and choosing a life without courage, without risk, commitment or love. A damn life without the creamy filling . . .

Chapter Eleven

Confused and, admittedly, sexually frustrated, Lily took the bit in her teeth and began a new portrait, this one of a man fully clothed who looked nothing like Daniel. She wanted to kill loneliness before it killed her. If Daniel was choosing another's company, then so would she. But the entire time she prepped the canvas, designed her composition, and roughed out the figure in chalk, she could hear her list of excuses to him squabbling like squirrels inside her head; *I'm not ready, I don't know how to love someone,* and her personal favorite, *Daniel, you deserve better.*

Four hours later she jumped back and watched her second perfect man, as classically beautiful as a GQ model, tear free of the canvas. He looked urbane, sophisticated, impossibly handsome, and Lily watched an astonished disgust twist his features when he looked around her untidy apartment. Shit, just the kind of guy she didn't need . . . a Madison Avenue snob!

Lily named him Rodney because of his aquiline features, his cultured hauteur and, after he'd watched BBC television for ten minutes, his posh British accent. But of course, he had no culture or sophistication, being only a mix of magic and oil paint. Within half an hour Lily was dying to melt him. What little personality she'd somehow worked into him was arrogant and full of disdain.

After she poured him a glass of the expensive Napoleon brandy Ellen had given her for Christmas, he snatched the bottle and began slugging it back like orange juice. When she refused to play strip poker with him, he refused to play Scrabble with her. He finished off the brandy bottle while strolling her apartment making offensive statements about her "plain" furniture and "childish" wizard lights before moving on to his assessment of her "unspectacular" face, her "stubby" legs and her "barely there" breasts.

When the booze ran out, he tore through her cupboards looking for more, cursing and throwing pots and pans on the floor. Not finding any, he swept out of her apartment to shout down the hallway, "Is there a chap in this mausoleum possessing a bottle of Napoleon?"

Mortified, Lily grabbed his arms and tried to physically drag him back inside. Her effort was ludicrous. He outweighed her by more than a hundred pounds and she ended up being swung about like a rat latched onto a terrier. The McCready sisters popped their heads out their door to ask in astonishment if Lily was all right and should they call the police.

"No, thanks." Lily levered her feet under her and strong-armed Rodney another step towards her doorway. "I'll get rid of him, believe me!"

Mr. Newton in apartment 30 across the hall thrust two beers out his door and told Rodney to shut his "bloody yap." Lily nearly had him inside her apartment when Daniel burst through his door snarling like a mad dog. Seeing Lily clutching Rodney's arm, his eyes turned to cold steel. "What the hell—"

"He's going, Daniel. Right now." She elbowed Rodney sharply in the gut. "I'm sorry you were bothered. Ruby downstairs must have called you. Tell her—"

Rodney twisted his arm from Lily's grip and in the process struck the side of her head, knocking her to the floor. Stepping over her, he shoved his face close to Daniel's and said, "Do you perchance have any brandy, old man?"

Daniel's fist smashed the perfect, super-model nose. Lily scrambled unsteadily to her feet. With a strength born of utter humiliation, she tackled Rodney backwards into her apartment and kicked the door shut behind them.

*

Through the door, Daniel heard a stream of male curses that cut off abruptly.

The sudden silence left him cold and he threw himself at her door. "Lily, are you all right? Damn it, let me in!"

"I'm okay," he heard her whisper from just inside. "He . . . he's passed out. Sorry for the trouble, I'll make it up to everyone, I promise. This . . . this should never have happened and I'm sorry."

But Daniel's blood was up. His fist smacked the wooden wall. "Open this door right now or I swear I'll break it down!"

The moment her door cracked open, Daniel snaked his arm through and dragged her into the hallway. His body, hard and unyielding, pinned her to the wall. Furious, Lily aimed a fist at his head, which he brushed aside with a disdainful sneer. Then his fingers were on her face, probing her hairline for bruises.

At his touch the fight went out of her. Her eyes closed, her knees buckled. Satisfied she was unhurt, he grabbed her by the back of the neck and brutally kissed her. She tasted his fury and reveled in it, parting her lips to him. His breath quickened, his teeth grazed her face, nipped at her jaw forcing her chin back. She cried out at the wet flick of his tongue under her ear and clung helpless to his neck. His body drove against her, his thigh thrust between her legs and he felt her experiencing the sudden rise of orgasm. Then he went still.

Both were shaking, fighting for breath. Lily forced her eyes open to see his face, dark with anger, inches from hers. "Daniel . . . " she breathed, part apology, part surrender, and he brusquely pushed himself off her.

"Christ, Lil, you could always pick them. Who is he, a client? A victim of your filthy love potion?"

"No! Yes! He's an ass—" She shoved Daniel further away, embarrassed and too mad to speak coherently. "I . . . I called the guy a cab. He is so gone, okay?"

Rage still burned in Daniel's veins, and a jealousy beyond reason.

He knew he could have her in his bed and stripped naked in less than five minutes. She was willing, the air between them practically sizzled. "What are you playing at, Lily? He isn't even your type!"

Lily barked a self-deprecating laugh. "He was a mistake, like so many others. Can't we just leave it at that?"

"I don't like him."

"Well, that makes two of us!" she snapped, still breathing hard.

Daniel looked away from her and quickly back. "I'm sorry if I . . . if I hurt you just now." His palm hit the wall. "But damn it, Lily, you make me crazy!"

He took another deliberate step back, drew an unsteady breath. He knew if he reached for her she'd be wrapped around him like a straightjacket.

Sensing that, his anger died. "Let him wait for the cab with me, Lil, please. I don't want him near you."

"No." She sidled towards her door, face determined. "Rodney was my mistake, I'll handle him."

"Am I a mistake, too? Is that why you picked him up?"

"I didn't pick him up!" Lily cried. "It's just, you stirred me all up inside, Daniel. Made me feel things for you I never knew I . . . and then you acted like I didn't exist!"

He stared at her, incredulous. "You said you wanted time! I backed off, gave you space."

Lily slumped against the wall. "Yeah, well, I lied. You know what that's like, you with your bloody secrets. God, you heat me up with a touch! And I'm all the way there with you. Then you're gone. How do you do it? It's like you can dissociate at will. Is there a twelve-step program for that, and can I join? Because I'm all sorts of foolish. But Daniel, who the hell are you?"

Daniel wanted to tell her exactly who he was . . . and couldn't.

Lily brushed tears from her face with an impatient hand. "Just tell me how you can say you love me and hide from me at the same time?"

His voice held a weary defeat. "What I am frightens people, Lily." He reached out and circled her wrist with his fingers. "Holding you like this, I could open my senses and know why, where, and for what reason you picked up that bastard, Rodney."

He let her go, abruptly. "I had to learn as a child to block people out or go crazy. I'm an empath, Lil. I can Read emotional vibrations as easily as people read road signs. That's a psychic's curse. When I met you . . . God, Lily, you were so wondrously unconscious of yourself, of others, of subjective need. It was refreshing. I could relax with you, something I've never been able to do with anyone."

His smile was wry. "How could I not want you? I'm empathic but I'm also a man. Try not to hold either against me." He took a step towards her and stopped himself, but Lily already had her arms clasped around his neck and her lips pressed to his. The kiss was long and full of promise, and when she left him to slip back into her apartment, she took more than just his breath with her.

The following morning, Daniel tacked a note to his apartment door:

Gone fishing. Brian in #26 is my Go-to-Guy. Be back on Sunday.

Then he skipped town for three days, sliding into a slot at the week long G-Fest comi-con in Greater Milwaukee. He wasn't afraid to admit he'd bailed for reasons of self-preservation. His iron will had failed, his self-control was disintegrating. He could sense Lily everywhere, smell her in his sleep, Read her coming from three blocks away.

The battle she waged inside herself tore at him through the walls of their apartments. He understood better than anyone her instinctive fear of magic. And her need to accept who she was turning into without sacrificing the person she already was. Best thing for both of them was to take himself out of the picture for awhile.

The episode over Rodney had left a dirty stain on Daniel's soul.

Not only had he treated Lily with brutish cruelty, the violence of his jealousy had shaken his belief in the kind of man he thought himself to be. He'd never lost his head like that before.

Then there was Rodney himself . . . something about the man chilled him to the bone.

*

Lily saw Daniel's note as she headed to work that morning and almost cried. Her sense of relief left her weak-kneed. She knew why he'd gone. Knew the entire mess was her fault, Rodney's existence, her lack of faith, her fear of losing Daniel, of losing herself. But now she had the breathing space she so desperately needed. A sudden thought had her clutching her chest. What if he'd gone off with that Megan girl?

Daniel would never play her false, Lily knew that. Yet she could not keep her feet from walking past Spencer's Gallery on her way to work. And there stood Megan, pretty as a calendar girl, personably flirting while guiding a customer around the showroom. Lily realized how ridiculous she'd behaved in coming and turned to make a hasty exit when the brunette saw her and waved. Inviting the customer to look around, Megan excused herself.

Trying for a nonchalant expression, Lily asked, "Is Gradyn around?"

"No." Megan's critical glance took in Lily's oversized jacket, khakis worn at the knees, and the stained satchel. "I can leave him a message, though. I know he's been anxious to hear from you."

"Has he? Been anxious, I mean?" Lily asked.

"Well, anxious is probably too strong a word, I admit. How's Daniel?"

Lily forced a pleasant smile. "Good. He's out of town for a few days."

"Are you and he . . . "

"We're very close, yes." Lily ground her teeth.

Megan leaned closer, oozing confidence with a challenge in her eye. "Gradyn's gorgeous, no question. But Daniel . . . I mean, Gods! Those eyes of his. If he didn't hide them behind glasses, women would drop drooling at his feet. Yeah, I'd let Daniel tickle me naked anytime."

Lily's mouth fell open, anger reddening her cheeks. Spinning on her heel, she left the gallery before a hailstorm of offensive responses escaped her. She didn't know whether to curse on Daniel's behalf, laugh at the woman's vanity, or feel sorry for her lack of professionalism! After walking a few blocks, Lily cooled off. By the time she reached the studio, she'd become captivated by the strangely opalescent fog shrouding the city. Her encounter with Megan had faded in the mist.

*

Lily waited in Ellen's office, curled in a luxuriant chair reserved for clients. Her boss was late, a thing unheard of. Lily realized she hadn't a clue what was happening in Ellen's life these days. Did her friend still date the futures speculator with the thinning hair who, Ellen claimed with a decided sparkle in her eye, made love more inventively than anyone she'd ever been with?

Drowning in her own problems, Lily hadn't thought to ask. Glancing around the small office, Lily saw new color swatches tacked to the wall. The room had no windows, so Ellen was constantly redecorating to keep the environment novel and stimulating. The shelves housed framed snapshots of her many relatives and a few interesting books for browsing. A small table held magazines about art, naturally, and international finance, business, celebrity gossip. Whatever a client might want to flip through if, heaven forbid, they were forced to wait on an appointment with a forgetful artist. Several easels stood folded in the corner next to a large artist's cabinet with long, flat drawers designed to hold photographs and drawings.

Lily loved Ellen's desk. It was huge, square, almost mannish except for the vase of freshly scented and very feminine flowers. Lily could move the vase, a lamp, the calendar blotter and have the entire surface to stretch full length on for a nap and, in fact, was contemplating doing just that when Ellen breezed in wearing her faux sable coat and a bright scarf and carrying two mugs of coffee that filled Lily with humble gratitude.

"I'm sorry I've been so self-absorbed lately," Lily blurted out, gulping coffee so fast it burned her mouth.

"Fear does that to people. Turns them inward," Ellen said with an astute lift of an eyebrow. "I've told you that, oh, at least ten dozen times."

"I'm obviously incapable of getting the point. But I do truly hate flitting around the edge of people's lives."

"Daniel's?"

A worry line appeared between Lily's eyes. "Always. But yours, too, Ellen. And I'm sorry."

For several minutes the two women bantered back and forth about the many lascivious reasons Ellen was late this particular morning until finally Lily spilled it.

"I painted another guy. This one was a total ass. I couldn't melt him fast enough. I'm a monster, Ellen, sick, twisted—"

"Psychotic?" But Ellen's teasing couldn't conceal her worry.

"Without question," Lily groaned. "Daniel went ballistic—"

"Daniel was there?"

"As apartment manager handling an obnoxious creep when tenants are threatening to call the cops? Yeah."

Ellen longed for details but hearing the fragility in Lily's voice, didn't press.

Grateful, Lily drew her portfolio onto her lap. "I brought the Wilson sketches and a couple workups in oil. Are you ready to see them? The girls aren't scheduled for another sitting until their parents decide."

Ellen took her time shuffling through the posed drawings, raising an occasional eyebrow or expressing a "mmmm" or "nice" before she reached for the small oils. An immediate smile blossomed on her face. "Oh, Lil, this one of them in costume is fantastic."

"Isn't it? The girls adore those dresses."

"And themselves dressed up. It shows."

"Do you think you could tweak the parents in that direction?" When Ellen looked up, Lily rushed on. "I'd never ask, except—"

"The poor darlings do look ridiculous in these frothy white things," Ellen agreed.

"And Lindsay and Carmen know it. They told me they'd rather give up ice cream for a year than have that hanging in their living room."

"I'll see what I can do." Ellen turned to the cabinet and laid Lily's sketches in one labeled "Wilson" before propping the two canvases on the floor.

With a beleaguered sigh, Lily laid her head down on Ellen's desk. "Since I don't have a sitting today can I go home?"

"Most definitely. But not yet. I want to know what you've done with my friend. You don't even look like the Lily we all know and love. Your socks match, for Christ's sake, your hair is brushed, you've been wearing color-coordinated outfits. It's freaking me out! Where are the pencils and breadsticks stuck in your hair, the paint all over your face, the gushing, bouncy fizz? And honestly, the dark circles under your eyes aren't doing you any favors. Blowing off meetings because you get lost in a painting or the park or even a magic shop is one thing. Consciously destroying the amazing woman you are is quite another. I won't stand for it, Lil. None of us want you certified the perfect woman, for pity's sake! Daniel doesn't, that's for sure. If he did don't you think he could have his pick of the beauties swarming around the rich, successful, and oh so pretty Gradyn Spencer? Use your brain, girl. We who know you best want the old Lily back."

"But why?" Lily demanded, astonished.

"Because we love you, stupid. And because you're amazing, and in your right mind you know it. You've just gone a bit love-buggy. Trying to remodel yourself into a person you think fits some *loveable* profile goes so far beyond insane you ought to be committed."

Lily slumped back in the chair. "What if I can't? Ellen, I'm afraid I'll never figure out how love works well enough for it to take."

"Take?"

"Grip, fit, become part of me like painting is."

Ellen rolled her eyes. "You seriously do need therapy. Lily, love is a force! It takes without permission, it fits whether you want it to or not. It sticks, it clings, it locks on like a sucking parasite. And it's already hooked you, sweet cheeks."

"Wouldn't I feel happy if it had?"

Exasperated, Ellen said, "Your painting phantom men and putting your heart into them instead of doing what you really want isn't making you happy, either. So snap out of it. For everyone's sake!"

*

Later that morning Lily was in the basement of the Lennox folding the last of her laundry when she heard the old elevator screech to a stop in the dark recesses behind her. Glancing back, she saw Ruby from the second floor push back the accordion gates. A year ago Ruby, barely eighteen, had gotten pregnant. She and her high school sweetheart, Brian, married and moved into the Lennox. Four months later, Ruby miscarried and fell to pieces. Her young husband couldn't console her and had gone to Daniel, who then sent Lily to Ruby. During the terrible days and nights that followed, the two women became as close as sisters.

Standing side by side at the work counter, Ruby sorted laundry and asked about the guy in the apartment the night before. "Brian and I were scared witless for you, Lil. It's why I called Daniel. I'm sorry, but Brian was about to liberate you with a baseball bat. Did Daniel totally freak?"

"Yes. And rightly so. I did something really stupid, the guy was a jerk and is gone forever, thank the Gods." Lily bumped an affectionate shoulder against the girl. "And thank Brian for me."

"So what's up with Daniel? He's not his usual, laid-back self lately."

Lily thought about fawning Ruby off with some half truth but the kinship they'd developed demanded honesty. She hadn't been honest with Daniel, to her shame, and it was still costing her. "It's a long, sordid story I'll tell you sometime when I can laugh about it. The short version is I'm losing Daniel. Our friendship means the world to me. But he kissed me and changed everything. Now there's this intense heat between us and—"

Ruby whooped. "It's about bloody time!"

"What do you mean?"

"What do *you* mean?" The girl countered. "You two are crazy about each other. It's obvious to everyone in the building. Lonnie has a pool going, for God's sake!"

"A pool?"

"On when you and Daniel will finally get down and dirty."

Lily stared. "Are you serious?"

Ruby laughed and wrapped her friend in an ecstatic hug. "Bedsprings will sing and soon, Lily! Can't fight the magic."

A shiver ran down Lily's spine. Little did Ruby know . . . and Lily wasn't about to enlighten her. She hefted her basket to head upstairs and hesitated. "Tell me, Ruby, is it possible to come on too strong with a man?"

"With Daniel?" The girl's eyes widened. "Hell, no! It would take a pipe wrench upside his head before he'd see beyond this pile of brick and mortar."

Lily laughed, a grateful sound of release. What Ruby implied wasn't true. Daniel didn't miss a trick with those sharp, perceptive eyes. Still, there was no mistaking his interest in her. The air practically burst into flame when they were together. But she didn't feel ready to spill that juicy tidbit. Even to Ruby.

She spent the next three days locked in her apartment painting for fun, flaking out over digi-movies, jacking in to music, and losing herself inside a sappy historical romance. As she began to relax, the voracious plants ceased their rampant growth and the jabbering flamingos quieted to only occasional murmurs. The days felt like a reprieve. She slept like a baby, ate three meals a day, and went back to work refreshed, rejuvenated, and reactivated.

Chapter Twelve

Ellen opened her desk drawer, pulled out a newspaper strip, and thrust it at Lily. "Another *Lost and Found* for you."

Groaning, Lily took the comic strip and recognized the character Ellen had affectionately nicknamed "Lesser Lil" because of the sometimes uncanny and always humorous resemblance. In the first frame of the comic, Lesser Lil and the guy she dated were in a video store, arguing over a movie to rent. He held up one, and she stood scowling, arms folded; then she held up one and he struck the same pose. Unable to agree, they left the store empty-handed. In the last frame they were in bed, obviously post coital, dreamily sharing a thought balloon that read, "I love a movie that ends well."

"And the point is?" Lily growled.

"You know the point, Lil. Stop messing around and jump Daniel's bones."

Lily stood up, jamming her portfolio angrily under her arm. "It's not that simple. I'm not ready."

Ellen released a frustrated sigh. "Just ask him to Spencer's grand opening. It won't be a real date. More like skidding towards a real date."

Lily often went to art shows with Daniel. They knew many of the same people, and it was never a big deal. Until now. Until this earthquake of emotions turned her love-stupid.

"It's next Tuesday." Ellen winked playfully. "And even I got an invite from the illustrious Gradyn Spencer. Must be 'cause I'm pals with a featured artist."

Lily rolled her eyes. "Yeah, right. I'm one of five featured artists."

"Have I seen these paintings?"

"No. No one has." Her brows furrowed and she dropped back to sit in the chair. "The paintings . . . Ellen, I'm nervous about them. They're, well, *strange* doesn't begin to describe them. They are unlike anything I've ever painted."

"I'm intrigued."

"What if Daniel doesn't like them? I couldn't bear it."

Ellen leaned across the desk to squeeze Lily's hand. "Gradyn wouldn't accept any work that wasn't brilliant, Lil. Not to mention passing the rigors of your own obsessive perfection complex. Stop hiding behind excuses."

Lily chest felt tight and then words exploded. "My internal glue has gone tacky, Ellen! I'm slip-sliding all over the place. Daniel and I kissed. My God, we more than kissed! He's not . . . he isn't simply a friend anymore."

Ellen crossed her arms in satisfaction. "Like I said. A force. Are you in love with him?"

"I might be. And now I'm afraid he's picked up a Megan!" Lily exclaimed.

"A what?"

"This Megan person came home with him the other night. I'd locked myself out, again, and was waiting and there she stood, all beautiful and tall and . . . well, Megany."

Ellen laughed. "You're ridiculous."

"I'd gotten bored waiting and started drawing on the wall—"

"You didn't!"

"I did. And he caught me."

"Was he mad?"

"No, he laughed." Lily looked up. "I've never been in love before. I've cared for a lot of things, even people, but never have I felt anything like this fluttery mad passion . . . . it must be love, right? I mean, it's sort of like how I feel about color. I want to wrap around him, melt into him, know his essence." She drew a breath. "Does that sound corny?"

"Not from you, oddly enough." Ellen came around the desk and dropped a kiss onto Lily's head. "Ask him to the opening, for pity's sake. Because when push comes to shove, a Megan can't hold a candle to a Lily."

Lily spent the day locked in her studio at Faces in Time, refusing admittance to one and all so she could finish her third painting for Gradyn's show. She'd promised him four new pieces and still hadn't a clue what to paint next. Which was why she hadn't left him a message. He'd asked her to deliver the work by Sunday, at the latest. Five days to go and no inspiration. Odd for her, no ideas tumbling like lotto balls inside her head. The empty space was driving her mad!

Standing back, Lily cocked her head at the painting perched on the easel, a large abstract oil. She blinked, drew an unsteady breath. Moving to her worktable, she flipped through a pile of sketches until she found her first conceptual drawings. She'd strayed completely from the clean lines and healthy delight of her original idea. The mood on the canvas had entirely changed.

Instead of a bright playful interaction with light, the painting projected a formidable presence in the undercurrents of color. When had this happened? Her painting style was intuitive, yes, but she'd always been a very deliberate artist with a tendency to over-sketch in order to develop just the right emotional context for a composition.

This painting resonated a darkness completely alien to who she was! Where had that darkness come from? Lily sat down hard on the stool. Never in her life had she painted anything that so utterly frightened her. And that included the two men who'd stepped from her canvases!

Sure, style and technique did evolve, but for emotions so out of character to show up in a composition . . . was Ellen right? In attempting to change herself into a more responsible person had she corrupted her spirit? Lily turned her back on the easel and paced the room, refusing to look at the painting while trying to clear her mind and think.

The emotion in the painting was despairing, the colors foreboding and bleak. Not unfamiliar to her, these emotions, this colored atmosphere, but they'd never dominated her to the point she couldn't manage them while she painted. Damn it, she had more strength and skill than this. Being an artist was more than just what she did. Creating defined the essence of her being, her soul. She was a painter! Not some depressed, despondent mope. And certainly not demented . . .

At least not until recently. Lately, she'd been driving blind down unlighted streets. Always when she painted, Lily knew her head and heart worked as one. Now both seemed powered by raw, unruly emotion more than intellect. Why? Had the magical love potion changed her that much? Somehow she needed to rediscover trust in herself and find a way back to her heart.

Lily closed her eyes and dove inward to sort through her most intimate thoughts. More angry than afraid of these dark feelings, she shoved and prodded at long pondered questions, unresolved issues and deep-rooted insecurities until at her center she felt a release of pressure like the cracking open of an egg. Warmth filled her chest and spread like liquid gold through her limbs, a thread of power not dark at all, but airy and light. It left her gasping and opening her eyes; she saw her skin glowing as if every pore leaked phosphorescence.

And that's when she understood. Her magic had at last slipped its leash! Once it had lived quiescent and contained inside her, in ideas, in technique and paint. Now, inexplicably, it beat with her heart, surged through her veins and folded around her bones. Waves of energy as capricious as the wind raced through her. Spreading her arms, Lily fell to the floor and in laughing defeat, surrendered to her power.

Time passed, she floated . . . maybe. Or simply disappeared

inside the magic. When eventually the room spun back into focus and she could stand, Lily opened her eyes to a new world. Every sensation felt enhanced, the droplets of rain whipping against her window pane, the smell of linseed oil and wet canvas thick on her skin. All objects, every sense, throbbed with a multi-dimensional brilliance she'd never imagined existed.

She turned then and looked at the painting, watched each detail pop out at her. For the most part the composition was sound, an abstract landscape with planets swirling in nebulas of color . . . no, not quite planets but eggs. Stepping back, Lily saw how adding dabs of warm ochre could turn the eggs into pebbles on a river bottom. A more definite light source might create effervescent ripples across a surface no longer murky but fluid and living, like river water. Planets, eggs, pebbles . . . all this painting lacked was a source of hope, a sense of cosmic optimism.

And that meant more light. Did she have the artistic skill to change murky chaos into beaming brightness? Reaching up, Lily pulled a clean paintbrush from the nest of her hair and without hesitation, lost herself in gleaming oranges, warm yellows, hot titanium whites. Two hours later she stepped back and for a moment stood breathless. She'd done it! She didn't know how, but she'd transformed a disturbing, desolate painting into one that uplifted and inspired.

Exhaustion hit her then like an avalanche, brutal, fast, nearly toppling her off the stool. Lily realized she was starving for food. So weak she could barely lift the painting off the easel, she set it facing the wall to dry overnight. It took forever to clean her brushes and palette knives. All movement had become a sluggish crawl but at last she pulled on her wool jacket and cap. Somewhere she found the energy to walk to the bus stop and dropped onto the bench to wait.

*

A last streak of daylight broke through the clouds, slanting in stark, horizontal beams between the downtown skyscrapers rising in rows of crooked teeth. And then night fell like soft velvet over New Chicago. Traffic sounds became manic as people poured out of offices to head home. The e-bus finally arrived and Lily sank into an open seat, grateful and for once unbothered by the press of bodies and smells that usually drove her to walk the long miles home.

Altering the painting had drained her utterly, and though she'd managed to fix it, she knew the darkness she'd seen on the canvas had come from a place inside her. If she couldn't recognize what had precipitated it and then come to understand it, Lily knew all that she loved, her vision, her passion for color, her restless need to create, would slowly bleed away. Her essence could dissolve as easily as her painted men.

Resting her forehead against the smeared window, she closed her eyes, heard the drone of voices around her and as ever these days, thought of Daniel. How was he able, with his psychic sensitivities, to live in such a rabid press of humanity? She remembered the gentle circle of his fingers around her wrist and wondered why, if he was her best friend in the world, had she never recognized that his reserve masked such penetrating isolation.

A sudden thought struck her . . . he must know some of what she felt for him. He'd certainly made no secret of his feelings for her. And yet he'd kept a careful line drawn between them. Even with her throwing sexual heat at him like lightning bolts. Which meant he also knew of her confusion and fear . . . God and Saints! She'd been torturing him for weeks and didn't even know it! No wonder his temper frayed so easily of late.

Lily walked the last few blocks from the bus stop and paused on the sidewalk to look up at the Lennox building. Granite stones rising in old-fashioned grandeur shone a pearly lavender under the halogen street lights. Her breath caught at the sweeping beauty of the building's art deco curves, the colonnade porch, the embrasures, louvered balconies, and long windows. It had been awhile since she'd stopped long enough to truly look at her home and haven.

She saw the shadow of a man, indistinct under the spreading branches of the towering spruce tree at the corner of the building. He stepped forward under the light. It was . . . Rodney!

Lily ran for the protection of the porch, her heart exploding with fear. Her mind screamed that Rodney did not exist! She'd melted him, she had! Under the safety of the porch ablaze in lamp light, Lily glanced behind her. Rodney hadn't moved. Only his head had swiveled to watch her flight. Now he simply stared, face indistinct, body a murky blur in the shadows of the tree. When he didn't pursue her, Lily stopped, took two hesitant steps down the porch towards him.

"You aren't real!" Lily found voice to say. "Go away. Leave me alone."

Rodney stood mute. His eyes burned red and hungry, scary as hell. A darker shadow shifted beyond him and stepped forward, and Lily stumbled with a cry. Her first painted man stood at Rodney's shoulder, blurry and paper thin. Scrabbling back up the steps, Lily slammed through the front door. She didn't stop until she stood behind the new security door and flipped the dead bolt with fingers that quaked. Squinting through the glass she waited, skin crawling, for the two men to suddenly press themselves against the door like androids gone haywire.

Quite suddenly her legs gave out and she collapsed at the base of the stairs. Her satchel and sketchbook fell from hands gone numb. Only then did it hit her. She hadn't been seeing the real Daniel in cafés and e-bus windows this past week, but his look-alike! The first man she'd painted and accidentally dissolved. Hysterical laughter bubbled in her throat. Gods afire, she was being stalked by the ghosts of her own portraits!

*

A visceral fear swept through her, the kind of fear that screams *Run!* in your nightmares. She couldn't think, couldn't breathe. How was this possible, this animating of something never real in the first place? The answer rose from deep within her . . . magic. Here was the sinister side of her new-born powers, twin to the strange, alien darkness she'd seen today in her painting and now manifested in apparitions standing on the Lennox lawn.

Lily remembered queasily cleaning up every speck of the painted men's existence. Were they now reconstituted, made of paint once more, or had they somehow become flesh and blood? Cold to the bone, she clasped her arms about herself. She never took her eyes off the rectangle of window framing a lit portion of the front porch, the steps, and a small patch of brittle grass. But Rodney and the disturbing Daniel look-alike did not appear. Time passed, endless minutes that helped her mind stop skittering about like bugs on water, though her heart still pounded loud enough to wake the dead.

Above her head, Lily heard the sudden rattle of the elevator's accordion gate open and then close. Under her feet, the floorboards began vibrating to the hum of the ancient motor. This familiar sound, heard so often she thought of it as the Lennox breathing, reminded Lily that Daniel, the true Daniel was somewhere in this building. Here she would be safe, protected. Loved. And he understood magic, was in fact a creature of magic himself. Like her. The sudden acknowledgement made her half sick. Yes, Daniel could help her.

Except constraints now lay on their once-easy friendship She could no longer burst into his apartment and flop down on his couch to tell him in an exaggerated whine that always set him laughing how she'd tried to paint a perfect man and ended up getting stalked by their ghosts instead. No, there would be no talking this situation through over companionable wine until, slightly sloshed and giggling, they'd begin competing with ever more absurd stories of past stupidities.

Looking up, she watched the elevator descend inside its polished cage of brass, dropping from the third floor. Which meant it carried the McCready sisters. She stood up, still unsteady. Her hand went to her unkempt hair. Eleanor McCready, sharp eyed even behind the thick glasses, would notice her shell-shocked disarray and start probing. Lily looked about for her hair clip and unable to find it, twisted her curls into a tangled knot and tucked them down inside her collar.

She had the presence of mind to unbolt the security door before seating herself on the bottom step, flexing her hands to stop them shaking. The elevator cage dropped towards her. Inside, two pairs of sturdy shoes appeared followed by four thick legs in support hose. Yes, the McCready sisters, dressed in fur trimmed woolen coats long out of fashion. Lily pasted a smile on her stiff face. Ruth waved through the grate as the elevator settled to a noisy stop. Lily stood to fold back the outer gate as Ruth wrestled with the inner one.

"Oh, Lily, you look terribly pale. Are you all right?" Eleanor's glance was sharp, but she turned to take her more fragile sister's elbow and guide her from the lift. "We're off to dinner. There's no electricity upstairs at the moment. Daniel's cleaning the chandeliers in our hallway, took them completely apart, you know. So we're using that as an excuse to dine out."

"Meatloaf special at Tappy's." Ruth smiled.

"Want to join us?" Eleanor asked. "We'd love it, Lily. Haven't seen near enough of you lately."

Lily tucked her arm through Ruth's elbow. "Thanks so much, but no. I'm beat and I'm looking forward to a long soak in a hot bath."

Eleanor said. "Don't worry, he's near done. And the chandeliers do look lovely with the bronze all polished to a shine."

"The glass sparkles like little suns." Ruth's pixie smile broadened.

Eleanor took Lily's other arm. "You do look done in, child. Be a good girl and take the lift up, let Daniel make you some tea."

"He needs tea," Ruth leaned to whisper. "He only cleans chandeliers when he's specially upset."

"Then I'll fix him tea." Lily hugged their arms close. "You two look very dashing tonight, all dressed up." Lily escorted them out the front door, her eyes scanning the shadows for the skulking Rodney. And there he stood back under the big spruce again.

Eleanor followed her glance. "Why, isn't that your loud friend from the other night?"

"He's not my friend," Lily stifled a shudder and raised her voice to call, "and he's certainly not welcome here. Go home, Rodney."

Beyond Rodney she could see the faint outline of the second apparition and quickly hustled the two sisters into the waiting cab before he, too, stepped into light enough to be recognized. How in Mary's name would she ever explain a man who could be Daniel's twin?

"Have fun!" She waved them off, watching the taxi cab disappear before turning back to the two men. But they had gone, dissipating like mist. Lily felt an enormous relief and with it, an equal wave of exhaustion that left her lightheaded. Stumbling back inside, she gathered up her fallen portfolio and satchel and dragged her weary body up the stairs to Daniel.

Chapter Thirteen

Lily decided for tonight at least, Rodney and Look-Alike could kiss her ass. Because she was home. Her family lived here. Every person in this building would dash to her rescue if she needed them . . . except maybe Lonnie Ranchero, who would expect some carnal reward. Pausing on the last stair landing to dig for her keys, Lily glanced up and saw Daniel standing high atop a ladder on the floor above her. She felt a rush of tender gratitude so intense she had to grab hold of the railing. More of the ache in her chest eased. He hadn't heard her, didn't even seem aware of her.

Knowing this, Lily allowed herself to just look at him and glory in the strong, lithe line of him from ragged tennis shoes all the way up to the dark hair curling out from under an old Cubs baseball cap he wore backwards. His hands were full of the cumbersome light fixture, his mouth sprouted half a dozen screws. Behind his glasses, his bold brows frowned in concentration.

God, he was beautiful with his striking dark looks; his long, athletic body; and large, capable hands. She wondered what other delights she'd discover in him with her new magically enhanced vision. As if in answer, an effervescent power stirred deep within her. With no idea what else her magic could do, Lily called on the fizzing energy. For a flashing instant she saw Daniel's aura, radiant blues and silver that quivered with a tremendous power. Then her senses slammed hard against the barrier of his own magic. Hurt, even knowing he used the barrier to protect himself, Lily wanted to smash all her own power against him.

Instead, she let her breath out slowly and eased up the last turn of stairs. He still didn't see her, his hands busy among the tangle of wires dangling from the housing box set in the ceiling. Lily's gaze moved up the length of his legs in frayed, faded jeans. A tool belt rode low on his hips, baring the flat muscles of his belly and a faint line of dark hair disappearing into the waist of his jeans. Heat exploded in her veins, a flash of pure lust. How the hell did a tool belt make a man look so damn sexy?

At that moment, Daniel glanced down and saw her.

"Hey, Lil, you're home." He grinned around the mouthful of screws and hefted the fixture higher above his head. His T-shirt hiked up, exposing more naked skin, and suddenly Lily wanted her mouth on him, there, just below his belly button where a fading tan ended and tender, pale skin began.

Her knees buckled and she caught herself against the rail. Sketchbooks fell at her feet. Unable to look away, her gaze slid up over the arc of his ribs and across his chest following the perfect curve of pectoral muscle into bicep. The man on the ladder had ceased being Daniel and became instead a throbbing pulse in her throat and a hot ache between her legs.

"Lily?"

She blinked stupidly at him.

"You okay? Electricity's out in your kitchen, but I'm almost done." He eyed her uneasily and moved to climb down the ladder.

She jerked out of her trance. "Okay, yeah, electricity, right." Somehow she gathered up her things, found her key and stumbled up the remaining stairs. When the door to her apartment opened, she fell headlong inside.

Daniel leaned out from the ladder. "Are you all right?"

Her head peeped out her door, eyes wide, pupils dilated. "I'm fine, really."

A taut line appeared at the corner of Daniel's mouth. "Then I take it you saw him?"

"What? Who?"

"That asshole Rodney."

With a dizzying rush, the blood drained from her face. "So you saw him, too."

"How could I not? Did he touch you, Lily? Because I swear, if—"

"No, he just stared at me."

Struggling to cool his temper, Daniel climbed a step higher and resumed working. "The jerk's been lurking around all day. You told me he was gone."

"I thought he was. Gone forever, in fact," she shivered. "I'll get rid of him somehow, I promise."

"Try a restraining order," Daniel said caustically.

Lily glanced up, wishing she could pour out the entire story to him. Instead, she ducked back inside the apartment and closed the door.

*

Daniel willed himself still, but the anger wouldn't leave his body. Damn, but she tied him in knots! And he was bloody tired of it. This weird restraint between them lately seemed as unnatural as . . . as wool on a bluebird! He lived his days no longer content and easy but consumed by thoughts of her. And Christ's army, the very idea of her with that pig Rodney . . . he'd never felt such a violent jealousy in his life. Or such savage joy at the feel of her pinned under him against the wall the other night. And Lily, she'd raged at him, feared and fought him . . . and loved him all at the same time.

The door to her apartment jerked open. "I was wondering . . ." She leaned out, tried to meet his eyes and couldn't. "You know how I hate art openings. The one at Gradyn's new gallery is next Tuesday. Is there a possibility you might not mind awfully going with me?"

"No."

"Oh, okay then. Well, no problem." She started to close the door.

"I mean, I don't mind going with you."

"Oh, good." Her large, unsettled gaze flitted to his face and away. "That's good. Thank you."

Daniel plucked the screws from his mouth. "What's going on with you, Lily? You're all fluttery. No, don't duck back inside."

He stepped down the ladder and approached where she cowered behind her half closed door. His frown turned to astonishment. "Are you afraid of me?" Dragging off his baseball cap, Daniel ran a hand through his hair. "I behaved like an ass the other night, and I'm sorry but—"

"Of course I'm not afraid of you, Daniel," she scoffed.

"Then what's going on? I'll take care of Rodney if he's frightening you." Face grim, he stepped closer.

"No. Yeah, he scares me, but it's complicated. I have to handle him myself, and that's the long and short of it. Otherwise, I'm fine, really. I'm just . . . nervous."

"Nervous? Of me? You've asked me to openings before, what's the big deal—" His eyes widened. "Are you asking me out, Lily?"

He jumped back as she slammed the door in his face. "Yes!" he exulted under his breath and grinning like a wolf, bounded back up the ladder.

Lily's door burst open again. "Don't you already have a date with Megan on Tuesday?"

Daniel's face went blank. "Megan who?"

"The Megan you were with last week. She said she'd see you Tuesday."

"You mean the Megan who works at Spencer Gallery? I wasn't *not* going to the opening, Lily. It's your big night, and Gradyn's. And I kind of assumed you and I would go together. We usually do."

"We do." Lily nodded and disappeared inside. This time she left her door open and Daniel heard her shoes hit the wall as she kicked them off. "Do I have electricity yet?"

"Give me two minutes." Daniel gave the wire connectors a final twist, fit the fixture tight inside its housing and placed the screws before stepping down the ladder to the breaker panel and flipping the switch. Light beamed clean and sparkling from the chandelier and in Lily's kitchen, he heard the faucet filling a hollow tea kettle.

"Ruth says I'm to make you tea," she called.

"Then I'll be sure to thank her." He gave Lily's open door a bemused look as he folded the ladder. Gods and favors, but the girl was a mind-tweak. He never knew what to expect from her . . . even with his almighty psychic powers! Then Daniel heard the techo-punk band Tired Treads singing from her comp-deck about how there's "no new thing under the sun." His heart tumbled in his chest, and he wished she'd offer him more than tea.

Daniel came in moments later, minus the tool belt. He cast a quick glance at Lily's face and caught a delicate flush there, so slipped into his best friend role. Soon he had her relaxed and laughing. Right where he wanted her, for the time being. She looked exhausted and Daniel, unwilling to overstay his welcome, left after one cup.

"Thank you, Daniel," she stood when he did, "for not going off about Rodney again. I'm sorry if . . . well, he'll be gone as soon as I can arrange it. For good."

"I can arrange some very imaginative ways for him to disappear." He flashed a malicious grin.

She looked up at him with her laughing eyes a radiant blue and he wanted her in his arms and kissing him more than . . .

Daniel made a quick exit and spent the evening working off his sexual frustration by repairing a broken dryer in the basement.

*

So exhausted half an hour earlier she could hardly climb the stairs, Lily now felt her blood zinging with a serotonin high one only got from love, sex, and rock 'n roll. Not that she'd had the sex yet. But if merely being in Daniel's company had her skin humming harmonics and her nerves sizzling, what other inconceivable delights awaited her? Her body loosened as she put on sultry jazz and danced around the apartment, wolfing down celery sticks dipped in peanut butter.

Imagination firing on all cylinders, faith and love leaking from every pore in her body, Lily started the final painting for Gradyn Spencer's opening. Not a portrait . . . well, perhaps a kind of a self portrait but only obliquely so. She began slapping paint on the canvas without a preliminary sketch and with an uninhibited pleasure she'd never experienced before.

Colors blazed to life, hot yellows and fierce reds that intensified the soft, moody blues of a shadowy form almost supernaturally taking shape on the canvas. Fueled by passion, Lily worked into the wee hours. When at last she called Gradyn, she caught him groggy on the phone and only then realized it was five o'clock in the morning.

"I'm sorry," she stammered, "I just realized how early it is . . . it's just I haven't returned your calls and—"

"Lily, it's okay. I had to get up in another half hour anyway. Let me flip on my coffee." She heard him moving about, and then his voice was back in her ear. "So, I'm guessing you stayed up all night painting."

"Yes. I hope you like the pieces I've done and feel they're good enough. You're giving me such a break," she gushed, "and I'm sorry I didn't call you sooner."

"Stop apologizing, Lil." He yawned. "Artists are notorious procrastinators. The downside of genius, I imagine. You're more than forgiven. I assume you used fast drying oils?"

"I did, but the final varnish—"

"It can wait. Are they standard sized canvases? I can get them framed if you bring them in today."

"Thank you," Lily breathed. "Two of them are already framed. The one at Faces in Time isn't, but I'll bring it by this morning. The rest are here. I'll box them up. Should I get Daniel to drop them off at the gallery?"

"Are you two speaking to each other?"

"I . . . he . . . " Lily could heard Grady laughing.

"I'll call him, Lil, ask if he'll bring them down for you. I hear you're doing a kick-ass portrait of two girls. I should talk to Ellen Reid about doing a show of her portrait artists. Do you think she'd be interested?"

"I think she'd be interested. But Daniel says I'm all fluttery and not myself these days. So you should ask her."

Gradyn laughed.

"Oh, one last thing." Lily hesitated. "One of the paintings, it's called *Paradigm*, can you not sell it? You'll know why when you see it. Is that a problem?"

"Not really. I'll just slap an outrageous price on it and a tag that says *Sold*. That'll give buyers something to think about. And Lily, don't stop painting. I want Spencer's to carry your work exclusively. This is just the beginning. You understand that, don't you?"

"I'm beginning to," she said, hanging up with a shiver of excitement tangled around more than a little fear.

Chapter Fourteen

Daniel had new pages from *Graffic Blues* to colorize and worked all morning in his office. He hadn't slept much, tossing and turning over dreams of Lily being pursued by shadowy figures, Lily lost in a labyrinth, Lily lonely and afraid. Getting up for a snack around two a.m., he heard her singing faint, broken snatches of song and knew she was painting.

The walls between apartments in the Lennox were more soundproof than most new buildings but once upon a time Daniel and Lily's apartment had been one big suite. Remodeling in the late twentieth century had divided it into two apartments with only a thin wall between. When she'd first moved in, he'd felt uncomfortably voyeuristic. The wall of his office and her bedroom wall were the same.

Working late at night he could sometimes hear her singing in the bath, dashing about dressing, or the tired squeal of springs when she fell into bed. He found himself working more at night because she slept only a few feet from where he sat at his drawing table. As he grew to know her and discovered she was a peculiar cross between the proverbial ship lost at sea and the bull in a china shop, he felt more protective and less like a peeper.

He heard no sound from her apartment all morning, then just after noon sounds of abrupt bustling came vaguely through the wall, followed by the slam of her door and footsteps skipping down the stairs. Daniel had finished his pages by late afternoon and was ready for a break when he received the call from Gradyn Spencer and agreed to play delivery man.

Lily had left her apartment unlocked for him. The moment his hand touched the doorknob he felt the emotional maelstrom whipping like a tornado inside the room. Her magic. Christ, conjuring up this much supernatural power went far beyond the skills of simple alchemy! All his psychic barricades trembled. He knew if he entered her apartment with the air charged by this much expressively worked magic, the synapses in his brain would surely fry.

He'd heard of instances where extra-sensory overload permanently damaged a Reader's telepathic powers. The whirlwind behind Lily's door could irreparably damage him. It had happened before. But sweet Gods, he wanted her! With all her quixotic moods, her joyous pleasure in simple beauties, her expressive, yearning pain . . . and from beyond the door he could feel her need for him fill his heart and blood with an answering excitement.

Daniel closed his eyes, mentally spiraled down into the well of his own magic where he began constructing a shield he hoped would be strong enough to block so much unbridled, magical energy. Murmuring a protective spell, he drew a deep breath, turned the doorknob and stepped into Lily's apartment.

An aurora borealis shimmered in curtains of vivid color, dancing in the air as if alive inside the room. It painted the furniture, walls, lush plants, even the fishbowl all the shades of Lily's complex personality: vibrant purples, lush greens, brilliant blues . . . and refracted, amplified a hundred times, through the crystals pulsing like a beating heart inside the geode on her coffee table. Daniel stumbled against the psychic blast. A lifetime of defensive constructs crumbled into ruin. Holy Gods and Saints! She'd told him she wanted in . . . he could no more block her out now than he could stop breathing.

With elated surrender, he let down his barriers and opened himself fully to Lily's magnificent power. For a moment all he felt was her joy zinging along his nerves. Then his sensory awareness deepened and the full impact of her jubilant passion exploded into him like a shredding grenade. Pain, fierce as blinding light, seared the pathways to his brain.

He fell to his knees clutching his head, panting against a scream rising in his throat. The air filled with the scent of her hair, the taste of her skin. His synapses flash-burned to colorless ash and still her emotional storm pounded him, demanding, racing through every nerve. He fought to stay alert long enough to magically bind his shattering abilities to her fledgling magic, praying the innocence of her power would be enough to save him.

Time stood still. Shivering and barely conscious, Daniel lay curled on Lily's floor and heard deep inside his scoured mind his grandmother's words from long ago. "Empathic magic is the most unforgiving of powers. You will know boundless ecstasy, suffer unholy pain, and discover more than you want to know about the human heart. Such is a Reader's merciless gift."

Gran had offered him the protection of her own magic twice. Shortly after his seventh birthday he began sensing other people's emotions while tackling them in play or brushing against them at school. It terrified him, feeling sentiments as real as his own but not of his making. So he ran, began skipping school, avoiding friends.

His mother came from a family of witches, her magic was culinary. His father despised magic and refused to acknowledge it in any way. All his life Daniel had suffered his father's impatient anger; now he learned the man thought him a freakish, unnatural thing. Life grew unbearable, his home a waking nightmare of atmospheric sensation he could not understand or avoid. He started sleepwalking, and when his mother found him half dead in the backyard one frigid winter night, she called on her aunts, healers all, and her maternal grandmother.

Daniel moved in with Gran while he recovered from a pneumonia that almost killed him. Her house was soothing, a quiet place of airy light scented with herbs. She kept her own emotions shielded, something she would eventually teach him to do and he knew a child's peace once more, anxiety free and healthy. Birds of all species flew loose and free inside Gran's house. They had their perches, favorite haunts.

Daniel learned, like his Gran, to carry a rag everywhere for wiping up bird droppings. It was part of life with her, a matter of course, and well worth the little effort to feel a handful of contented sparrows nestling in his hair while he studied or a finch affectionately tweak his ear as it sat his shoulder while he bathed or brushed his teeth.

Daniel spent two months recovering. During that time Gran began his training. He learned spells of focus that enabled him to build the all important "constructs," those mental barriers that protect a Reader from *seeing* too deeply and feeling too much. He worked daily on the mundane disciplines of magic, calling fire, conjuring, scrying, as well as learning the basic elements of clairvoyance before he began studying magic more specific to his own case, spells of defense and protection that provided shielding and internal shelters. He even learned charms of self-healing. And all the while he wore a fluorite crystal talisman Gran made to protect him from emotional overload.

By the time he moved home again, he'd learned to survive in public. He went back to school and developed thicker skin after scuffles over the fact that he wore a necklace like a girl. By the time he was ten, he no longer needed the crystal charm.

Then puberty struck and Gran saved his life a second time. Full power came to him suddenly at thirteen, bringing with it hyper-sensitivities that lit his body like a torch. Not only was his body in hormonal upheaval, but every day he felt the onslaught of everyone else's confusion and pubescent turmoil. And he no longer needed to touch someone to Read them.

Girls . . . Glorious Gods! Their scent and their awakening female energy permeated every classroom in the middle school. They were everywhere, the sudden center of the universe with their alluring shapes and flitting, shadowed eyes. They frightened the wits out of him and every other male in seventh grade. But Daniel felt more than their interest. He was at the mercy of every hormonal nuance the girls projected and suffered irritating, frightening arousals over their budding and often aggressive sexuality. He began skipping classes again, dropped out of football and basketball, which pissed off his dad. He brought home a report card full of Fs, which just about killed his mother until she realized his every waking moment was spent scrambling together emotional barriers no longer powerful enough to protect a boy now becoming a man.

Once again, Gran came to his rescue, first with a new, more powerful charm to wear, and then the study of new spells, these more potent, more specific, and taught to him by witch women of his own blood. By the time his boyish face thinned to heart-breaking good looks and the girls began competing for attention from his beautiful, thick lashed eyes, he no longer had to retreat unprepared.

Pain piercing every joint and muscle finally roused Daniel to the present and full consciousness. He could *feel* every person in the Lennox as if they lived inside his head; Lonnie Ranchero on the first floor, angrily punching coarse, cliché sentences into his computer. The McCready sisters down the hall discussing Hercule Poirot's clever deductions, and just below him, the teenage newlyweds tumbled together making love. Great, Daniel moaned, just the kind of heat he didn't need in his head at the moment. He flexed aching fingers, then wrists and arms until he found, after a bit, he could push himself onto his knees. His body felt as if he'd been struck by lightning and stripped of skin.

When at last he opened his eyes, he saw the pulsing color in Lily's living room had dissipated. The geode sat quiescent and blank on the table near his head. Outside, night was falling with autumnal speed . . . Lily would be home soon. He absolutely could not be here when she arrived.

His brain felt like splintered wood. Hundreds of synaptic explosions had left his senses as raw as open wounds. Bloody gouges from his clenched fingernails covered his palms. But he could think. And he could feel . . . feel his love for Lily drowning under a panicked need to gather protection against her. Though the geode no longer amplified her emotions, he still sensed them swimming the room like spectral fish, ravenous and needy. Crawling towards the door, his ankle brushed against one of the boxed paintings leaning against the couch. A burst of pain dropped him gasping to the floor again. One of the paintings radiated blistering, psychic fire. Daniel rolled away from it, senses blasted anew.

*

Once outside her rooms with the door closed behind him, he could rise on half dead legs and shuffle into his apartment where his phone was ringing.

"Hey," Gradyn shouted into his ear. "Where the hell are you? I thought you were bringing Lily's paintings by an hour ago."

"Yeah, about that . . . " Even his voice hurt. "I need help."

A silence echoed through the phone. "Okay, sure, be there momentarily. Are you all right? Did something happen to Lily?"

"I'm not all right. And yes, something most definitely happened to Lily. She's okay, just come. I'll explain when you get here."

Gradyn arrived within ten minutes to find Daniel curled on his couch as if he'd been gut shot, lines of pain etching his clammy face.

"Christ, Daniel!" Gradyn didn't touch him, apparently remembering from the past that any touch would feel like burning coals in his condition. "Even I could feel her . . . Lily, everywhere, as soon as I entered the building!"

"Yes." Daniel drew a shuddering breath, forced himself to sit up.

"A drink, I think." Gradyn went to the cupboard, poured a tall glass of scotch, tipped half down his own throat before taking the rest to Daniel who automatically reached for it before snatching his hand away as if singed. Gradyn set the glass on the table.

Gradyn's mouth was grim. "So, she possesses more magic than just the simple enchanting of pigment."

"To put it mildly," Daniel shivered. "She woke a damned

geode, which should have been my first clue."

"She can't have known how you would—"

"No. But I should have."

Gradyn lifted the glass Daniel hadn't touched and, pressing it to his friend's lips, forced him to swallow down a good portion of the liquor.

Daniel choked, gasped but within moments his shaking eased and he sat up straighter. "Christ, Grady, I want her so much, and she burned me good! I can't be near her, not until . . . "

"You'll heal, Daniel. You have before. We'll call your Gran, she can make you one of those talismans—"

"No! If I back away now, she'll run. From herself, from loving me. Which I forced on her before she was ready. Gradyn, she's opening up her heart! For the first time. How can I offer her less?"

"How can you offer her more and survive, Daniel?" Gradyn pulled his sat-phone from his pocket. "You look like Dante's Death crawling up from Hell. I'm calling your Gran."

Daniel pushed himself off the couch and staggered into the kitchen where, with trembling hands, he grabbed the bottle of scotch and tipped most of the contents down his throat. He then guzzled two glasses of water. Behind him, he could hear Gradyn talking.

"Yeah, he's on his feet, barely. Tell me he can come back from a stripping like this, Gran, please. He . . . " Gradyn glanced over his shoulder and lowered his voice. "He's afraid. I've never seen him afraid before." A pause. "For her, yes. Really? She has to be there? Okay." Gradyn shut the phone with a snap. "I'm packing you a bag, buddy. You're staying with me tonight. And your Gran's sending out a summons."

"Shit," Daniel cursed. "A damn coven of witch women to heal me."

"Including Lily."

"No! She mustn't know what she's done. It'll destroy her."

"Your Gran commanded, and I'm not one to argue with her." Gradyn disappeared into Daniel's room and came back moments later zipping a duffel closed. "Wait here. I'll load the paintings;

we'll drop them at the studio. Unless being in the van with them is too painful for you."

Disgusted by his weakness, Daniel shrugged. "I'll survive."

Gradyn quickly loaded the boxes in his van and returned to help Daniel make his slow way down the stairs. The pain in his body had steadied to a persistent throb. He thought perhaps soon he'd have the strength for a simple healing spell. Then he could begin constructing barriers again, at least enough to protect him while he talked to Lily, explain what had happened, and tell her that he loved her, that they could still be together . . .

Except he didn't know if they could be together. Sometimes a stripping left the senses so damaged that an object, or person, in close proximity acted like a toxic poison. He'd read about such happenings, though he'd never experienced them at their worst. And he wouldn't, he promised himself. He wanted Lily more than he wanted to live. She deserved him healed and unafraid, committed to her heart and soul. That's what she would get, by God. Stumbling on the steps outside the Lennox, Daniel froze.

"She's close, I feel her . . . " He turned to look down the street where she would soon appear.

Gradyn grabbed Daniel, ignoring his cry of pain, and shoved him into the van. In seconds, they were driving away. Frantic, Daniel spun to look behind them and saw Lily rounding the corner, head down, kicking at leaves as she walked. He couldn't leave her, not this way . . . he snatched at the car door handle. Quickly, Gradyn punched the auto lock. Lily's head snapped up. Daniel felt her sudden awareness of him slam into his chest and knew she felt his pain as vividly as if she lived inside his psyche. Gasping, he clutched his head when her panic hit him. He saw her books fall to the ground, saw her bolting towards the Lennox.

"Call Gran, quick!" Daniel spat through gritted teeth, "Tell her to phone Lily right now and explain . . . explain something. Gradyn, she's in my head! Merciful Gods, what have we done to each other?"

Chapter Fifteen

By the time Gradyn skidded the van into the alley behind Spencer Gallery and backed up to the loading dock, Daniel's white knuckled grip on the armrest was all that kept him upright. Fumbling open the passenger door, he half fell out of the seat to stumble quickly away from the vehicle. He watched from a distance, defeat in every line of his body, as Gradyn carried the three paintings in through the back of the building.

The evening air held the taste of winter and a murky sleet had begun to fall. Daniel lifted his face to it, relishing the cold relief on skin shivering with fever. His senses on high alert, he could smell the city's dusty exhaust, taste the dank, moldering flavor of the lake nearly two miles away.

For a long time he stood in the darkening alley, eyes closed, trying to block the sound and feel of people locking up their shops for the night. When a woman stepped out a back door on her way to her car and he felt her urgent need to beat traffic home like a torch against his skin, he walked to the gallery, climbed onto the loading dock, and went inside.

The back room was in chaos, unusual for the meticulous Mr. Spencer except when he was putting up a new show. Framed and unframed watercolors and oils lay on work tables, sculptures stood in crates with the packing pulled loose. A holo-board stood on an easel near the door leading onto the gallery floor. It was covered with overlapping lists, sticky notes, and a roughed out floor plan of where artwork might best be displayed in the show room and upstairs galleria.

Daniel stood with his back pressed to the wall and tried to find a place of calm inside himself. Forcing deep, even breaths, he focused on the wooden floor beneath his feet and made it his ground zero. He Read, through the pounding in his head, the lingering impressions of visitors to the gallery over the past few hours: a woman's excitement at buying a special gift, a husband's pressure over an anniversary, a girl's longing for a coveted necklace.

Time passing would take this razor's edge off his sensitivities. All he needed was a little patience. And a way to avoid being in a room with someone other than Gradyn, who'd been taught as a child how to shield his emotions. The faint sheen of sweat on his friend's upper lip- and Gradyn never sweated -told Daniel just how hard the man was working to block his concern. He'd placed Lily's boxed paintings in another room behind a closed door. Daniel could still feel her magic, though the violent immediacy was fading.

Or he'd finally managed to build something of a shield.

Daniel came inside to find Gradyn talking to Megan in the door leading out to the gallery. "Close up now, will you, Megs?" Gradyn said when he saw Daniel. "Daniel and I will be back here getting privately intoxicated."

The girl laughed with a breezy toss of hair. She peered around Gradyn to flash a brilliant smile at Daniel, who cringed from her heated interest. Gradyn, noticing, closed the door between them before he moved to the mobile bar he kept stocked for art openings. The large work room was laid out with every efficiency. Against the wall behind the rolling bar ran a short counter with a sink, cupboards, microwave, a large restaurant-style coffee maker, and a mini fridge. In the far corner sat a round table surrounded by four comfortable chairs. The rest of the space held tool benches, racks, nicked shelves, and long, heavy-duty tables.

"No more scotch, please," Daniel groaned as he dropped into one of the chairs. Gradyn was twisting the cap off a bottle of Walker's Blue Diamond. "I'll be no use sloppy drunk."

"You'll be senseless, which is the better point." Gradyn poured a full glass and set it on the table, standing above his friend for a moment with a worried scowl. Ignoring Daniel's sarcastic thanks, he moved back to the bar to pour a glass for himself.

Daniel hated scotch; he'd be passed out in half an hour and Gradyn knew it.

"Remember my last stripping?" Daniel asked after swallowing a mouthful. The grin he directed at Gradyn was loose and starting to show no pain.

"Lords, yes." Gradyn snorted a laugh as he dropped into a nearby chair. "In seventh grade, wasn't it? A terrifying experience. You are referring, I assume, to the stripping that lusty slut Susan Lerner planned for you under the football bleachers? As a matter of fact, you collapsing comatose on the ground with blood streaming from your nose was your best and only defense against her."

"Coulda used a bottle of this stinking stuff that day. Susan Lerner was a she-tiger."

Gradyn laughed. "So I learned when she took my virginity instead of yours."

"Like you were sorry. You gloated for months, then tumbled Elsie Swanson, who'd been dying for you since fifth grade."

Gradyn placed an offended hand over his heart. "I'll have you know Elsie was my first and truest love. And we waited until sophomore year . . . well, almost waited. I did show some restraint, though nothing compared to your cold-hearted control."

"Yeah, that's me. Heartless and cold." Daniel rolled eyes no longer focused. "You know I couldn't—"

"Yeah, yeah," Gradyn said, "you couldn't afford to let anyone close. I've heard that song and dance a jillion times. But damn it, we're talking about Lily. Lily, in all her glorious innocence busting you wide open with the wanting of you. So now what, Danny boy? Another Gran charm to protect you? From Lily, for God's sake."

Daniel's eyes flashed anger. He stabbed a finger at the closed door leading into the workshop. "Open that painting, the one labeled *Paradigm*. Then maybe you'll get the picture."

"Ha, ha," Gradyn said and crossed the floor to disappear inside the other room. He slid one of the boxes out through the door. "Is this the one she painted last night?"

"Yep." Daniel emptied his glass with a gulp.

"She warned me it might not be dry yet."

Daniel barked a laugh. "I can guarantee it's not dry yet. You know she asked me how I could love her and hide from her at the same time? Then she spent all night immersed in magic, and painted her frustration and loneliness and a love bright enough to light the universe onto that canvas there. She wanted me to know her heart like . . . like she knows paint! Intimately. And the geode came to life, absorbed all her amazing passion, and released it like a supernova."

Gradyn, ripping staples from the end of the box with a pair of pliers, straightened to stare at him, shocked. "How is that even possible?"

Daniel shrugged elaborately.

"She asked me not to sell this one, you know. *Paradigm,*" Gradyn said.

Daniel, feeling the sloppy slide of alcohol thick in his blood, threw up a hasty barrier fragile as spider's silk as Gradyn drew the canvas from the box and lifted it onto a nearby easel.

"Christ Almighty!" Daniel whispered, shrinking deeper in his chair. Even from across the room, the painting throbbed with savage power. Dazzling light and rich, intense color shifted in a sensual entwining that struck him full force. *Paradigm* was breathtaking, a masterpiece, a radiant overture of friendship and longing, and hot, pulsing lust.

Gradyn stepped back, mouth falling open. "There is a bit of almighty in it, isn't there? It's . . . it's overwhelming! Eager, vehement, and . . . Jesus H., throbbing with passion!" He turned to see his friend dabbing absently at blood trickling from his nose.

Daniel couldn't take his eyes off the painting even though they burned as if he stared into the sun. The fertile greens and rich blues, the highlights of sizzling yellows all reached out to glide over his skin in sweet, unbearable pain. The resonating composition coalesced, ultimately, into a fantastical central figure draped in streams of color. Exquisite of face and delicate of limb, the creature reached out of a living darkness like some ethereal demon on wings spread to escape the canvas.

"Gods on high . . . the girl is over the moon for you," Gradyn murmured. "It's obvious even to me, a magic illiterate. This painting screams of secret cravings, haunted vulnerability. And Danny boy, she doesn't just want you in a biblical way."

Tissue pressed to his nose, Daniel stood and staggered to the bar to refill his glass, choking half of it down on the spot.

Gradyn crossed the room. "You okay?"

"I am, actually." Daniel felt his fragile shield slither away and no longer cared. Liquor having numbed his senses, the vivid palette in the painting enchanted now instead of burned him, and he found the joyful hunger on the figure's face more tender than provocative. "The pain's going. D'you think that's the scotch or the fact that I'm the damn luckiest man on the planet?"

"It's the scotch. Probably. Hell, Daniel, I had no idea Lily was this . . . this good! Did you?"

"Oh, yes. But not until recently. See, Nila made her this love potion . . . oops, that's supposed to be secret. An' the potion, it awakened . . . well, all of her. She wanted me stripped naked of every defense an' did it simply by baring her soul." Daniel smiled woozily in his chair. "An' I'm okay with that. I want her just as bad. And just as naked."

"Hold on there, big guy. You can't go near her. Gran's sent for Lily. She'll be part of creating the protective talisman, I imagine. Still, even a hocus pocus stone won't keep her from burning your senses blind. Not until you've healed."

Daniel frowned, suddenly ferocious. "I will not wear a talisman against Lily. I'll never place another barrier between us again, I swear it."

"You're too drunk to think straight." Gradyn took the glass away from him. "Being near her when you're this stripped will . . ."

"Yes!" Daniel laughed jubilantly. "It will. I'll feel everything, all unlocked and vulnerable and aching for her! You ever been in love, Grady?"

"Not, well . . . perhaps. Somewhat."

"Now that's a spot-on Gradyn Spencer answer if I ever heard one." Daniel snatched his glass back and drained it. "You can tell Gran and Nila and the whole damn coven to kiss their fucking talisman! I *want* to be with Lily. Can you imagine? I want all of her, and when I touch her—"

"You'll feel agonies you can't imagine, you dolt! I know, I've seen it happen to you."

"Not this time." Daniel pushed shakily to his feet, sweeping his arms wide like a prisoner shaking off chains. "Look inside your gut, Gradyn, then look at that painting. *Paradigm . . .* means a conjugation, a coupling. Can't you see it in the textures, the perfect contrast between dark and light? A uniting of two into one. Only Lily can heal me. At this moment I feel her in my head. She's miles away with Gran. She's just met Madame Bagasha and the rest of the coven. And she's really, really pissed off. Have you ever seen Lily mad? It's so God damn intense! I've seen her laugh with wild abandon, cry as if all the color has bled from her universe, and I've felt her love like hot lava in my veins. But oh, how glorious her rage is! What I wouldn't give to be one of Gran's little sparrows in that house right now." Daniel wobbled to the bar and grabbed the half empty bottle of Blue Diamond before collapsing back in his chair hugging it to his chest.

"Just look at that painting of perfection, Gradyn Spencer. Those witch women've got my Lily and they don't have a clue who or what she is. 'N' guess what else? There ain't a blasted thing you or me can do about it. 'Cept wait. 'N drink. Where'd that bottle go?"

Disgusted, Gradyn pulled the bottle clear of Daniel's loose hands. On impulse, he poked him in the cheek.

"Ouch." Daniel flashed a goofy grin. "See? I'm already healing. Hey, d'you remember Harold Greenway, back in ninth grade?"

"Hard-on Harry? Lords, yes. He walked around with a perpetual erection and—" Gradyn sent an astounded glance at Daniel who waved a drunken arm at the painting across the room and shrugged with sheepish eloquence.

He snickered. "Remember how we fixed Harry?"

"You want a blow-up sex doll?" Gradyn asked.

"'Course not. I already got a sex doll if I can just catch her."

Gradyn looked back at *Paradigm*'s resonating bold shapes and explosive color. "Somehow, I don't think catching her'll be a problem, bud."

Daniel's brows furrowed. "Yeah, well, Lily's complicated. We've barely kissed."

"You can't be serious! You mean, in all this time you haven't . . . what the hell's the matter with you two?"

"Oh, so many things . . ." Daniel's eyelids drooped closed, then popped wide. "She's afraid if we're lovers our friendship will be ruined forever."

Gradyn belched a laugh. "She's ridiculous."

"So she keeps telling me. Warning me." Daniel looked at the painting again and whispered. "Like I don't know her better than I know myself."

"That I do believe," Gradyn said affably. "Have you told her yet what you really do for a living?"

"No. Can't. She'll hate me. Feel betrayed."

Gradyn slapped a hand on Daniel's shoulder, gripped him. "You look at that painting, dude. She couldn't hate you if you were the devil calling her down to Hell."

Daniel stared at *Paradigm* for a sobering moment. "Tell me, Gradyn, do you see Lily and me surviving my little secret? Blessed Saints, I have so much to tell her . . . " He sat silent for a long time before suddenly leaning forward with a loose grin. "By the way, that Megan girl wants to jump my bones. And if not mine, then yours."

"And any other male who happens into a room," Gradyn snorted. "I've noticed a definite 'I'm yours for the taking' vibe about her."

"See, you are magic!" Daniel's face lit up, then suddenly blazed with anger. "You bastard, get that thought out of your head this second! Lily is mine."

"Gotcha!" Gradyn sniggered. "Like I didn't know you'd Read me."

"Lily's not your type. At all."

"She truly isn't. All that delicious naiveté." Gradyn took another drink and smacked his lips. "On the other hand . . . "

"Knock it off!" Daniel came out of his chair with his fist heading for Gradyn's face. His toe caught the edge of the chair and he went down, wacked the table with his elbow, and knocked over the bottle.

"You missed," Gradyn laughed.

"First time for everything." Daniel scrambled back into the chair and clutched his spinning head. "Damn," he moaned. Together they watched the expensive scotch drip an amber waterfall over the edge of the table.

After a moment Gradyn kicked his shoes across the room and asked brightly, "So Chinese take out, do you think?"

Chapter Sixteen

Lily sat hunched in her living room listening to the cold, steely voice speaking over the phone. Daniel's Gran. And she sounded about as "milk and cookies" as Medusa!

"Nila will pick you up in twenty minutes. I don't know what you did or why, but Daniel is in terrible pain. You will help us create a talisman to protect him while he heals. Bring the geode." The sat-link went dead.

That was all, an oblique accusation, a command, no identification. Of course Lily knew who'd been speaking. As she waited on the steps of the Lennox, edgy with fear for Daniel, she hated the thought of meeting his grandmother under these circumstances. He rarely talked about her or his relationship to the community of witches he called the Cohort. But since Lily had rounded the street corner twenty minutes earlier and slammed her senses into Daniel's pain, she continued to feel his thoughts and emotions like a humming inside her head. And even lost in pain, Daniel's concern was for her. Waiting on the front porch, tears mingled with the icy rain dripping down her face.

*

Nila's little e-car squealed to a stop against the curb. Lily ran to jerk open the door and fell into the passenger seat.

The young witch's face was stiff, closed off. "I'm not to tell you anything, Lily, so please don't ask. But take warning. Gran is livid with me, and with you."

"Why is she mad at you?" The anger at Daniel's gran that had begun over the phone now swelled to active dislike.

Nila twitched her shoulders as if her skin hurt. "I was supposed to have recognized your power and reported it. Especially when you woke a geode."

Lily swore under her breath. "I haven't a clue what I've done, and you aren't allowed to tell me? So you're as damned as I, is that it? By witches, no less! How freaking ironic. Nila, I am responsible for myself and my actions. Not you. And not a coven of women, no matter who they think they are. If Daniel wasn't getting plastered with Gradyn Spencer right now, nothing on this earth would keep me from going to him. Especially his great and powerful Gran."

Nila grimaced in the eerie light of the dashboard. "You don't understand."

"Of course I bloody don't! And if you won't give me answers, who the hell will?"

"Madame Bagasha. All the other women have gone mad, I swear."

"Can you tell me where we're going, at least?"

"To Gran's house."

"I'm supposed to help make a talisman to heal him," Lily said. "What does that mean?"

"That's what I can't tell you. And I'm sorry, Lil. Truly. But Madame is there, she will help you. She's, well, less vulnerable within the Cohort."

"More unbiased, you mean?"

"Not afraid of their power, political and . . . otherwise. " Nila sent Lily an unreadable look. Crossing her arms, Lily sat back to fume as the younger girl refused to say another word. They headed northeast through the dark, the electric car quietly humming. Another ten minutes had them skirting block after block of burned and blackened buildings, scarred metal beams rising like twisted skeletons in windowless high rises. Beyond them the splintered shells of collapsed, dead homes stood like phantoms. A high, barbed security fence wrapped these war torn ruins.

They drove down rubbled streets with large *Danger: Radiation* signs posted every twelve feet or so. Nila explained the area had been condemned and never rebuilt after the riots. Lily stared in dismay. She'd never been in this part of Old Town before, hadn't realized this many once thriving communities had been destroyed so utterly and completely.

"Mostly Hispanic, Italian, and African American neighborhoods," Nila explained. "Burnt to the ground by the police during the race riots. Those who survived now live out in Valley Town, mostly."

"That was more than ten years ago. Why is nothing rebuilt?"

Nila was silent a moment and then said, "They used nerve gas. And other chemicals."

"So you're telling me that beyond those fences, the ground is toxic?"

"And all the technology and magic in the world can't cleanse it."

"Are there other places like this?"

"In every major city in America. Almost sixteen million people died, did you know that?"

Horror twisted Lily's face. "But I remember, the newspapers said two million. And most of those were terrorists. Or illegal immigrants."

"Yeah, right."

The little car finally left Burn-Out Central, as Nila called it, behind, and they were once again purring down streets lined with trees, houses, apartment buildings, and corner markets like Lily's own Little Belfast. A few minutes later Nila pulled over to a curb and parked.

"Where are we?" Lily asked.

"Island Park. Most practicing witches live here where they aren't so . . . noticeable. Not that tolerance toward them isn't better, it is. The more people who discover and believe in magic, the less prejudice there is towards it. And the Cohort."

Lily had heard rumors about the Island Park district, strange stories about ghosts, UFO sightings, unexplained lights, and ground tremors. Free Grace Hospital, the most accessible and illustrious hospital in New Chicago, was in Island Park. A community of healing witches explained a lot.

Nila got out of the car. After a stubborn, angry hesitation, Lily followed. The stinging rain hadn't begun to fall here, but Lily felt it creeping in, bone-chilling cold.

*

She discovered Gran's house was charming. That surprised her. A large, two-storied house with a bright blue front door, a wraparound porch and sprawling yard was enclosed inside a thick hedge broken by an archway of woven dogwood that supported a climbing rose, now dormant. Nila opened the gate and, following her under the arch, Lily imagined the air in summer must smell divine. Then she noticed the spiked thorns and recalled why she was here.

The yard grew like a crazy quilt in patchwork gardens of herbs, flowers, and strawberries, all tidily clipped and winterized. On another occasion, Lily might have found the grounds delightful with its dozens of bright bird houses and birdfeeders high on poles, bird baths, benches, and whirly-gigs in all shapes and colors. As the two women approached the house, the blue door opened. A needle-sharp shadow shot across the yard towards them. Lily stumbled, suppressed a shiver.

Lily approached the tall, spare woman waiting in the doorway, swallowing a tightness in her throat. She felt a bleary faith and love pouring into her through the psychic link she shared with Daniel. Her chin lifted as she crossed the porch and stepped into the house. The cloying smell of incense filled her nose.

Lily's stomach tumbled uneasily. Nila shrugged out of her coat, handing it to Gran, who'd stepped aside for them but did not speak in welcome. Lily refused to give up her jacket. A loud whirring noise grew in strength as dozens of birds flew out of doorways and down stairs to circle Lily's head in noisy, chirruping welcome. Enchanted, she lifted her hand to invite a tiny sparrow to clasp her fingers, felt feathers brush her face as three finches squabbled for a perch on her shoulder, while others settled on her head to tweak her hair.

She sensed Daniel's pleasure at her delight and was suddenly less afraid. What could she fear in a house full of birds, Lily decided, and turned to face Gran. All confidence died at the look on the old woman's face.

Eyes lowered, Nila said, "Lily, this is Magdaline Gilmore. Daniel's gran."

The witch woman did not smile, made no move to touch her. Lily could tell Gran was irritated by the birds' uninhibited welcome.

Her own anger quickened. "Were you expecting horns and a forked tail, Mrs. Gilmore?"

Gran's mouth tightened and her answering stare was both arrogant and rude. The woman had once possessed great beauty, Lily realized. Daniel had inherited her dark, slashing brows and large, long-lashed eyes. But where his always shone with humor and warmth, hers smoldered in hard bitterness. She turned abruptly to lead Nila and Lily across the foyer into a large living room filled with women who ceased talking the moment they appeared.

The room was brightly lit. A pleasant fire burned merrily in the grate. The scene might have engendered a cozy atmosphere but for the angry tension Lily felt as palpable as hailstones in the air. Nila introduced her around the room and each of the five women took her hand in an almost brutal grasp before speaking in a patronizing drone, "Our creed is *do no harm.*"

Lily choked on a laugh. No harm when the air crackled with aggressive dislike? Shocked by their obvious assumption that she'd hurt Daniel on purpose, Lily glanced around the room for escape and found herself looking into the eyes of a tiny, round woman she knew immediately was Madame Bagasha. Even without her flamboyant television costume.

Madame had a plump, rosy-cheeked face framed by gray brillo-pad hair. Her eyes, black and bright as a raven's, locked on

Lily as she pushed her way through the crowd, impatiently clicking her tongue. Reaching Lily, she took her hands as if she'd been waiting an eternity to meet her. They were the same height, and looking into Madame Bagasha's sweet, intelligent face, Lily felt her fear for Daniel diminish. This woman had kindness written in every wrinkle on her aging face. She would know what to do, she would help Lily save him.

Lily spoke through stiff lips. "I'm relieved to meet you at last, Madame Bagasha. And thank you for at least pretending to welcome me." She flicked a glance towards Gran standing erect and disapproving of Madame's greeting.

Madame tucked her arm through Lily's, drew her across the room to sit beside her on a faded floral settee. "Lily," she said, her voice deep and oddly rough. "You can understand, I'm sure, why Daniel's grandmother is less than pleased with you."

"But I don't understand anything!" Lily exclaimed in a low tone. "I have no idea what's happened, only that Daniel is hurting and somehow I caused it. He's feeling no pain at the moment, of course, because that damn Gradyn Spencer's getting him stinking drunk—"

Daniel's Gran cut in abruptly. "You can sense Daniel? Now?"

"Yes." Lily looked baffled. "Will someone please explain what's going on? Whatever I've done, I can fix it."

"You cannot fix a thing," Gran stated in her cold voice. "Nor will you be allowed to. But you can be sure we will." Her gesture took in the women standing silently about the room.

Lily's anger flared and she leaped to her feet. Startled birds flew up only to resettle quickly, as if eager to soothe her. "You don't know me, Mrs. Gilmore, or my relationship with Daniel. Whatever I've done I have the power to undo. I know it here." She pressed a fist fiercely to her chest. "Please, tell me what's happened to Daniel."

Gran stepped closer. "Your self-indulgent ignorance stripped him, burned his empathic senses like a wildfire burns grass. He may never recover."

Lily's eyes widened. Her hands flew to her mouth with a horrified cry. Madame eased her, trembling, back onto the couch, and sent Gran an exasperated look.

But Daniel's grandmother would not be stopped. "His nerves, psychic and otherwise, are now as sensitive as the tissue of someone with third degree burns."

Lily couldn't breathe, knew she must escape this room, and this woman, immediately.

Gran opened her mouth again, but Madame cut in. "Enough, Maggie. The girl did not hurt him on purpose, that's clear. Read her if you like, but stop this bullying. Now."

In the next instant, Lily was slammed back by the force of a raging alien will inside her head. Instinctively, she threw up a shield.

"We who are innocent hide nothing from each other!" Gran accused.

Lily hissed a furious breath. "And I believe one asks permission to Read another before invading." She felt Daniel's joyful support flowing warm in her blood, tasted the flare of her own magic and her vision suddenly tunneled. The scene before her sharpened. She saw each woman outlined in colors discordant and harsh. They were backing away from her as if they sensed some cataclysmic instability in the air. Nested in the crook of Lily's arm, the geode flared to pulsing life.

"Rogue magic!" Gran raised her hands to cast a counter spell.

"No!" Madame cried, throwing herself in front of Lily. "Maggie, stop this, I beg you! We're here to find answers. To work together to help Daniel. I am telling each of you right now this girl is under my *aegis*. Magdaline, do you understand?"

Gran's eyes burned with something close to hate, and Lily shuddered under a spike of power that raised the hair on the back of her neck.

"Magdaline!" Madame's voice cracked like a whip. She turned to Lily. "No one here means you real harm, truly. These women are stirred up by half-truths and anger just as you are stirred by frustration and fear. Please, Lily, pull your magic back, my dear. You haven't control over it."

Lily dragged her glare off of Gran and instantly the air cleared. The geode quieted and Lily sat down in the circle of Madame's arms.

Madame half closed her eyes and her lips parted as if she were tasting the nuances of magic fading from the room.

"Maggie, did you sense him in the Quickening just now? Daniel's magic, wrapped with hers?"

"No!" Gran spat. "She possesses Rogue magic and must be shackled immediately."

Lily felt Daniel's hot anger flick through her mind and stood suddenly. In a voice that shook, she said, "I came here in good faith, desperate for answers that have not been forthcoming. I've been judged and condemned without a single question asked of me. But know this. What you do to me, you do to Daniel. If you can help me heal him, I beg you do it. Otherwise, I am leaving."

Every face in the room turned to Madame Bagasha whose cheeks flared with embarrassed shame on their behalf. "I apologize, child, for all of us. Your . . . your power, it is not a magic we know. Nor are we comfortable with it. Quite frankly, you've frightened us as much as we've frightened you. Stay, please. Gran knows a way to help Daniel and she needs your cooperation. Will you forgive her enough to help work a talisman to shield him while he heals?"

"I forgive her, of course," Lily said, voice steadier. "I know she acts out of love, as I do. But Daniel will not wear a talisman against me."

Face purple with frustration, Gran stepped forward and snatched the geode from Lily's arms. For a moment pain flashed on her wrinkled face. Lily watched her brow furrow and her eyes glaze in concentration. Stroking the geode with thin, knobbled fingers, Gran closed her eyes. All color in the crystals faded, doused by a magic Lily felt as real as fingers closing around her throat.

"Tell us what you see," Madame Bagasha demanded.

"She's painting," Gran spoke, her voice no longer cold but almost lyrical. "Swirls of color and . . . and emotions. Such emotion. She wants to know him, wants inside his heart. Wants him to see and know her. Oh, her frustration, her confusion! And tenderness, desire that overwhelms. It seeps from her hands, spills into the canvas . . . too intense for paint to hold. The geode burns!" Gran's eyes flew open and she threw the rock at Lily as if it were on fire. In a shattered voice, she said, "You love too much, girl! An empath cannot survive such a devouring, restless passion!"

"Daniel would argue that with his last breath, Mrs. Gilmore. He opened me up, showed me love like I never imagined. Love like a living organism, too omnipotent for one heart to hold! Who are you to decide what he and I can share?" She turned to Madame Bagasha. "Why isn't Daniel here? He'll tell you."

"He cannot be near you without suffering great pain." Gran said, sympathy draining the rage from her voice. "Not for a long time. He must heal. A stripping leaves—"

"He is not stripped!" Lily cried. "If he is as vulnerable to raw emotion as you claim, then how can he tolerate me inside his head? The power to heal him lies inside my magic, inside what I feel. Daniel knows this, he's always known. And he's not afraid, he's rejoicing!" Impatient, Lily wiped away her suddenly falling tears. "Just who do you think is keeping us linked?"

A stunned silence filled the room. Gran spoke, "You have felt this connection with him before?"

Lily blushed. "Only once, briefly. We were . . . kissing."

"The love potion she drank. Would it . . . ?"

Madame Bagasha shook her head. "Nila hasn't such power yet. The potion was nothing more than a *séduction*. It merely enhanced Lily's more appealing attributes, nothing more. But there have been curious side effects."

"Side effects?"

Madame glanced around the room warily before saying, "It seems to have awakened Lily's latent powers. There were . . . manifestations. What Lily painted became animated."

Frightened exclamations greeted this announcement.

"How is that possible?" Gran's panic paled her skin.

But Madame smiled reassurance. "When she and I sit down for our first lesson, we'll discover more. Does the girl have more power than Nila and I assumed? Obviously. Did she hurt Daniel on purpose? No, clearly the girl's crazy about your grandson. So, Maggie, can we please relax, perhaps share tea together? After all, if Lily has magic, she will become one of us."

"We must still create a talisman," Gran said with an obstinate lift of her chin.

Madame took Lily's face between both hands and looked deep in her eyes. Nodding, she said, "The girl speaks true, he will not wear it. None the less, we will make one." Her smile, as her hands slipped from Lily's cheeks, was ironic. "It is what we do."

Chapter Seventeen

Madame gripped Gran's hand in hers as the two women walked, heads bent close in talk, from the room. The level of tension barely diminished. Nila dashed from her solitary stance in the corner to collapse on the settee beside Lily. Hands shaking, the young witch tempted a few birds from Lily's shoulder onto her own and stroked their downy breasts until Lily felt the girl's body, pressed close to hers, relax as well.

Lily expelled a deep breath. "Tea. Who needs tea? I need freaking whiskey!"

"If only I could conjure." Nila attempted a shaky smile. "Can you sense booze nearby? I could float a bottle in if I knew where it was."

"All I sense is scotch. Poor Daniel, he hates scotch." Lily unclipped her hair to run nervous fingers through it. "He'll be so sick. Gradyn may be a class act in most things, but he's also a sadist."

Nila sat hunched and silent. After a moment, Lily whispered, "What is Rogue magic, exactly?"

The girl winced, reached to take the geode from Lily's lap and turning it in her hands, watched the crystals catch and reflect the firelight. "Rogue Magic is very rare," Nila said. "A very strong, volatile, and unpredictable magic. Most of the horrendous things witches have been condemned for down through the ages were done with Rogue magic."

Lily felt sick to her stomach. "And you believe I have it?"

Nila said nothing, just turned her cheek to rub against a finch fluffed near her ear.

"Does Madame think so?" Lily persisted.

Carefully Nila placed the geode back in Lily's lap. "Yes. It . . . it explains so much, you see. The geode waking, the love potion gone awry, the painted man coming to life."

Lily clamped her mouth shut on a compulsion to tell Nila that not only one, but two painted men had come to life and rather than disappearing, roamed the earth haunting her. But in this hostile environment, if these women suspected Lily of one more magical malfunction, she'd be lucky to escape a lynching.

She glanced at them all talking in groups of twos and threes about the room. "If my magic is Rogue and they so dislike me, why am I still here? The currents in this room, magical and otherwise, are making my skin crawl."

"You and me both." Nila shivered.

"Are you afraid of me, Nila?"

"Yes," the girl said immediately, then, "No, not especially. You have a good heart, Lily. And a conscience, thank the Gods and Goddesses. But Rogue Magic terrifies witches and that's a fact. It's not easily categorized so it's often misrepresented and misunderstood. And it, well . . . it possesses a dark side which one has to work hard to keep leashed. My magic has Rogue elements, as does Madame's. I was raised knowing this and received rigorous training and discipline because of it. I still can't always predict what it might do."

"Like with the love potion?"

Nila grimaced. "Like with the love potion. But you . . . Lily, there is reason to fear your magic. You don't have the knowledge or skill to contain it. And power without knowledge is . . . "

"I get the picture," Lily cut in brusquely, staring down at the geode in her lap. Oh, yeah, the signals were coming through loud and clear. She didn't need Second Sight to feel it. Yet none of these women knew her, even Nila. None here realized that as an artist, she possessed great discipline of craft and a devoted technical skill. Her magic might be Rogue but it manifested first in her paintings and her relationship with art. It was born of her creative spirit and was as essential to her existence as the beating of her heart. No one here could convince her that her power wasn't as it should be and therefore good and true.

An uneasy truce had settled over the room. Looking around, Lily realized Madame Bagasha must have cast a calming spell-not a bad idea considering each of these witch women carried an *athame*, a not always dull, ceremonial knife used in ritual magic. Eleven heads lifted in relief at the sound of the tea cart.

The mundane had arrived in the shape of tea and thick slices of pumpkin bread. Steaming mugs were passed around by Nila's cousin who had to force herself to extend a cup to Lily. Lily mumbled her thanks without looking up, curling her hands around the mug as if a deep breath might shatter the delicate china. At Gran's presence in the room a band of tension had tightened around her chest and she wondered again why she had to be here.

Talk buzzed among the women, who perfunctorily ignored both Nila and Lily sitting on the settee. Lily could understand being left out, she being the offender in their eyes. But Nila was one of them, a trained healer and probably related to most of these women. Did this snubbing have to do with Nila being Rogue or was it part of her training as an apprentice? Either way, no amount of coaxing would ever compel Lily to become a member of this group!

Madame wandered the room, casually touching each woman as if measuring their mood. She approached the two girls pressed together like so much refuse tossed on a beach.

"Nila, dear . . . " The tiny Hungarian woman cast a quick glance at Gran who, by the speculative gleam in her eye, was also measuring the merit of her chosen witches. "Keep a sharp eye, will you, dear? You'll be inside the circle, I will not."

Nila nodded, once, quickly.

"What's going on?" Lily said. Nila hushed her with look.

When the tea—which, Nila explained, was actually an herbal concoction meant to promote harmony for the working of joined magic—was finished and the cart wheeled away, two women bent to roll back the large rug in the center of the room. Gran rose to her feet, at once imposing and austere. Lily saw her already dark eyes darken further and felt a sullen drift of magic across her skin. The birds took flight all at once, to roost on lampshades and curtain rods at the far edges of the room. The staccato flap of wings echoed the rapid beat of her heart.

"Lily, you and Nila stand here." Gran positioned them near an empty table pulled into the center of the room to serve as an altar. On this table Gran placed a bowl hollowed from a burl of wood. Beside the bowl she laid out a chain holding a set of gemstones wrapped in an elaborate filigree knot of burnished silver.

Nila breathed in Lily's ear, "The dusk-colored gemstone is fluorite, for psychic protection. The other stones are lapis lazuli and amber to enhance psychological healing, all worked together with silver to secure the spell."

This then, was Daniel's talisman . . . his protection against her. Lily's heart felt like a lump of lead in her chest and unwanted tears rose in her eyes. The room seemed to shrink around her, stifling, too warm from the fire. She gagged at the Sandalwood incense clinging to her hair, her clothes.

"I can't stay here," she said suddenly and took a step towards the door. But Gran had already closed the circle of power she'd been chalking in one continuous stroke around the wooden floor. Her voice, low and musical, chanted a spell as she moved. Lily saw rich burgundy light sink into the curved line at its closing. The eleven women of the coven, along with Nila, *athames* in hands, walked the circle of power, one following the other. They too, chanted.

Lily watched their magic drip off their knives in colors as individual and varied as themselves and sink into the chalked line. Pain began pounding at the base of Lily's skull as a surly power thickened inside the circle. Within the chalk line, Gran marked out a large, five-sided pentacle. Lily saw her glance once, rather furtively, at Madame standing outside the circle before she sketched a fleeting pattern in the air with her fingers. For the briefest instant, Lily thought she saw a dark shape in the air before it sank into the pentagram.

Panic snaked up Lily's spine. Something was not right. The magic rising was too sharp, too oppressive. Even the sense of Daniel, loose and easy inside her head, did not reassure her. Nila moved, still chanting with the others, to stand beside her once again. The girl had relaxed into a ritual as familiar to her as prepping a canvas was to Lily.

The remaining women took their places at each compass and pentacle point. One stood like a guard on each side of Nila and Lily. They all watched Gran light candles a translucent maroon with a simple pass of her hand. She handed them around until each witch except Nila held a candle in their left hand and their *athames* raised in their right.

Gran then moved to stand at the northern most compass point, lifted her chin and closed her eyes. Every lamp in the room blinked off. The candles cast eerie glows over each of the thirteen female faces, etching chins, noses and hollowed eye sockets in a ghostly light. Gran's voice spoke out of the near darkness.

"We ask the holy Goddess to bless and guide the work we do here this night."

Thirteen voices spoke as one. "Bless us. Guide us."

Lily heard Nila's voice added to the others and shivered as she saw magic shimmering at the edge of each ritual knife before it began to drift, pulled in individual strands like colored thread by Gran, who gathered up the strands. She began to weave them into a complex ball of power.

"This coven takes action only to protect and to heal," Gran intoned again.

"To protect. To heal," the voices echoed.

"And do no harm," Madame spoke firmly from outside the circle. Not one of the coven members echoed her words. Nila's eyes snapped opened as if she'd been slapped. Her gaze sought Madame's in the dark. Nila muttered a hasty spell under her breath and hearing it, Lily panicked. And ran. She dashed three steps before slamming into the circle's magic barrier as if it were a solid wall.

"You cannot leave the protective circle," Gran said, her voice matter of fact.

Lily picked herself up off the floor and leaped again at the wall only to fall once more. Dazed, she lay looking up at the curtain of power, woven with the colors of each witch, vibrant and beautiful and alive. At another time she might have been fascinated by this tapestry of different magics tangled together into one. Now she scrambled back from it in terror.

Inside her head, Daniel's attention sharpened. She felt a surge of his empathic energy sweep through their link, a wary protection she clung to. Nila reached down to help her up and as they touched, a spark jumped between them. Magic flowed beneath Nila's skin. Lily could see it, a sunny gold not part of the power Gran worked with the nimble fingers of a master weaver.

"The colors . . . " Lily gasped.

Nila's grip on her arm tightened. "Lily, there are no colors."

Only then did Lily realize none of these powerful women could see magic. Only her vision revealed which strands belonged to which witch. It steadied her, gave her a sense of her own autonomy at last. Still, she watched in growing dread as the weave thickened between Gran's hands into a dark, brooding red. The brilliant threads, stained and turgid, no longer shone with beauty.

As the magic darkened, each strand twisted tighter around the next until they swarmed together like a nest of writhing snakes. Lifting her hands, Gran threw the spell at Lily. It struck with a force that arched the girl's back and tore a scream from her throat. Then Lily couldn't cry at all, couldn't move as the thick band of dark magic whipped around her, tighter and tighter, squeezing her heart, her organs, her ribs, binding her like rope.

Lily struggled in claustrophobic terror as the binding became as rigid as cold steel.

"Magdaline." Madame's voice was livid with rage. "You will not shackle her!"

"It is done," Gran spoke with an odd note of sadness. Then she crossed the circle to where Lily stood stiffly immobile and laid her Reader's hands on her shoulders. Lily felt again the alien force of another in her mind, very briefly and this time, gently.

"The Rogue magic is bound." Gran turned back to resume her place at the head of the pentacle. Lily felt the steely grasp of the shackling spell like iron, heavy, ice cold. Her blood thickened, slowed. Her heart beat harder, struggling to pump warmth to her limbs. Colors dimmed, outlines faded and she felt her happy, impulsive magic curling in on itself like a dying leaf.

Closing her eyes, Lily tried to visualize it back to life. She tried whipping it with anger, inspiring it with creative excitement and dizzying ideas. When even Daniel's power, raging like a furious storm down the link, proved unable to draw even a spark from her dying power, Lily sank to her knees in despair. Her sobs filled the stunned, silent room, a heartbreaking death knell that had the rest of the coven keening in sorrow and wiping tears falling down their faces.

Nila, her face a ghastly white, turned on Gran. She had never raised magic against this woman who taught her but a need to retaliate had her hands lifted and her voice calling up vengeful power.

"No, Nila." Madame's disembodied voice came out of the flickering dark. "Enough harm has been done this night. But know this, Magdaline Gilmore, there will be repercussions."

"As head of the Cohort I have the authority—"

"No!" Madame snapped back. "As a Reader you have the skill. But you used the power of these twelve women." She glanced at the stricken faces of the other witches inside the circle. "Did they agree to help Shackle another's magic? You know it is what each of us fears above all things, Maggie. How could you? Your actions were premature and selfish, to say the least. Now finish this travesty, create your damned talisman, and let the girl be."

Only Gran's unflappable force of will gathered the witches back to order. Only her skill as a Reader drew their magic into a unifying force once more. The chanting restarted, grew louder, faster. Lily sat curled on the floor, silently crying. She no longer cared what they did to her.

"Grab her arm," Gran commanded Nila, who hesitated for a defiant moment before plucking up Lily's limp arm to hold above the wooden bowl on the altar. The chanting quickened, the power recharged. When the voices suddenly stopped, Lily felt an unbearable pressure inside her head like nails being hammered through her skull.

"Do you offer your blood willingly to bind this protective talisman?" the coven recited in unison.

Nothing on earth would drag acceptance of this travesty from Lily now . . . nothing but the knowledge that Daniel would stand by her and all would be well. That knowledge held more power than all the magic in the world.

"I offer it willingly," Lily whispered through stiff lips. Nila made the slash quick and shallow across Lily's lower arm. Blood bright as rubies swelled from the wound to drip into the waiting bowl. Lily felt nothing, not the blade's edge, not the painful cut. She'd disappeared into Daniel's drunken tenderness, singing through their link like an angel inside her head.

The bowl filled quickly. Nila pressed a gauze bandage tight to the wound. Still on the floor, Lily looked up to see Daniel's grandmother lift the talisman above the bowl. Her voice cried out,

"Healing grace infuse this charm, protect the wearer from passion's harm!"

Lily felt the brush of a phantom kiss tasting of scotch, felt each witch's power coalesce above her before diving into the wooden bowl. Gran dropped the talisman into the pooled blood. Lily screamed as her link with Daniel was abruptly severed.

Not a soul moved in the terrible silence that followed that scream. Power still raged inside the circle. On Lily's lap the geode blazed to fiery life. Arrows of angry light shot out of its crystal heart in every direction. From the roosting corners of the room birds rose in shrieking flight. Nila threw herself across Lily's body as the protective circle shattered. Magic gone wild ricocheted like bolts of lightning around the room, knocking three women to the floor. In a panic, Gran tried to harness the violent energy and was tossed like a rag doll across the room.

The pressure in Lily's head had eased, leaving only a trickle of blood seeping from her nose. The room boiled with magic that pricked her like a thousand needles. Clutching the geode close, she scrambled to her feet and stumbled out of the house.

Chapter Eighteen

"Lily, for pity's sake, stop! Please!" Nila yelled out the open window of her little car, her face wet and cold from the sleet pouring out of the dirty sky. She was driving down unfamiliar, unlighted streets, shadowing Lily, who ran heedlessly through the dark. The windshield wipers at full speed barely cleared enough visibility for Nila to see. She was terrified of hitting Lily with the car.

But Lily refused to stop, in fact could not even hear Nila yelling. She simply ran, feet blundering through puddles, hair plastered in icy strings to her head. The geode glowed like white fire under her arm. Her only thought was to reach Daniel. And so she ran as if the hounds of hell snapped at her heels. Towards the last place she'd felt him before their link had shattered.

Losing patience, Nila skidded into a swerve across the road and slammed on the brakes, effectively stopping the girl. "Get in the car, damn you!"

Lily fell to her knees beside the car, choking for air, sides stitched with pain. "I'm so pissed!" She gasped a scream. "So mad! How could they? I curse them—"

"No!" Nila leaped out of the car. "For goodness's sake, do not curse them!" She hauled Lily up and forced her into the passenger seat.

"Like I'd do any harm . . . " Lily coughed raggedly and curled into a shivering ball. "The bloody bitches killed my magic! I need Daniel," she said, then, "Oh, God, I think I'm going to be sick."

"You don't have time to be sick." Nila flung herself back behind the wheel and flipped the heater on high. "We have work to do. At this moment the talisman is heading Daniel's way. If Gran has her wish, he'll be forced to wear it."

"She can force him?" Lily's teeth chattered against blue lips.

Nila rammed her foot down on the gas. "She'll try. Or hadn't you noticed Gran likes things her way?"

The inside of the car reeked of the hateful incense, making Lily's stomach heave and her head spin. She felt hollow boned and weak as a baby sparrow. "My magic is dead, Nila. She stole my joy, my painting . . ."

"No one can steal another's power. Gran only bound your magic, made it inaccessible. And it can be unbound."

Lily turned her dripping head towards the girl, recalling Nila muttering quick words just before the Shackling spell struck her. "You hexed the spell?"

The girl shrugged. "You heard Madame warn me. I think I managed to deflect some of it."

"Deflect it where?"

She flashed a grin both macabre and nasty in the glow of the dashboard light. "Let's just say Gran's electricity will be sporadic for a few weeks." Anger twisted her face. "Shackling is forbidden except in extreme cases. And after a hearing in front of the entire Cohort. Your magic, though not in the least bit normal, doesn't seem close to extreme."

The rain drumming like impatient fingers on the car roof echoed the pounding ache inside Lily's head. Peeling off her sodden jacket and sweater, she wondered if the young witch would revise her opinion when she found out the men Lily'd painted to life were now stalking her like the walking dead.

Another shiver wracked her body. "The minute that damn talisman touched my blood, my link with Daniel died. And he's so far beyond angry. If Gran thinks her will is stronger than his, she's delusional."

"She might very well be delusional," Nila said icily. "To attempt a shackling . . . holy shit! And with witches who had no clue their magic would be so used? She'll lose her position in the Cohort at the very least." The girl wrenched the wheel as the car hydroplaned towards a gutter full of roiling water.

"Then I'm sorry for her," Lily said. "But only a little. I know she is only trying to protect Daniel."

Nila reached across to squeeze her hand.

"I can heal him, you know. Or I could have, before." Lily's voice broke.

"I believe you can, Lil. I've never seen magic like yours. Madame Bagasha usually senses a new power in the city and seeks the person out before, well, before mishaps occur. But she missed yours. Rogue magic is an Elemental and, like I said, unpredictable. Highly intuitive, spontaneous, and creative. Like you. With Elemental witches, the magic is part of their essence. I know you can undo what you've done. Just like you can paint over a canvas you don't like. But you'll need help and supplies. And Madame Bagasha."

"I need Daniel," Lily sobbed through another teeth clenching shiver. "Now that my magic is Shackled I can't hurt him, right? Take me to him, Nila, please?"

Face grim in the meager light, Nila nodded. "I will. But there's something you need to know, Lily. Since you are an Elemental, magic is substantive, of your essence. A shackling can mean death to an Elemental. It will slowly drain you until, well . . . until you're nothing but an empty husk."

Lily began to cry. She felt the cold weight of the binding inside her chest. Her ribs hurt from the swollen thickness of the spell. Her heart ached as if massive fingers were squeezing the life from it, beat by sluggish beat. She'd feared her magic, yes, even rejected it. At first. Only now did she understand. She was made of magic. As much as skin and bone, beating heart, thought, and emotion.

Nila had it right. From inside her shriveled innards that once held light and joy and love, Lily felt a hatred building against Daniel's grandmother. And it frightened her. If she could hurt Daniel through love, what despicable, unconscious acts might she do for vengeance? Another shiver shook her, this one of fear.

Maybe Gran was right to shackle her . . .

"You can shield, can't you?" Nila asked suddenly. "I saw you block Gran when she tried to Read you."

"Yes, a little. It was instinct. And I used anger, not good, I know. Nila, I can . . . I could see magic. In color, I mean. Weaving and swirling through the air. I could mix the colors of every witch's magic there tonight. Gran's is a deep, bloody burgundy."

Nila's mouth dropped open. "But of course! That makes perfect sense, your medium is color."

"You know that if I'd any idea I could hurt Daniel, I never would have . . ."

"Like you had any choice," Nila smiled at her. "Either in the waking of your magic or in loving him. Daniel's not just a Reader, he's a babe magnet. Always has been. And the way he tells it, you belonged to him the moment he first laid eyes on you. Which is a lovely bit of magic in itself, if you ask me. All his life, Daniel's kept his distance from people. Never allowed anyone to get close. Except maybe Gradyn, a little. Gran did her job well."

"What do you mean?"

"She taught him an empath can be destroyed by too much emotion. Isn't that the saddest thing? When her abilities manifested, her parents had her committed to a sanitarium. She grew into a cold, calculating woman with no patience for emotion. Which explains her immediate dislike of you, wearing your heart on your sleeve. To Gran, lack of control is a weakness. That's what life taught her, poor soul." Nila slowed to turn the little car up the expressway on-ramp and eased into traffic heading through downtown. "She's forever pressuring Daniel to join the Cohort, hates that he won't use his abilities for their benefit. But he refuses to have any part of us, thinks we meddle. And he's right. We do meddle. We always think we know what's best. A Cohort of witches is like any other cooperative, a beehive of power grubbing politics and personal agendas."

"I won't be part of them either, ever. Those women tonight treated you like a leper, Nila. Why? You're one of them."

"I'm not, actually. I am Madame Bagasha's, and they resent it."

"That you train with her and they don't?"

"I guess. But also because my magic is in some way Rogue, too." She glanced at Lily. "They have a right to be angry with me. I failed in my responsibility by not discovering you have Rogue magic. Thank the Gods you're a loving soul, Lil, or more than Daniel might have been hurt."

Glancing at the geode on Lily's lap, now a rippling purple, Nila smiled. "That thing gives a whole new meaning to the term *pet rock*. See those colors it's flashing? They're typically soothing."

"What can I say? It loves me." Lily gave the rock an ambiguous look. "I'm not sure the feeling's mutual. If it amplified my feelings enough to strip Daniel, then . . . "

"It'll work the same way to heal him. I have faith in you, Lil. You should too."

"Faith, yeah, about that . . . I'm only sure of two things when it comes to my magic. It's more forceful hooked up to love. And love uses it for its own purpose. Can I put faith in that?"

Nila grinned. "More than anything else, I should think."

They drove in silence after that. The rain streamed from the sky hard and fast. Nila concentrated on keeping the car steady in the growing traffic. The strong musk of incense still clung to their clothes and coated Lily's throat with sick dread. She was exhausted, freezing, and afraid of what she'd done, what she could no longer do and what would become of Daniel. Every muscle in her body ached. Every nerve screamed as if she'd imploded in on herself.

Nila began talking again, about magic and about the workings of simple spells and techniques. Lily knew she was just trying to distract her. But it worked. After a few more minutes, Lily uncurled. She actually felt the heater warm her skin as it began to dry her cotton shirt. Bit by bit, her body unclenched and she concentrated more intently on Nila's words. If her power ever lived again, Lily knew she would need all the knowledge she could get to make it work safely.

Twenty minutes later, Nila left the expressway and turned down a side street to stop in front of a squat little building dwarfed between towering downtown office buildings. She turned off the engine and the hot fan died. Lily immediately started to shiver. "Gradyn lives here?"

"Hardly," Nila laughed. "Look closer."

Lily's jaw dropped when the Madame's magic shop materialized before her eyes.

"I told you we needed supplies." Nila motioned her out of the car. Lily plucked her soggy sweater off the floor and tugged it back on, cursing as the clammy wool stuck to her skin. She loved this wool sweater, a shrunken hand-me-down from Daniel. She buried her face in the sleeve for a moment, trying to draw in his scent and got only a dose of wet sheep. She stepped reluctantly from the warm confines of the car and found that even wet, the wool protected her from the worst of the wind as she ran towards the purple door with its dragonhead handle.

*

Inside the shop, the air swept over her with golden color and an astounding warmth, as if it knew what her draining spirits needed most. The room hadn't changed, prisms still danced on beaded strings and an invisible breeze swept the scent of sage, camphor, and gardenias across her skin. But tonight, standing behind the counter packing a woven basket, was the diminutive, bright eyed, and bristly haired Madame herself.

She smiled like a fairy godmother caught out on the town when she saw Lily's eyes fill with grateful tears. "Surely you didn't think I would send you off on your first healing unprepared? I've packed candles, crystals, herbs for spells and healing teas." Madame's eyes twinkled. "And a few extras for whatever else might come up."

Nila cackled, Lily blushed, and Madame pretended her words weren't as obvious as the spangles glittering on her wrists.

Nila glanced inside the basket. "Lavender candles instead of green ones? But you know Daniel's a Taurus."

"Taurus?" Lily asked.

"The bull," Nila whispered a lurid grin.

"She and Daniel won't have the time, nor much inclination I suspect, for fun and games." Madame pushed Nila out of the way with a flap of her hands. "Now, Lily, though I impart this knowledge quickly, do not doubt that it is important. As rules go, these are sacred. Rule Number One: Always keep your use of magic simple and confined to what you know."

Lily looked confused. "But the shackling worked. I have no magic."

Madame's mouth thinned into an angry line. "And I do apologize for Daniel's gran, my sweet child. She had no right and she'll be dealt with. But your magic isn't dead. See how the geode still pulses? As a Reader, Daniel can undo the shackling when he's had some healing time."

Lily felt a glimmer of hope. "But Gran insists Daniel is stripped. Can he even work magic?"

A sly smile crossed her face and was instantly gone. "Love is as powerful a magic as any, dear girl. Which leads me to Rule Number Two. Remember to take into account both the light and dark sides of magic. Never doubt that all power has two faces. Every working has the potential for good as well as evil, as you learned tonight. Never forget that. Rule Number Three: All the power you call must be directed into a spell, a working, or a charm. Something specific. No energy must be left lingering. When your geode broke the magic circle at Magdaline's house tonight, the power went wild. I had to harness it, which made me more than a little cranky, I can tell you.

"And that was the reason I could not help you at the time, Lily. I am sorry. I placed that harnessed power inside three gemstones I have added to this basket. Their potency should improve Daniel's healing process. When you set out your triangle of healing, you must place a candle and one of these stones at each of the three points. This," Madame held up a cluster of purplish crystals, "is an amethyst. For protection. The golden amber is for focusing. And this dark stone, hematite, will enhance a working harmony between the two of you."

"Where's the rose quartz for love?" Nila teased.

"They need no help in that area," Madame said in a tone implying Nila was an idiot child. She wrapped the gemstones in scraps of flannel and tucked them back inside the basket along with a much worn book of healing spells. Behind her back, Nila plucked a pale red quartz from under the counter and with a broad wink Lily couldn't miss, dropped it into the basket.

"Rule Number Four," Madame continued. "This is magic's most precious, unbreakable rule. Harm none. Anger generates . . . well, you were a victim this night, Lily, but you also inflicted pain. When the geode blasted the circle, we remaining witches ended up with aching heads and a valuable, long overdue reminder that negative energy has absolutely no place in a weaving. Now," Madame gave the basket a final pat, "I've tried to think of every possibility, my dear, and added a few things Daniel can use."

"Like condoms?" Nila grinned.

Madame cupped Lily's face between her small hands. Lily felt a tingling buzz run through her body. "There is to be no physical contact between you and Daniel, Lily. Even if the boy insists."

Blushing yet again, Lily nodded.

"And about the geode . . . " Madame Bagasha mused.

"Should I leave it behind?"

The little Romany witch shrugged. "You'll have to trust your heart to guide you now, little one. Just try not to love the boy to death."

Behind Madame, Nila grinned shamelessly. Lily reached to take the basket . . . and jerked away as a wave of revulsion filled her chest.

"Oh my weary stars! I forgot! The blasted talisman is in there," Madame Bagasha dug into the basket and pulled out the gemstone necklace. Lily turned her face away with a shudder as Nila quickly found a lead box. Madame dropped the talisman inside and carefully latched the lid before placing it back in the basket. "I'm sorry, child, but Maggie insisted it reach him. Just in case. It's Daniel's choice to wear it or not. I insisted on that."

"Do you think . . . " Lily began and then gushed. "Do I have love enough to heal him?"

"Oh, my dear, yes. And how I envy you this adventure." She pressed a kiss to Lily's cheek. "Be sure to ask the Goddess's blessing, and always give thanks as well. It's the polite thing to do. And good luck. You'll need that as much as any blessing. Or maybe not."

With a wink, she shooed the two from the shop.

Chapter Nineteen

Outside the magic shop once again, the sleet hit Lily with a frigid blast that had her diving thankfully into Nila's car.

Nila had the heater on high before they'd fastened their seat belts. "Sorry we didn't have dry clothes at the shop for you, Lil. Gradyn will probably have some female thing you can change into. Can you imagine the parade of women through his life?"

"Do you?" Lily asked, surprised. "Imagine his women, I mean? I've known him almost a year, and I've never seen him seriously pursue anyone. He is a champion flirt, though."

"I wouldn't know," Nila said with feigned disinterest. "I stay out of his sights. The man scares the wits out of me, all gorgeous and fancified. Makes me twitchy."

"Is that so?" Lily cast her a long look. "Daniel makes me twitchy. Among other things."

Nila frowned. "Madame Bagasha was serious about no physical contact. Right now touching Daniel would be like pressing a fresh burn. Pure agony. Do you think you can keep your hands to yourself or should I take you home right now?"

"Do I really need a lecture, Mom? I was linked to him for hours, I know what kind of pain he's in."

"Sorry." The girl had the grace to grimace. "What was that like anyway? Could you, like, hear him speaking in an echoing, ominous voice or what?"

Lily laughed, "No." She clutched the basket nervously on her lap, once more unsure of what she was doing and who she imagined herself to be in order to do it. "He was just a reassuring presence in my head. I could feel his stronger emotions."

"You keep saying he isn't stripped."

Lily looked at her in the dim light. "Could he maintain any emotional link if his paranormal senses were burned as badly as Gran claimed? Mostly he was drunk out of his gourd, all mushy and drifty. At least until . . . God, he must have felt the shackling spell hit me because he got suddenly mad as hell. Then he just held . . . well, he just sort of held me. With his mind."

"What an awesome gift to share." Nila let out an exaggerated sigh. "I wonder if there's a tall, dark, and handsome Reader with a link out there for me."

Lily groaned. "I think you and Gradyn Spencer should pair up and have a flock of mocking, sadistic babies. You two deserve each other."

"He is gorgeous," Nila sighed. "I'd split the sheets with him, no hesitation, if I was drunk out of my gourd."

"Then come to the opening Tuesday night at his new gallery." Lily turned to her. "If you're there I will know . . . mmm, let me think, four people I can talk to. Gradyn said I could invite anyone I wanted. Say you'll come, Nila, please? You and I can gaze at the unparalleled gorgeousity of Mr. Spencer from across the room. And across glasses of very expensive champagne."

"I'll gaze. You'll be attached at the hip to Daniel."

"I won't, you know. I'll be whisked off to meet dozens of people I won't remember, be asked about inspiration and ideas as if I just pluck paintings out of my brain like they are on an assembly line."

"Don't you?"

"Hell, no. Ideas just come. Like magic . . . "

"You'll get your powers back, Lil." Nila reached to clasp her arm and give her a shake. "Daniel is a very powerful Reader. If anyone can undo Gran's shackling, he can."

Lily leaned her head back and closed eyelids suddenly too heavy to hold open. "I feel all caved in. And lost. Have you ever been in love, Nila?"

"Gods, yes. I've been in love with Gradyn Spencer since the day I was born. Hurts like hell, doesn't it?"

"I never imagined," Lily sighed.

Ten minutes later Nila turned the car into a sweeping drive that led up to a large, magnificently restored Victorian house. "Ta-da! Gradyn Spencer's domicile. Spectacular, huh? The man has class, I grant him that. I'll walk you to the door and then, Lily dear, you are on your own."

Lily panicked. "You can't leave me! What do I do with all this . . . stuff?" She gave the basket a rigid shake.

Nila laughed. "Well, first you set the candles out. Preferably upright. Then you light them with a blessing. After that I guarantee instinct, and Daniel's particular magic," she did her eyebrow waggle again, "will kick in."

It wasn't until Nila rang the doorbell that the two realized the time was well after midnight.

"Damn." Nila poised to run.

*

But the Gradyn who opened the door was dressed and, though drunk and unshaven, appeared wide awake. "Ladies!" He beamed and blinked in alarm when Nila vanished back into the dark. Then he had Lily by the arm and was dragging her inside the house. "Good Lord, Lily, you're soaked to the skin!"

"I'll drip all over your beautiful floor," she stuttered as he forced her into the foyer and with a last bemused look after Nila, closed the door against the rain.

"You, silly child, will take those clothes off this minute. And if I must, I'll bring you a robe." His grin was far from sober, or paternal. Already his nimble hands were stripping the wet jacket from her shoulders. She hadn't the energy to fight him.

"How's Daniel? Is he . . . "

"Asleep. After puking his insides out. I assume you brought the talisman . . . wait! Shit, Lily, you can't be here!" Gradyn cast a wild eye up the stairs and tried to shove her back out the door.

"It's okay, Gradyn. Believe it or not, I'm Daniel's healer tonight. With Madame Bagasha's blessing. But I have the talisman." Distaste flared on her face. "I'm just praying like hell he won't need it."

Gradyn's brows lifted in comical confusion. "You're a . . . ? You can . . . ?"

"Yes." The half-truth and another shiver shook her weary body. She lifted her arms like a child as Gradyn peeled off the sweater and dropped it in a sopping heap on his perfect parquet floor.

He started on her shirt buttons. "Daniel never has to know, love." He smirked as she slapped his hands away to undo them herself. He grinned incorrigibly. "Now there's some color back in your face. Through that door is a hot fire waiting just for you. I'm off to make you tea, which you will drink, before you can see Daniel. No arguments." Gradyn dashed away to find the promised robe. "Just leave your clothes there, I'll toss them in the dryer."

By the time she'd stripped down to clammy skin, a thick robe had floated down from the balcony above. The robe, a man's, naturally, was huge but dry and warm. Lily wrapped it nearly twice around herself before knotting the belt. It sagged open at the neck. She clutched it close, shooting a grateful smile at Gradyn when he came through a door carrying a tea tray and kicking a laundry basket ahead of him. Lily threw her wet clothes in the basket. Tucking the geode inside one of the robe's giant pockets, she gathered up the dragging hem before following him into a large room of male heaven complete with game consoles and both a pool and air hockey table.

Lily ran to the hearth to curl as close to the flames as possible. Gradyn handed her a steaming mug of tea. He had to cover her shaking fingers with his until he was sure she wouldn't spill and burn herself.

He was suddenly all seriousness as he folded his tall frame to sit on the floor beside her. "Now, Lily, you understand about shielding, don't you? Because emotions are like poison to him in his state."

The hot tea burned her mouth but she gulped it anyway, closing her eyes at the heady spread of warmth through her limbs. She flashed him a grateful grin. He'd liberally doctored the brew with brandy.

"I can shield," she said after another sip. "And Nila taught me a few simple spells on the way here. I swear I won't hurt him again, Gradyn. In fact, I'm probably the only person who can give him peace enough to heal himself. He needs me now as much as I need him." Tears sprang to fill her eyes and she put up a ready shield against the emotion. "Did he tell you? Gran and her coven shackled my magic."

Gradyn's face paled. "She wouldn't dare!"

"She did. Madame and Nila say I'm a Rogue Elemental. Which means my magic is as much a part of me as these painter's hands or my blue eyes." She met his horrified gaze. "And only another Reader can undo a binding spell of this magnitude."

"Christ, Lily, are you saying . . . the shackling can't kill you, can it?" He reached as if to take her in his arms but at her negligent shrug, forced a smile instead. "You should have seen Daniel bolt for the door the second your link broke. I had to tackle him and he fought like a lion. Then the scotch got the better of him. Finally."

Lily stared miserably into the flames and finished her tea in silence. What good she would do Daniel with her magic bound, she hadn't a clue. And he couldn't work magic until he was healed. What a vicious cycle of events. She knew nothing of power, hadn't any technique or skill. In fact, Lily realized with a fragile draw of breath, she really only had the will of her heart to guide her. She stood and handed Gradyn the empty mug.

"Lil, are you sure . . . "

"I am sure, absolutely." She walked to where she'd set Madame's basket and, picking it up, headed towards the stairs. As Gradyn moved to lead the way, she shook her head. "You don't have to show me." She flashed a sudden smile. "I know where he is."

Gradyn looked down at her. "How come tonight you're all self-assured and growed up? It's a bit of a shocker, I don't mind saying."

"I hurt the person I love most in the world today," Lily said with unforgiving terseness. "That will bring the most wayward spirit down to earth pretty damn fast."

Gradyn brushed a knuckle across her cheek and said gently, "I'm at the end of the hall if you need anything."

Looking up the curved stairway, Lily sensed Daniel asleep above her like a faint breath cruising her skin. She took the stairs two at a time, the geode heavy in her pocket, the basket clutched under her arm. Pausing outside his closed door, she felt the link between them strong again, lilting in her veins. She took a moment to rejoice at its return. Then with a frown of concentration, burrowed inward to rope all her turbulent emotions like wild horses, corralling them inside a mountainous vault made real in her mind before she slipped inside the room.

The link vibrated, brimming with emotional harmonics, Daniel's semi-conscious acknowledgment of her, her awareness of him in the bed, the scent of him sweet on her tongue. Drawing a steadying breath, Lily struggled to think of him only in soothing terms while she stood waiting for her eyes to adjust to the dark. The room was minimally furnished with a large bed, a bureau, a tidy desk, and night tables on both sides of the bed. Cool air smelling of rain and wet leaves drifted through a barely opened window, fluttering the flame of a single candle burning on the desk. In the dusky light Lily saw clothes scattered across the floor where Daniel had drunkenly shed them.

She tiptoed closer to the bed, clutching the basket to her chest and saw him lying curled on his side under blankets bunched at his waist. His skin was pale as marble and sweat gleamed on his shoulders. His chest rose and fell in irregular huffs of pain. Dark hair spilled across the pillow and curled damp at his neck.

Seeing him so tortured, Lily felt the rise of guilty tears. Knowing such feelings could undo whatever self healing he'd managed, she slammed her self-control more securely in place. No more hurt, she promised him in a fierce whisper.

Digging out the candles Madame Bagasha had packed, Lily noticed the magic symbols carved into the wax. They would enhance whatever spells Daniel was strong enough to cast. Lily remembered Madame telling her this and was grateful the little gypsy witch had allowed her to come. Few would have trusted Lily near him, especially knowing she possessed an untrained Elemental magic. Lily was determined to live up to that faith . . . even if her own belief teetered as precariously as a crystal in a hurricane. Bare feet silent on the thick carpet, Lily set about placing the candles, the first on the night table at Daniel's back, the second on a cedar chest at his feet and the third on the table near his head.

He lay very still, deep in some meditative trance, Lily suspected. She couldn't take her eyes off him glowing ghostly white against the dark sheets. His naked back curved long and slender, his spine a wonderland of shadowed hills and valleys. Lily wanted to fold herself around him, feel that strong back solid against her and bit her lip against a need to touch him. Placing the last candle, she stepped back, checking the alignment of each to see that they enclosed him inside an upside down triangle. Madame had explained that an inverted triangle represented the womb, a vessel of creation. Female power, the little witch had added with an enigmatic smile.

Lily held a match ready to strike and hesitated. Nila had described how to light a candle the magical way, all the while laughing over how difficult it had been for her to master the task. With her own magic shackled, Lily realized she'd fail if she tried. But standing in the dark at Daniel's back, Lily felt his presence like lyrical notes in her head and imagined his magic trickling like clear water through her veins. And she sensed, suddenly, another energy in the room, a magic faintly drifting in the air, feral and untried.

If she could see this magic's color, then perhaps she could work it like she painted, one brush stroke at a time. Closing her eyes, she stretched her mind out and felt the strange, untamed power respond. A golden light bloomed like a dawning sun behind her eyelids. This power was not of the geode and not of Daniel. Lily briefly wondered where it came from, then was only grateful for its presence. She curled her hands into a cup beside the unlighted candlewick and visualized the cup filled with restorative water.

In the barest of whispers, Lily spoke, "*Gentle powers, bless this flame, undo the harm where I'm to blame,*" and gently blew across her cupped palms towards the candle. The wick burst into flame. Lily straightened in disbelief. She'd done it, first try! Moving quickly, Lily lit the candle at the foot of the bed, and then moved to the one nearest Daniel's head. Whispering the blessing a last time, she breathed the flame to life. And across the lighted wick met Daniel's eyes open and watching her.

Chapter Twenty

Lily simply stared at Daniel for a long, breathless minute. His glasses lay on the nightstand. Without them his beautiful eyes shone an intense golden brown, alive with delight and promise and passion.

"Am I hurting you?" she finally managed to whisper.

"Not even a little." He rose on one elbow with an amazed laugh. "It's a freaking miracle. And you're shielded. When'd you learn that?"

"I've always known. You know, how to hide bothersome things. Hide myself. I just never did it with you. I never had to. Oh, Daniel . . . " Her smile faded. "I am so sorry."

"I'm not." His teeth flashed white in a grin of drunken cheerfulness. "God, to feel you in my head, Lily, in my blood. It's fantastic! I must be dreaming because you can't possibly be here. The witches would never allow it."

Lily took a half step closer. "So my nearness, it isn't agony?"

"Ah, babe, it's ecstasy!" He reached out to her. His grin died and his hand fell. "Are you all right? You . . . you feel different."

"You don't remember? Your Gran, she used the coven to shackle my magic."

He sat up, face stricken with horror, disbelief, and finally outrage. "No . . . " His whisper nearly broke her. When he moved to get out of bed, Lily thrust out her hands.

"Stop! You can't touch me. I'll . . . I'll fall apart if you touch me, Daniel. And I can't fall apart."

Her panic slithered past her shield. He grabbed his head as shots of pain peppered his senses. He fought it, sweat beading his forehead. Lily stumbled back. "I shouldn't be here, I'm not strong enough! Oh, Daniel . . . "

"No, stay." He lowered his shaking hands to look at her. "I can undo the shackling spell. Only a Reader can. And I must." His eyes darkened with fear. "You're an Elemental, Lily. Your magic is your essence. If you stay bound too long . . . "

"I know, Nila told me. But I have time." With a visible straightening of her spine, she nodded. "I'll stay, but only if you promise you'll tell me when my presence becomes too painful."

Quickly, she finished setting the gemstones, amethyst and agates, at the base of each candle. Daniel watched her every move. When she finished, she folded to a sit on the carpet a few feet from the bed where he could see her face but stay beyond his reach.

She smiled sadly. "Needless to say, your Gran and I aren't friends."

Anger tightened Daniel's mouth. "She had no right, Lily, and I'm sorry."

"She was only trying to protect you."

"I wish that were so, but with Gran it's never simple. She's always got an agenda. I knew you two wouldn't get along. You are sunlight and crazy color, she's shadow and hard discipline."

"I could have healed you, Daniel, before she . . . I could see in my head just how to undo what I'd done." Lily tugged the geode out of the robe pocket and held it up. "Can you feel the energy inside these crystals?"

"Yes. I feel you, your magic! Wait . . . how is this possible?"

Lily shrugged. "I have Rogue magic. Who can say what's possible? Nila managed to deflect some of the power behind your grandmother's spell. With the geode . . . well, you know it's more than just a rock. It amplifies power, as you discovered," she sent him an apologetic look, "and seems to reflect and channel energy. I think it can help you heal."

"But you don't have that much time, Lily. The shackling will—"

Her voice cut him off, tranquil and steady. "I have time, Daniel. Just tell me how we can help you." She grinned, hefting the geode. "Me and my pet rock."

Daniel leaned his head back against the headboard. Fear for her and a seething anger strained his face. After a moment his shoulders heaved as if he'd shifted a great weight. He closed his eyes and smiled dreamily.

"I can feel that drifty stillness you become when you disappear into a slant of intriguing light or a pattern in the clouds. An emotion, by the way, completely you, Lil. And so magnificently different from the storm of passion I walked into in your apartment this afternoon. Which is you since I kissed you." His eyes opened and he leered at her. "So I'm thinking you should shed that ridiculous robe already half falling off anyway, and climb in here with me."

"No!" Lily snatched at the gaping robe and scuttled further back. "No physical contact. Madame Bagasha was definite about that!"

Daniel sat up, eyes darkly serious. "Listen, Lily. Tonight there is no Madame. And no Gran. It's just you and me. I saw you light that candle with magic, yet yours is shackled. And you empowered a geode, filled it with your heart, and I walked into it. Maybe the geode protected me and forged this link we share, I don't know. I don't care! All I want is you, now. I think we should ride this as far as it takes us."

He laughed at the stubborn lift of her chin.

"No." She scowled. "I'm here to take back what I caused, that's all."

"Don't you dare take back a thing. I've waited too long for you, for this!" His anger shot blazing color around the room and bent him double in pain.

She was halfway to his side before she could stop herself. "I'll only take the hurt, Daniel. Can't it be that simple for now? Please?"

With a caustic laugh, he said, "You and I passed simple a while ago, Lil." His body slid to lie flat on the bed, every muscle, nerve, and bone blistered and hot.

"We'll get through this, I promise," he reassured her before his eyes closed again. Whispering a protection spell, Daniel stretched his senses out to touch Lily's pet geode. And he found her there, inside the crystals, loving and strong and determined.

He laid an arm across his aching eyes, heaved an easier breath. "No matter what Gran said, I'm not stripped, Lil. Scorched, yes. Hurting? Hell, yes. But I felt all your amazing power before I stepped into that apartment and I went freely, with my heart wide open." He lifted his arm to look at her. "Tell me something, do you know how to draw pain using magic?"

"No. But—"

"I do. I can show you. All I need is you in this bed, wrapped around me. Please, Lily." Another spasm twisted his face. On the carpet in front of her, the geode pulsed a brutal red . . . not a reflection of her feelings this time, but his. Lily wrapped her hands around the stone and imagined easing it into cool lake water. She heard Daniel's sigh of relief. Beneath her fingers the light dimmed to a kaleidoscope of muted blues and silver. He rolled over on his side. She saw his fingers move, shaping and reshaping spells in the flickering candlelight.

Through the link, she felt him struggling to gather power and wanted to weep. What was she doing here? Even if her magic were free she still hadn't a clue how to use it properly. God, she hated learning in baby steps! One couldn't get to where one needed fast enough. All she wanted was to crawl in bed with him as he'd asked. But Madame Bagasha had been adamant.

"Trust me," she heard his whisper. "I need you in this bed, Lily."

Every instinct cried out to hold him, smooth his hair, brush reassuring kisses on his damp forehead. And Madame Bagasha had also told her to trust her instincts. Perhaps if they didn't touch she could lie, just for a bit, beside him. She stood and, moving carefully to keep her hands from brushing his skin, she pulled the comforter up over his shoulders, encasing him in a cocoon of blankets until only the dark of his hair showed on the pillow.

Then she climbed onto the bed at his back. She thought she heard him groan and froze for a long moment before stretching out to lie curved in his shadow, not touching him. Daniel's breath hitched in response to her. She felt the geode's power surge again. The scent of apple blossoms filled the air and then the geode changed its rhythm to match her pulse.

Lily lay stiff and carefully unmoving for a long time, holding tight rein on her awareness of Daniel so close, the male smell of him, the heat of his body. And lying so still, she was suddenly, starkly aware of the shackling spell swelling into a thing large and deadly in her chest. She could taste an acidic metal on her tongue, feel a spiked darkness coiling through her organs, sucking the warmth from her limbs, from her blood. Lily remembered this sense of losing cohesion, of shredding to pieces, a memory from long ago when her parents died. Now she had the same crumbling sensation. As if her heart hadn't the strength to expand and contract. She bit down hard on her lip and used the pain to keep her focus sharp. The last thing Daniel needed was terror leaking through her shield. And so she lay stiff, still, while her spirit bled from her like paint dripping from a canvas.

Daniel's magic touched her first as a tentative breeze on her cheek. She saw it against the candle light, a drift of blue mist. Her heavy heart leaped eagerly towards him, and he shrank away. Self control, she reprimanded herself and soon felt him hesitantly seek her again. He was directing his magic through the geode, letting the crystals act as buffer from the emotional forces his psychic nerves were too tender to tolerate. So they were both learning in baby steps, Lily thought.

Knowing the geode helped shield him only made Lily more desperate to reach him. But she waited. Feeling another sweep of his magic, she slowly lowered her shield. And finally understood. He'd been trained to link magic with others, as all witches of the Cohort did. He was trying to show her what to do. She opened herself further, felt the probing of his mind in hers like fingers playing music she already knew how to sing . . . a sweet touch that left her gasping.

*

Only then did Daniel realize how fast the shackling was draining her.

His eyes snapped open. Ignoring the pain, he rolled to pull her into his arms. His synapses blistered when his skin touched hers. His magic ricocheted out of control. The geode blazed with light and Daniel felt a mighty tug as the power inside the rock began to draw the worst of his pain.

Then Lily's body went limp, her skin turned a pale cold, her lips too harsh a red. Her eyes, a blue as clear as a morning sky, shone on him as if all the life left in her was his to take. Daniel shook with rage at the impotency of his weakened state, at the abusive power his Gran had wielded just because she could. His lips brushed Lily's icy cheek . . . and he tasted a strange magic swarming the room, free and wild as a mountain wind. Opening his senses to it, Daniel caught his breath and laughed.

"Bless the Powers!" he cried in a broken voice. "Lily, you won't believe this. In her single-minded rage, Gran missed something incredible when she shackled you. You, darling girl, have more than one magic!"

Lily blinked blearily at him. "Is that possible?"

In the dim candlelight, Daniel's eyes glowed. "It seems for you nothing is impossible! Your magic isn't singular . . . it sort of splinters off, like a fractal. You know, how water crystallizes in all directions when it freezes? Gran never realized that. What she shackled was like an arm, a piece. I've never heard of such a magic! And, man, is it beautiful, Lily. Wild and creative and courageous. Like you!" He grinned like a fool and covered her face with kisses. Which burned like hell, the softness of her under his lips, the flavor of her in his mouth. But he didn't care.

"This magic, Lil? It's free. Unbound. I know it sounds impossible. Yet now I've Read it, I realize I've been immersed in this energy since you walked in the room. It's a power so elemental, it defies restraint!"

"But can it heal you?"

"Oh, yes!" He let her cocoon him in blankets again but when she lay back down, tugged his arms free to wrap loosely around her.

At her scalding look, he said, "Give me a break, Lily. I can't *not* hold you."

Unafraid of the pain and impatient now, Daniel sank his magic into her again. As his empathic gift glided through her body, a sigh escaped her. Her wild magic raced in ecstatic circles around his, and after several tries, he managed to tame it enough to join his in testing the bonds of the shackling spell.

*

Lily marveled at the fluid, confident way his power moved through her, probing and curious and possessive. At some point she fell into a place beyond thought . . . beyond all need for thought, where only impression and sensation ruled. Her skin flushed. She stretched in dreamy, sensual pleasure. Magical threads wrapped like arms around her and desire stroked her nerves as if his tongue, and not his psychic skill, caressed her.

"Oh God, oh God, oh God . . . " she moaned, her body arching beneath a mystical touch more erotic than any she could imagine. She felt the flush of rising orgasm and stiffened, embarrassed.

"Damn it, Daniel, stop playing with me!"

She heard his breathy laugh.

"I'm sorry, sort of. I'll be good now. I just wanted . . . well, you know what I want."

"But you were inside me. And it was almost as good as the real thing."

"Not even," Daniel growled. After a long moment where he gathered his wits, his discipline, and some self-control, he was able to pull her magic into a joint weaving. He let her explore the give and take of their two abilities working together. Later Lily would try to describe the intimacy of the experience, how she opened fully to his Reader's sight, how his magic, so masculine and yet gentle, tangled around hers. How, with her own magical sight, she saw her verdant greens and his iridescent blues soaring and diving together like musical riffs in a symphony, too delicate and beautiful for the naked eye. Oh, if she could but paint the colors they created this night . . .

Needless to say they blew Gran's shackling to bits. And while their two magics learned each other, their bodies strained together, her fingers playing in his hair, his hands sliding over the robe to stroke her back, fit her hips tighter to his.

At one point Daniel quoted softly in her ear, "*To wake the soul by tender strokes of art, to raise the genius, and to mend the heart . . .*"

Lily laughed and burrowed closer to trail kisses down his throat.

She heard his sharp intake of breath. "Jesus! Cool the magic, darling girl, or I'll be shagging you senseless in another minute, burned nerves be damned."

Lily drew away and looked at him. "Could you . . . ?"

"No. So for pity's sake, ratchet back that amazing energy a notch or two."

"Sorry."

"You're not."

She hooked a leg across his blanketed hip. "You could be more accommodating, you know. I can't get in to heal if you stay shielded, Daniel."

He groaned. She got an impression of extreme sexual frustration and, with a sigh, gentled her magic to drift about them like rain. Reluctantly, Daniel unblocked his senses. His pain, sharp-edged and visceral, snapped at Lily's mind like a rabid dog. But her concentration held. Praying her lack of finesse wouldn't harm him, she released a soothing current down his sensory pathways and found the epicenter of nerve damage ablaze with jagged pain. Instinct kicked in. She felt a force both primordial and timeless rise up from her womb. The geode flared on the table beside them. In her arms, Daniel whimpered before all tension drained from his body as he surrendered to her.

Using the geode as vessel and transmitter, Lily whispered her spell. *"Untried power that caused this pain, help me draw it back again."*

Magic crackled in the air like static, stirring Daniel's hair. He whispered her name, tightened his arms around her. She felt a wild surge of love and calmly, confidently banked it into a usable force. Cheek settled against his chest, she let magic swell from her like an operatic aria, ripe, fertile, ebbing and peaking, rising and sweeping. Whispering the words over and over, she let her spell fall into him and began wrapping each burnt synapse in comfort as soft as goose down.

Daniel's fists uncurled, his legs straightened and he fell, at long last, into a natural sleep. Lily, deep inside the beauty of their entwined mysticism, murmured tender words and drew his pain like a syringe draws blood from a vein. All the while she matched him heartbeat for heartbeat until, after a time, she too drifted to sleep.

Chapter Twenty-one

Lily woke in the pre-light of dawn with a hangover, Daniel's hangover, throbbing in her temples. As if she'd been the one slogging scotch the night before. She lay in a tangled nest of blankets. The room smelled of cooling beeswax, wet leaves . . . and Daniel, tangy sweet and warm nearby. Memory rushed in and with it, a sharp intake of breath. Opening her eyes, she saw him propped on his elbow grinning down at her.

He brushed a delicate kiss over her lips. "Gods help me, but I love you."

His eyes were luminous in the soft light, intent, vulnerable, and hiding nothing without his glasses on. Lily wanted to sink to the bottom of their melting depths. She reached out a finger to trace the arc of his dark brow, then curved her palm around his stubbled jaw before resting her thumb at the corner of his mouth.

"Do you hurt?" she asked.

"Only a little. You are magnificent, Lil. Heaven knows what other miracles your little body holds, but I plan on claiming every one. Will you mind, do you think?"

"Hardly," she laughed and stretched in lazy satisfaction. "I hurt, too. I seem to have your hangover."

"And is your skin super sensitive?" Daniel rubbed his rough cheek lightly over hers. She shuddered with pleasure. "The aftereffects of magic, I'm afraid." His voice hitched as she nuzzled his throat.

He pressed her back on the bed to kiss her again, long and deep, teasing her lips open with nips of his teeth. Her fingers buried themselves in his hair. His mouth slanted harder across hers, a sliding wet flame that drew a whimper from her. She trembled and sighed and clung to him as if only he could give her what she needed.

He sank deeper into the kiss and gasping as if in searing agony, broke away. "Christ! I can't . . . wait, Lil, can you shield, at least a little?"

With his magic riding her and his breath gusting against her skin, Lily couldn't think, let alone visualize a mental barrier. She turned her head away from him and tried, tried to block out the scent of his skin, the staccato beat of his heart, the needy clasp of his arms. But her senses had been opened so completely by him the night before, all she could see behind her closed eyelids was the alluring blue of Daniel's magic filling her inside and out.

"Can't," she managed to gasp under the impatient graze of his teeth along her jaw. She turned to meet his mouth, drawing his breath into her as her arms locked around his neck, and had the sudden, dizzying impression of being inside his skin again. She felt his elation that her desire equaled his, then only an awareness of the thrust of his mouth against hers. Magic roared in their blood, hot, commanding, irrepressible.

*

Daniel could no longer tell where her emotions ended and his began. Their hunger generated an insistent energy that urged them closer, desperate for each other. Both fought to untangle the blankets separating them, and then Daniel's knee was free and between her thighs.

Pain exploded in his head once more. He tore his mouth from hers with a curse and rolled off her.

Lily lay quivering beside him. "We must wait, please. Until you're fully healed."

"I'm done waiting." He turned his head to look at her. Resolve glowed as fiercely as passion in his eyes.

She grinned shakily. "Are you thinking what I'm thinking?"

"That you've spoiled me for any other woman for all eternity?"

"There's that, yes," she laughed. "But last night, your magic, it moved inside me as if, well, as if you were inside me. And now . . . Sweet heaven, with both you and the magic touching me . . . will sex be as—"

In answer, he moved over her again and took her mouth in a groaning, open-mouthed kiss, teeth biting, tongue probing until her body gave in to pure sensation. She tasted of innocence and carnal bliss. Her hands glided over the curve of his shoulder, down the long line of his back.

"I can't shield . . . oh, Gods!" A shiver rocked her as Daniel traced his lips over the curve of her shadowed breast. His magic drank her in as he drove his hips deeper. Neither of them had the strength of will to fight a craving more demanding than the necessity to protect themselves.

Passion pounding in his blood, Daniel peeled the robe off Lily's shoulder and let his hands feed greedily on her soft skin. He knew she burned even as he burned, with pain more ecstasy than agony. She was so pliant, so receptive beneath him, aquiver at the wet thrust of his tongue in the hollow of her throat, whimpering as his hand roughly cupped her breast.

"My power!" Lily gasped, fingers digging into his back. "It's rising. Daniel, I can't control it!"

Daniel felt her wild magic explode into him more violently than it raced under her skin. Only his quick shielding kept his nerves from sizzling to ash again. Once more, he tore himself from her. "Damn it!'

Lily fell back, panting as if she'd run ten miles and clutched the bed clothes to keep from reaching for him. "I'm sorry . . . " Her voice shook with tears.

For a long moment they lay side by side, fingers barely touching. Then Daniel rose above her with grim determination. "Let your magic out, all of it. Now. Even if it hurts me. I want all of you, Lily." His quick fingers were already loosening her belt, sweeping the robe aside until she lay naked to his view. He sucked in an awed breath as his gaze moved over her small breasts, rosy pink with desire, her petite waist, the fine bones of her hips and legs.

"God, you're so tiny," he breathed. "So perfect . . ."

Her skin flushed beneath his skimming hand. His fingers teased one nipple to tortured bliss, then the other before they spilled down her body to splay possessively over her flat stomach. A frenzied ardor built in Daniel's eyes before he lowered his head and tasted with his tongue where his hands had been. His mouth on her was relentless, suckling her breasts, biting the heaving arc of her ribs. Every inch he tasted and she melted under him, weightless, buoyed only by his magic and his delighted investigations.

Her fingertips dripped flames of their own down his chest, across his belly to trace the soft line of hair disappearing under the waist of his boxer shorts. Before she could dip further, he snatched her hands to drag them above her head, stretching her beneath him. He groaned at the torment of her nipples hard against his chest, her belly slick under his. Never had he let his power loose. Never had he allowed himself this freedom to dive into another being so fully and with such unprotected abandon.

*

Lily felt metaphysically stripped, every nerve crackling under a sensual onslaught too intense for her body to contain. Her heart, open and vulnerable, filled with his cry of triumph and as his magic rushed to meet hers, she gave him all of her. Their combined power, so forceful and creative, began to spin his excruciating pain into an exuberant joy. Heat rose, primal and desperate, between her legs. She tore at the blankets between them and begged him to take her, no longer caring of the cost. Her fingers dragged at his boxers and suddenly she found herself unable to move.

A spell held her immobile! The shock to her aroused senses felt like a bucket of ice hitting her face. Abruptly, sanity returned. She knew at once the spell came from Madame Bagasha. Lily's arms fell from around Daniel. Gasping for breath, she asked him to stop.

"I feel it, Lil, a bloody command spell." His lips brushed her shoulder. "And it's pissing me off."

Lily, equally pissed, raged once again at being manipulated by another's will. Her magic, swollen with his, reared up and smashed Madame's spell to pieces as if it were made of eggshells. Unstoppable now, she pressed closer as his demanding hands danced over her hips, teasing the inside of her thighs. Daniel's mouth crushed hers as his fingers slid inside her. She cried out, exploding in a climax of blazing, brilliant color. She felt her orgasm pour searing pain through Daniel's veins. Still he did not stop kissing her, stroking deeper with each thrust of her body. She could no longer breathe, knew pain throbbed in his head because it throbbed inside hers.

Lily slammed her fists hard and sudden against his chest and rolled off the bed. Angry tears spilled from her eyes as she snatched her robe closed with a jerk. "Damn you, Daniel, you ruined everything!"

"It was worth it . . . " he gasped, face down on the bed.

Lily leaped on his back and, grabbing a handful of hair, dragged his head up. Shaking with fury, she sank her teeth into his ear, not gently.

"Don't you get that I want you as much? Holding nothing back, taking you like you take me? So until we can both enjoy, keep those clever hands and . . . that amazing mouth off me."

Quick as a flash, Daniel flipped her over and beneath him. His eyes were bright with feverish pain and insane delight. "You taste so good, Lily, like rain and springtime and you feel . . . Gods above, all giving and open and wet."

*

His pain was diminishing, bizarrely enough. He wondered if somehow their combined magic healed as vigorously as it hungered. Cupping her face between his hands, he kissed her once, and again, and again until he felt her furious, unbending body yield to his. He laughed against her mouth. Oh, yes, the psychic pain was definitely less torturous, and less demanding, than his physical need.

"The pain, it's fading, Lil. Let me make love to you, right now. I'm begging and I've never begged for sex, ever."

"Oh, Daniel, I want to but—"

"We'll go slow. Maybe we can spell the magic and it won't rage so out of control."

"No." She pulled away and sat up to tighten her belt with a prim jerk. "When we're touching each other neither of us has any will of our own. This crazy hunger takes over. I want that, don't get me wrong. But I also want slow caresses and magic fed by love, not just greed. We need to step back from each other, Daniel. Can't you feel the magic whipping around us, snapping with lust?"

"Gods, yes," he groaned, reaching for her.

Lily scooted away.

Growling his frustration, he rolled onto his back. "All right. Just don't leave, Lily. I shouldn't have pushed, and I confess it hurt like bloody hell for a while. But please, let me hold you. I need to hold you." He sat up, curls tumbling over his eyes, and pulled the blankets chastely up around his waist. With a shameless grin, he patted the space beside him.

"No touching," Lily commanded sternly as she crawled back to him.

"Only a little touching."

Laughing, Daniel pulled her down to spoon into the curve of his body. Folding his arms around her, he threw a leg across her hip for good measure. Lily wriggled deeper into his lap. He buried his face in her neck, heaved a great sigh. Lily twined her fingers in his, settling for the precious feel of her skin shifting soft against his.

She half turned to him. "Maybe if we tried shielding the more intense emotions . . . "

"Never," Daniel murmured against her cheek. "In for a penny, in for a pound. That's how we are together. Haven't you noticed?"

Lily kissed his knuckles. The magic stirred restlessly around them. "You feel that?"

"Mmmm." Daniel slid his hand inside the robe to cup her breast.

"Madame said that once magic is called, it must be used."

"This magic is too hot for healing. Let's see . . . " Daniel settled more comfortably around her. His sudden and forceful focus snapped their psychic link tight as a rubber band. The errant magic leaped to his bidding. The colors of their power, his blues and her greens, expanded in the air above the bed like a super nova before sifting down over them in a tingling cloud of fairy dust.

"Happy?" Daniel snuggled closer. Lily laughed, content. They were asleep within moments of each other.

Chapter Twenty-two

Lily floated in a vacuum of blue twilight. Hot water pounded her body, sluiced through her hair and down her face to swill at her feet on the tile floor of the shower. Except she lay in a bed with thick blankets tucked around her. Was she dreaming the hot water slicking her skin, the tension easing from aching muscles? She clearly remembered earlier that morning, watching the pre-dawn light play across Daniel's features, the feel of his dark curls falling over her face as his mouth moved across her skin.

Those memories were her own. But tangled alongside were emotions belonging to Daniel, his excitement at drawing her magic into him, the taste of her on his tongue, the fever burning in his veins when his hands roamed her body.

Gods afire, his magic had bound them too close! Instead of delighting in it, Lily felt a rise of claustrophobia squeeze the air from her lungs. The hot water, the dripping hair . . . his sensations roared more alive in her head than the sheets warm beneath her legs and the pillow soft against her cheek. Adrenaline searing her brain, Lily kicked at the strangling blankets.

Then Daniel's hands curled about her face and his mouth clamped down on hers, solid and forceful and real. Her mind snapped back into her own body. She felt his damp fingers on her face and the slick wetness of his skin under her grasping hands.

He pulled her close and trembling against him. "Jesus, Lily . . . I'm sorry. This sense of invasion? It won't last."

"You're burning me." She began to shake.

"No, babe, you're burning me. Look at me, Lily. See my eyes?" His hands clasped her head, smoothed the hair back from her face. "It's aftershock, that's all. It'll pass."

"You're all wet," she said through chattering teeth.

"Yes." He kissed her again and pulled her with him under the blankets, holding her close. Still she shivered and with regret he severed the psychic link.

"No!" she protested, but weakly as once again she felt only her own thoughts and emotions inside her head.

"Better?" Daniel heard the rapid beat of her heart slow as his body's warmth poured into her. Soon her shivering stopped and she relaxed.

"The magic, it bound us too tight," he explained in apology. "I should have broken the link while you slept. I just couldn't bring myself to let you go. I'm sorry. Your magic is so intrinsic to who you are, Lil, of course it would perceive mine as a threat."

"Never." Lily pulled him into another kiss. "My magic adores your magic. In fact, our magics had more fun than we did. Well, I got off, but poor you . . . am I still hurting you?"

"Only like a scab prickling. Which doesn't mean we can go at it like rabbits." His teeth grazing her shoulder and his hands sliding down her hips spoke differently. Moments later he pulled away with an unhappy sigh. "We have to figure out how the magic took us over so completely. Maybe try to cool it off or something. We're like a—"

"Nuclear explosion?" Lily stretched against him. "I never imagined you were so . . . so volatile. I've always had this image of you as self-contained, reserved, even cold sometimes." She laughed, played her fingers across his mouth. "Not anymore. And since self-restraint isn't even in my vocabulary, how will we keep off each other? Because I want you touching me all the time. Is that the magic or just being in love? I've never been in love, but maybe—"

He stopped her musings with a kiss while his fingers slipped inside her robe to trace the intriguing ridge of her spine. "Maybe we need help." He pulled back suddenly. "You know, counseling for magic that's too hot to handle."

"No!" Lily said when she realized he was serious.

"It would be like lessons, but in magic. With Madame Bagasha. Unless you prefer my Gran." Daniel teased and pulled her on top of him. Her resistance vanished as desire flared in her belly. She spread her legs to straddle him, aware that only a towel separated them from . . .

His hands circled her waist and he forcibly lifted her off him, setting her on the floor. He sat up and reached for his glasses. "God knows I want to spend this glorious Saturday with nothing on me except you, Lily, but . . . ."

"I know. Sorry," she sighed and retightened the oversized robe around her. "We have a forever of sleep-in Saturdays ahead of us. With sleep optional." She slanted him a smile and began pulling at the blankets on the bed. "Have you seen our geode?"

*

Our geode . . . his heart flipped over in his chest. He nearly pulled Lily back into bed. But he too wanted more than just frenzied passion. He wanted long, lazy love making on weekend mornings and nights spent cuddling, talking, sharing ideas, shopping for groceries, working side by side on projects, laughing, teasing . . . just caring for each other.

But with their magic, hers wild and unstable and his fiery and passionate, now joined into a new unruly power . . . well, they needed advice, at the very least. He'd rather not go to Madame Bagasha. She represented authority, rules, and the damn Cohort almost as much as his Gran did. But Nila, the only other witch he trusted, hadn't the knowledge or the experience to help them.

Lily watched him, her eyes large and troubled. "I hate that we're not linked anymore," she said in a small voice. "I don't know what you're thinking."

He dragged her into his arms. "Which makes us no different

than other lovers. Our bodies will have to do the talking."

"How much talking?" she laughed, pressing closer. "And how often?"

His magic leaped in gut-clenching need. "I'll never shut up, even when I'm old and doddering."

"Promise?" Her voice wavered, insecure.

He Read her now as easily as he'd always Read the magic in her paintings. She was afraid. And at last he understood. She'd told him the literal truth when she said she'd never been in love! Never felt whole-hearted passion and commitment and need for anyone. Never felt cherished and protected and adored. Not since her parents died leaving her alone with strangers.

Relationships with others had always been hard for her to maintain. With men they'd proved impossible. Time and again, he'd seen her say or do some quirky thing and watched a guy dump her. More often she ditched the guy. Until now, until him. Now, when she wanted to give him all of her, she didn't know what to do. And atypical of other women, Lily wasn't afraid of getting hurt as much as she feared her ignorance and lack of experience would hurt him!

Daniel drew her close. "I promise nothing you do or say will make me leave you, Lily."

With a deep sigh, she nodded and let him go. "Then we best find that bloody rock. Because unlike me, it has the knack of knowing exactly what to do and when to do it."

But the geode could not be found, not on the nightstand, in the bed, fallen to the floor or under the curtains. They searched the entire room. Their pet rock of supernatural, sentient power had vanished after a job well done.

*

Not wanting to disturb Gradyn so early, Lily searched out her clothes and found them in his dryer. Typical guy, he'd tossed the wool sweater in with her jeans and shrunk it even more. Pulling it on, she was happy to find it still hung past her butt. They called a cab and after only twenty minutes of random driving found the magic shop on Wessex Road East. The sign on the door said closed. Lily sagged with relief. Completely exhausted, she didn't feel up to facing Nila or anyone just yet. But before they could escape, the purple door of the shop swung open, and Madame beckoned them inside. God's sake, she'd been expecting them!

The shop prisms were reflecting a more brilliant shine today. The voices sang with greater verve and every gemstone in the shop sparkled with an uncanny radiance.

"The shackling is gone, I'm happy to see." Madame spoke in a noncommittal tone.

"I'll never forgive my grandmother for casting it," Daniel said.

"But you did break it when barely healed," Madame added temperately. "And my spell as well, it seems. Tell me, was my block even a challenge?"

Lily blushed and Daniel tucked her closer under his arm. "No."

"I don't hear an apology for breaking it either."

"I hate interference, and you know it," he snapped. "Lily and I will make our own decisions about our magic."

"And yet here you are," Madame smiled. Lily felt a soothing charm drift the room. Daniel scowled and twitched irritably under its effect. Then he gave a terse, diluted explanation of their problem.

"The magic between you is too *hot*?" Madame's bristly eyebrows shot upward.

"Yes." Daniel's mouth tightened.

"What do you mean by 'too hot,' exactly?" Laughter gleamed in her black eyes.

Daniel's cheeks reddened. "You were right, Lil. Coming here was a stupid idea."

Then Madame's laughter bubbled over in a whole-body-shaking, tears-running-down-her-face guffaw that left her gasping. "Oh, my . . . if that's not the cat's meow and the bee's knees all at once!" She slapped her thighs. "Most people can't create *enough* magic in their relationships. And yours is too 'hot'? Oh, that's rich, it truly is. No, Daniel, don't storm off. I'm sorry. Just . . . just give me a minute."

Watching the little witch doubled over with the giggles, Lily felt her own anger rising. But Madame was finally drying her eyes, cheeks aglow with the pleasure of a good laugh.

"Oh, don't look so put out, loveys, please?" Madame reached a hand to each of them. "I adore the fact, truly I do. Restores my faith in the wonders of the universe. And such healing, Daniel. That is truly a miracle."

"I'm not the only one to heal." Daniel pushed back the sleeve of Lily's sweater. "See where Nila cut her for the talisman blooding? The wound is gone. It seems once commanded to heal, our powers, or at least Lily's, never stopped. Does this make her a healer?" Daniel glowered. "Because I hate the thought of her in the hands of the Cohort."

"Now Daniel, we aren't all manipulative, scheming, and bossy." Madame's eyes shone with humor. "The girl will choose her own path, you know."

"I'm not so sure," Lily spoke hesitantly. She'd been keeping herself tightly shielded at Daniel's suggestion. Both were a little afraid to reveal too much of her new, wild power. "This magic Daniel and I generate together, it sort of takes over. And the more emotion involved, the more power it creates. I think it ate my geode." She sounded fearful.

Madame didn't press. Instead, she drew the same large book Nila had consulted days ago from under the counter but didn't open it. "Perhaps all it comes down to is your lack of experience and technical skill, Lily. Daniel himself knows very little about his powers, having spent his life resenting his psychic gifts rather than studying them. No, I'm not judging you, dear boy. I understand why."

She brushed gentle fingers over his cheek. Tucking the heavy tome under her arm, she led them down a short hallway to a large kitchen workroom bulging at the seams with scarred tables, benches, distilling apparatus and two cooking stoves, one of cast iron fueled by wood and another electric. Shelves and cupboards lined the walls, mundane cookware was stacked alongside more arcane magical objects. Other shelves overflowed with bottles and crocks of God knew what. The room was warm and smelled homey with wood smoke, hot wax, and something yeasty rising on the shelf.

Madame chattered, trying to put the two at ease. "I know that one can draw on another's magic to weave spells or build power. But a mingling, a joining that then becomes a new kind of magic? I have never heard such a thing. It was incredible, this joining, yes? Oh, how I love investigating new phenomena," she clapped her hands like a child. Pressing them both to sit, she continued. "And when your magics combine, Daniel, yours is more dominant? Even though Lily possesses greater power?"

"Yes."

"And then it spikes out of control," Lily added. "It's beautiful, though. The colors, I mean."

"Colors?" Madame asked in surprise. "Ah, you can *see* magic. I smell it, taste it. Daniel, did you see color as well?"

"Yes." He kissed the top of Lily's head. "Fantastic colors. Probably because I was so deep inside her. Metaphysically, I mean," he added quickly.

"Of course." Madame turned away to hide her grin. In a practical voice, she said, "This is all rather amazing, I must say. And truth to tell, a bit beyond my understanding. So some tea, I think. Then we experiment."

Madame set the large book down on the table, filled an iron tea kettle with water and placed it on the electric stove. Then she dragged a small ladder from under the sink and climbed up to sort through jars full of herbs.

"Let's see, something incendiary." She opened lid after lid, taking long sniffs, cocking her head in thought before either passing the jar to Daniel or replacing it on the shelf. When she was done selecting, she climbed carefully down and began crumbling pinches of each ingredient into a wooden bowl. Occasionally she stirred the mixture with her finger, bending to sniff the rising aroma. Lily, smelling cinnamon and something more pungent and unpleasant, slid closer to Daniel.

"A quick lesson in the basics for Lily," Madame talked while she worked. "As is right and proper, the universe holds as many different kinds of magic as there are kinds of people. But all magic falls into one of two categories, the Sensitive and the Elemental. Sensitive magic is the most common. These folk have power based on a perception, or sensitivity, that can be refined and controlled through study and technique. Daniel, being a Reader, is a Sensitive. Other Sensitives include Intuitives, Clairvoyants, Dreamrunners, Mesmers, Water, and Weatherwitchers, to name a few.

"You, Lily, are an Elemental. Your magic is intrinsic. Not of perception but of essence. Power is drawn from within and can be magnified or enhanced by organic objects possessing power of their own such as stones, herbs, bones. Elementals include Conjurers, Diviners, Sorcerers, Rifters, Timestriders, and Shapeshifters."

"Shapeshifters?" Lily shivered, thinking of her painted men.

"Oh, yes, dear," Madame went on. "But not to fear. They are the shyest of folk in my experience." The witch started to lift the steaming kettle from the stove. Daniel jumped to take it from her and pour the boiling water into the bowl of mixed herbs. The air filled with a dizzying scent and Lily found herself yawning, abruptly sleepy.

"Both Elementals and Sensitives enhance their magic by calling on earth energy. You know the lore, I'm sure. How witches use the elements of life: air, water, earth, fire. Some Elementals can draw power from more specific ores, like iron, magnesium, silver. You're aware of this, Lily, having drawn from your geode. Hence the natural use of stones and powders in many spells. A Conjurer, for example, can use particular elements to weave say, a flower or a hat or even a cookie.

"A working coven of witches needs both Elementals and Sensitives to perform a truly balanced magic. Sensitives rarely master the use of earth elements, though they can learn to manipulate them. The elements, after all, are pure energy and life is teeming with the stuff."

"Then you and Nila are Elementals?" Lily asked.

"Oh, yes," Madame Bagasha answered, "with a little Sensitive on the side, a not uncommon thing. Many witches have attributes of both. You do or you wouldn't be able to link with Daniel. I imagine that's partly why your magic's mixed so . . . intimately with each other."

Both Daniel and Lily blushed.

"This tea I'm brewing will dampen your powers."

When both looked apprehensive, she tutted. "Don't worry, the effects are short term. I want you both to drink the tea. Then I will test you. If my theory is correct, your control problem can't be solved with a simple tincture, sadly enough. Or perhaps, not so sadly." She gave them a wink and headed out of the kitchen, leaving them alone.

"So?" Daniel drew her close for a kiss. "Are you okay with doing this?"

Lily spoke in a shaky voice. "Shapeshifters? Conjurers? Gods' sakes, what's a person to do with this information?"

"Afraid you might have a bit of Shapeshifter in you?" Daniel teased and when she went pale he pulled her onto his lap. "It'll be all right, Lil, I promise."

But Lily wasn't reassured. Did painted portraits coming to life constitute shapeshifting? She'd never told him Rodney was more metaphysical than asshole. And now it was too late . . . Gods, how she hated secrets. The longer you kept them the less they wanted to be told.

"This power between us, Lily," Daniel said, sensing her fear as if they were still linked, "we'll get a handle on it. Or we won't. So what if it's all consuming? I don't mind if you don't."

She drew back to see excitement and acceptance in his eyes. He shrugged, "We are who we are. And we're together. Nothing else matters. Hey, is this tea making you sleepy, because I—"

"We'd best get cracking." Madame bustled in. Lily slid off Daniel's lap. "Okay, Daniel, I want you to open the link between you and Lily. Can you?"

"Yes," both said simultaneously.

"Close it back down. Lily, can you link to Daniel? Without touching him?"

Lily turned to look at him, saw his eyes darken and go soft. She felt the tug of his lips on hers as if he'd kissed her. He grinned shamelessly.

"That's cheating." Lily slugged him and looking away, opened her heart to find the rhythm of his. And there he was singing in her blood, his heart beating alongside hers, his happiness bursting inside her head.

She glanced at Madame, who rolled her eyes. "Like I can't tell by your face, child. So you're linked together, mind to mind, heart to heart. Now Daniel, try to break the link. Lily, you keep him from breaking it."

It was a battle of more than wills. Within minutes the room throbbed with a turgid, explosive force.

Madame took an unconscious step back. This magic tasted of mountain storms and ozone, felt unwieldy and more than a little dangerous. "Try harder, Daniel," she commanded.

But try as he did, Daniel could not severe the link as long as Lily wanted it open.

"Enough," Madame finally said.

It was clear they'd frightened Madame, which caused Lily's own fear to increase.

The little Romany's face seemed less ruddy. "You both no longer have the same magic you had before you joined to do the healing."

Daniel nodded. Lily bowed her head as if ashamed. Her panic raced through the link into him like a bolt of lightning. All three could sense her feral magic prowling the room, unbound and waiting.

"You'd better explain what it is I'm tasting in the air. And I mean now." Madame Bagasha demanded in a strained voice.

"It's not Lily's fault," Daniel said quickly. "In fact, I think Gran may have triggered it when she cast the shackling spell. Lily's core magic, the . . . well, the cataclysmic magic you're tasting, it must have lain dormant until last night. It's Rogue, of course, and probably more elemental than any category Elemental magic. What Gran refused to understand or see clearly was that Lily's source magic is intuitive and highly creative."

"You're saying it is . . . ?" Madame couldn't bring herself to speak the word.

"Evolving. Yes."

Lily held her breath. The power in the workroom spiked, lifted the frizz on Madame's head.

"I need your geode, Lily, to trap whatever is in this room."

"I told you, the geode's gone. It disappeared," Lily said. "Teach me how to call this power back and I will."

So Madame Bagasha did. And Lily raised her hands, spoke the sing-song words to entice and bind. For a moment, both Madame Bagasha and Daniel watched jagged flashes fly about the room before the light thinned, became a nimbus of gold around Lily's body, and sank under her skin.

Madame sat down abruptly on the bench, hands shaking. "After drinking that tea you shouldn't have been able to work magic, either of you. What just happened, what we all saw . . . it isn't possible!"

Hearing a strangled cry behind them, the three spun around to see Nila standing against the door jam, her face a rigid white mask, her fingernails digging deep into the wood. And in the dim shadows behind her stood Rodney and a man the spitting image of Daniel.

"What the bloody hell are you, Lily?" the young witch cried.

Chapter Twenty-three

In one swift move, Daniel leaped to his feet, thrust Lily behind him, and had Nila safely across the room away from the two strange men. To Lily, the kitchen suddenly seemed a box she'd locked herself inside during a forgetful moment. Oh, why hadn't she told him about the apparitions back when it would have been humorous, back when they could have laughed? Standing behind him, she reached trembling arms around his waist, pressed her face between his shoulders and whispered, "Forgive me, Daniel."

Then she stepped out to face Rodney and her Look-Alike man. Both apparitions hovered between the bright kitchen and the dark interior of the store. They looked almost human in the shadows. But when Lily beckoned them forward and they drifted eerily into the warm light, it became obvious the two were anything but flesh and blood. Their faces, hair, skin, clothes were the color of gray mud, not transparent but not quite solid either. Nila, one hand clutched in Madame's, had the other raised to cast whatever spell might prove necessary against them.

Lily half turned to the two witches before forcing her gaze to meet Daniel's. "It's all right. I don't think they're dangerous or anything. This one is Rodney, the other I call Look-Alike because, well . . . " She gestured at Daniel.

The apparitions didn't react to Lily's words, in fact seemed not to hear at all. They simply stared at her with a pleading hunger in their eyes.

*

The look frightened Daniel. At the same time he felt a deep jealousy whip up his spine. With no thought to protocol or protection, he extended his psychic senses to Read them.

Color drained from his face as he swept both arms out to protect Lily. "Gods and Saints! They're empty! There's nothing to them but—"

Lily nodded sorrowfully. "Oil paint and magic. I know."

Madame's voice cut in. "You told Nila about the one. You said he melted and disappeared. Now I see two. Explain yourself, Lily."

"Can't you make them go away first?" Nila begged. "They're really creepy."

Lily barked a sarcastic laugh. "What, like this?" She made shooing motions with her hands. "I can't make them do anything, Nila."

"But the way they look at you . . ." The girl shuddered.

Lily turned to Daniel with a disturbingly similar look in her eyes. "Please don't be mad, Daniel. At me or Nila. Neither of us knew."

Daniel stood ready to launch himself at the two apparitions, jaw clamped tight, his blood seething with anger. He wasn't surprised to feel the drift of Madame's calming spell in the air.

"It's just, I was so lonely." Lily reached for him. He stepped away, an unforgiving scowl on his face.

"Start at the beginning," Madame commanded.

"That is the beginning." Nila tossed a scurrilous look at Daniel before drawing Lily, now standing isolated and alone, to sit with her on the bench. "Lily had an appointment, you see, at the dating service next door. But she couldn't bring herself to go in. That's when she found the Magicke Shoppe. And me. I'd *seen* her coming in the crystals and knew . . . well, knew how little credit she gave herself. And how much she truly deserved. So I made her a love potion." She glared at Daniel. "If I'd known you were her perfect guy, pud-head, I'd have tried to talk her out of it."

Daniel tried to calm himself while Lily told the rest of the story in rapid-fire sentences like punches from a fist. She avoided everyone's gaze. "I know how pathetic and desperate I sound. I am so sorry, truly." She darted an unhappy look at Daniel.

"Well, you're right about one thing, Lily. They don't seem dangerous." Madame spoke in an almost dismissive tone. Going to the counter, she began putting together a pot of coffee.

Daniel backed away from the two ghostly incarnates to straddle the bench where he could watch them and still keep an eye on the women. "Why does one of them look like me?"

Lily's face flushed a deep red. "I painted him first. The night I drank the potion."

Daniel slid towards her. Very gently, he took her face in his hands, forcing her to look at him. "But I was right next door, Lily. Aching for you, damn it."

"I didn't know, Daniel, not then. And he wasn't meant to be you."

"Not consciously, anyway," Nila muttered while rustling for muffins from a cupboard. Madame elbowed her with a hiss.

"He was just a portrait I worked up from sketches," Lily explained miserably. "Then he was suddenly alive, and I . . . I was terrified. He got aggressive and while trying to get away from him, I accidentally bumped the table. Paint thinner splashed on the canvas. And then," she half sobbed, "he just melted into puddles of dripping paint! I thought he was gone forever."

Daniel nodded. "I remember. I asked if something happened in your apartment. I touched the drop cloth and—"

"How could I tell you, Daniel? *What* could I tell you, for pity's sake? I was scared silly."

"Then why Rodney?" Daniel asked, now hurt more than jealous.

Lily buried her face in her hands. With a rueful twist of his mouth, he pulled her into his arms. "You wanted someone else, Lil? Even after . . . "

"No! I just wondered if it could happen again and . . . Daniel, you were my best friend! I never wanted us to change. I told you that and still you—"

His face broke into a grin. "I knew it! I knew you were in love with me before I kissed you!"

Nila snorted. "Of course she was, idiot boy. But that didn't mean it made her happy. Confused, overwhelmed, frightened, yeah. But hey, aren't we all overlooking the more pressing matter? Like how these two walking *personas non grata* happened in the first place?"

They all looked at Lily who stared at them, dumbstruck. "You think I know? Two weeks ago magic didn't exist in my world! Am I responsible for hurting Daniel? Yes. Did my paintings leap to life? Yes. Do I have power even you experts are scared of . . . yes? I'm out of control, I get that. But I'm also terrified. These guy-things scare the crap out of me. You can't imagine how I felt when they melted. I'd . . . I'd killed them! So believe me when I tell you that being haunted by them is *not* the worst part of this nightmare."

"Which is why, Lily," Madame turned suddenly brisk, "you, Nila, and I are going to spend the rest of the afternoon learning about magic." Madame serenely set out cups and saucers. She poured coffee as if nothing else in the world was more important. She added a plate of scones, and asked if anyone wanted bacon and eggs. Daniel, cradling Lily between his thighs, shook his head. No one but Nila seemed to have an appetite. Madame sat down, sipped her coffee. Daniel nipped Lily's ear, felt her relax against him and the tension in the room disappeared.

"By working together," Madame continued, "we'll take some of the mystery out of Lily's magic and help her gain some control. We'll teach her the basic spells, words of power, how to focus. By the time we're done I, for one, will feel . . . well, a bit less uncertain about the mystical world I thought I knew so well."

Daniel opened his mouth to declare he was staying, too, but Madame cut him off. "You, dear boy, must go to your grandmother. She's half-sick over what she's done."

Daniel snarled his doubt.

"And needs reassurance that you are healing and Lily is unharmed. She'll Read you and understand what you and Lily are to each other. She'll *know* the power you share. Talk to her, Daniel. You have become strangers over the years. But despite her sharp-edged stubbornness, your gran is a woman of wisdom who can forgive. And more importantly, admit when she's wrong. Give her that chance. Please."

He finally agreed, reluctantly. Every instinct told him not to leave Lily alone with these two witch women. But he could find no rational argument not to let her stay. Madame and Nila had proved themselves allies.

And he owed Madame for allowing Lily to come to him the night before. Madame Bagasha was, without question, the only Elemental he trusted to teach Lily what she needed to know . . . and by doing so would probably save them all. Daniel knew better than anyone the nearly limitless power Lily possessed. And though it no longer frightened him, he understood the dangers of a magic so creative in the hands of one uninitiated.

*

Lily walked with him through the unlit shop to the purple door with the sign still turned to *Closed*. She held his hand in a death grip. The thought of existing without him after the hours they'd spent so physically and magically bound seemed more than she could bear. At the door, he gathered her close, buried his face in her hair to breathe her in. Her arms circled his neck, her little body pressed tight to his. He kissed her hard, with an almost desperate uneasiness.

Lily realized that like herself, he feared being separated would create a self-consciousness between them that would erode the closeness they'd created together. The very idea left her devastated. She'd learned her magic through his, learned not to fear the unpredictable energy that was her power . . . as long as Daniel was near. She certainly wasn't ready to share that energy with anyone else. Not this soon. All her original fears and uncertainties rose again. She knew an afternoon Working with Nila and Madame Bagasha would change her as deeply and irrevocably as the night she'd spent with Daniel.

"I will see you tonight?" She clutched him close as he pressed a last, deep kiss on her lips.

"Thirteen mad witches couldn't keep me away," he promised. With a brush of his fingers across her mouth, he left the shop.

Lily stayed with her hand pressed to the closed door until the last tinkle of the overhead bell died. Already her sense of him through the link was fading . . . like everything, too good to last. In the darkened room at her back, she sensed the objects of magic cluttering the shelves; globes and jars and crystals, withered roots and knotted sachets and intricate charms, all teasing her as if they were living, animate sprites.

They waited neutral, uncommitted, and she wondered if they might become, in time, tools as comfortably fitted to her needs as a sable paintbrush or a rich vermilion red. Gods afire, she wished she'd never discovered magic existed! Then she recalled the playful warmth of Daniel's power moving inside her and changed her mind. Stomach in knots, Lily drew a deep breath, screwed her courage to the sticking post, and walked back through the shop to the lighted room where Madame and Nila waited.

Rodney and Look-Alike shadowed her, never closer than five feet, never further than twenty. To Lily's eye, they appeared more substantial than before, less gray and filmy. She wondered if the magic inherent in the shop somehow infused them with more solid form . . . and shivered at the thought. What if they became real enough to haunt her the rest of her life?

Very soon Lily was too busy to worry about anything, literally, beyond the magic of the moment. She learned first that Madame's power glowed a lovely warm lavender and felt comfortable working with it simply because she liked the color. When Nila's turn came to play with Lily, her magic felt as whimsical and spontaneous as orange Jell-O. Lily had a hard time co-coordinating her magic to Nila's and the girl kept apologizing as if she was the rank beginner, not Lily.

Madame worked with Lily on techniques of control, patiently teaching her how to draw magic out in measures as deliberate and aesthetic as musical notes. And as soaring, Lily discovered, once again sensing magic as harmonics and full bodied chords. At one point Nila jumped off the bench unable to keep from dancing to the sinuous rhythms throbbing in the room. Barefoot, faded jeans loose on her willowy hips, she looked like a Bacchanalian wood nymph, laughing in wild abandon, long braid flopping at her waist.

In one of their more maddening revelations, the three found Lily's magic was not compatible to basic spell weaving.

"How you and Daniel managed to work a healing, I can't imagine," Madame exclaimed in exasperation.

"I can," Nila murmured and Lily's cheeks bloomed a dazzling red.

Even the simplest charms wreaked havoc when fused with Lily's magic. She melted candles, caused the hands of a cuckoo clock to spin backwards, made a pot of soup boil over, and at one point had the stove dancing like an animation from a Disney movie.

"Am I over-thinking this or what?" Lily asked, hands tearing at her hair.

"Maybe Daniel tempered your spells with one of his own," Nila suggested.

Lily shook her head. "No, he gave me a sense of what was needed. Then I just made up my own words."

Madame grinned triumphantly. After that Lily "designed" her own spells. Some worked. Some didn't, and Lily found that her many failures didn't bother her that much. She'd already made up her mind she would never work magic as part of the Cohort, a coven, or anything that wasn't part of Daniel. Not that she said so out loud. Everything Madame and Nila taught her that afternoon she gobbled up as eagerly as a newly hatched bird. Every moment they worked her on technique she appreciated with the same exhilaration she got when she obtained the perfect light and color balance in a painting.

At one point, awkwardly juggling four spells at once, she promised herself and the world in general that never would her magic, as volatile as it was boundless, hurt another person. The afternoon wore on, the work room filled with the tantalizing smell of vegetable soup and baking bread. Lily wove and unwove magic, raised power, learned to spin it into a charm or spell that left no lingering, potentially harmful energy behind. After nearly three hours, the women took a break. Only then did Lily realize her psychic sense of Daniel was gone.

Seeing her suddenly strained face, Nila asked, "What's wrong?"

"My link with Daniel. It's gone again!" She turned to Madame in panic. "Would Gran . . . ?" She couldn't finish the dreadful thought.

"Would she force him to wear a talisman? No. He's mostly healed and has no need for one."

Nila set a bowl of steaming soup in front of Lily and gave her shoulders a reassuring squeeze before sitting down beside her. "I imagine the link's gone because you're exhausted, Lil. Gods afire, the things you've accomplished in the last few hours, the power you've generated? I mean really, no one should get to sense the guy they love twenty-four-seven, for pity's sake."

Lily felt suddenly ill. "Do you think Daniel resents the link?"

"No." Nila rolled her eyes at Lily's obtuseness. "You and Daniel share this amazing connection, a ton of incredible power and, adding insult to injury, you're insanely in love with each other. I'm saying give it a rest already."

"You're jealous?" Lily stared at her.

"Like, duh!" Nila said through a mouth full of bread.

"Me, too." Madame smiled giddily and suddenly there were stars in her eyes. Literally.

Both girls choked. They begged her to teach them the spell. All through the meal, the two girls tried one ridiculous spell after another on each other. One caused uncontrollable blotches, another curled hair and eyelashes. A third created a temporary allure the opposite sex found irresistible.

Lily refused to do that one. "Glamour spells and I don't mix.

I've got these two to prove it." She tipped her head at the gray specters hovering like pegged laundry in the corner. "Besides, Daniel wasn't affected by the love potion."

"So he claims." Nila sneered smugly. Finishing her soup with a last hearty slurp, Nila, visibly "girding her loins," approached the two apparitions and placed a hand on Rodney's shoulder. And found him a solid . . . something.

"Not flesh." She snatched her hand quickly back. "He's colder than cold. So how do we dispel them?" She directed the question to Madame.

Madame cleared the bowls from the table before going to the giant, tattered book she'd carried in hours before. While she turned pages and jotted down notes, occasionally mumbling an unintelligible word and staring off into space, Nila and Lily washed and dried the dishes. Bored, they began to splash playful spells at each other. Lily's hair turned a florescent pink, Nila suddenly sported elephant ears.

"Oh, gosh!" Lily apologized, mortified. "I meant that for your feet. Sorry." When she couldn't undo the spell, Madame had to intervene. The fun went out of the game for Lily. She refused to rise to Nila's challenges no matter what color the young witch turned her skin or how many extra fingers she gave her.

"Did you find a way to get rid of my guy-things?" Lily collapsed on the bench after conceding a towel snapping fight to Nila.

"Not specifically, no. What I have discovered, Lily, is that only you can do it. Not me, not Daniel, not a coven. The power that created them is within you and so is the power to drive them away. How, I do not know. But I'll investigate more, maybe experiment. In the meantime," the tiny witch grinned, "try and think of them as . . . well, oversized puppies."

As Lily was about to leave the magic shop, Madame Bagasha said. "It might be wise, Lily, if you and Daniel stayed away from each other for a few days. Give him a chance to fully heal. And perhaps give the . . . um, *ardor* time to cool."

Nila did her eye roll thing. "Like separation ever cooled passion."

"None the less." Madame took Lily's face in her hands. "Love is all powerful. Mix love with an all powerful magic and, well, you don't want to hurt each other."

Lily nodded, tight lipped and pale. Nila turned from where she was dipping candles. "Is that still possible?"

"What isn't possible?" Madame shrugged. "I did not know until today that one magic could melt into another to create an entirely new force."

"Isn't that the way love works?" Lily asked.

Madame laughed, pressed her wrinkled cheek to Lily's smooth one and whispered, "How could I have forgotten, huh?"

*

Lily left the two side by side, dipping candles. Stepping out the door, she realized that while she'd been inside, the shop had changed locations again. Had she felt movement, a slight shifting of the floor, a wobbling nausea like one experiences during small earthquakes? No. Now that's powerful magic, Lily thought. No matter what qualms Madame had about her power, Lily knew that even with Daniel, she could never move an entire building!

She glanced up at the darkening sky to take her bearings only to find she was within three blocks of the Lennox. A bone-deep weariness suddenly struck her and she found she could barely place one foot in front of the other. She'd have to use a spell just to get herself up the three flights of stairs to her apartment! Half a block from home, Lily's mind filled with the loving presence of Daniel once more. She had a strong sense of his fury, barely restrained, before the link once again faded into an awareness as soft as baby's breath.

In essence, Gran had kidnapped Daniel. Lily practically fell through the door of her apartment and saw the answering machine blinking red. His recorded voice was livid:

"Yeah, well, I'm sure you got the lecture too, Lil. That we should stay away from each other 'til I'm fully healed. Damn them all." He heaved a gusty sigh. *"I've been hijacked for a family dinner tonight and if Gran has her way I won't be home until very late . . . I'd sell my soul just to sleep beside you tonight. Every night."*

Lily dug out a scrap of paper, scrawled the words, "Come anyway, even late," and slipped the note under his door. Too tired to eat, she dozed off in the bathtub only to wake shivering in the cooling water, pulled on flannel pajamas, and was asleep before her head hit the pillow.

Half waking in the dark, she felt the mattress dip beside her, then Daniel's lips warm on her cheek before he wrapped her in the curve of his body, nesting his face against the back of her neck. Within moments both were sound asleep.

*

Daniel woke in the early morning light with a pounding headache. And fully aroused. He rolled out of Lily's bed as if she were on fire and stood looking down at her, blond curls spread across the pillow, her fist tucked against a rosy cheek. A possessive hunger filled him. But he only kissed her sleeping lips before grabbing his clothes and tiptoeing from her apartment to his.

Chapter Twenty-four

For two days, Lily didn't see Daniel, even though they slept together every night. She'd feel him slip into her bed in the deep dark and try like hell to wake herself up. He would fill his arms with her. His magic would drift like warm honey across her skin and she'd fall more deeply asleep. In the morning he was always gone. She'd wake, roll to press her face into his pillow, and breath the lingering scent of him, her chest aching with loneliness, and cursed his restraint.

She did see Rodney and his companion at odd, disorienting moments as if they were strings tied around her fingers like ragged reminders. No matter how much she pretended, Lily could not think of them as puppies, innocuous and devoted. They hounded her for days. She'd glimpse them outside the apartment or through a window on the e-train. No one else seemed aware of them, and no one strolled unknowingly through their incorporeal bodies.

Lily woke alone again on the day of the Spencer Gallery art opening and lay near tears wishing Daniel had stayed, this morning above all others. Nervous and scatter-brained, she dashed to work without her portfolio and the sketches for the Wilson girl's final portrait. Ellen rolled her eyes when Lily told her and asked if they needed to cancel today's after school sitting with the two girls.

"No." Lily rubbed her tired eyes. "I'll do a cold sketch on the large canvas, and hopefully they won't turn into little savages and skin me alive."

Lily met Lindsay and Carmen that afternoon dressed like a medieval jester, leering from the middle of her studio, legs splayed, hands on her hips like Peter Pan. Except she wore a harlequin tunic garishly beribboned and a three-pronged hat strung with bells. The girls stared in drop-jawed astonishment.

"Today is a day of torture." Lily shook her jongleur stick at them. "You must sit unmoving for excruciatingly long, painful hours frozen in whatever position I put you in. No twitching of hands, no tapping of feet, no disrupting the folds of your costumes that I will have elaborately and decoratively arranged."

The two nodded, higher than kites, giggly and extremely pleased with themselves in all their radiant magnificence. Lily gave them a thumbs up, put on the music they'd brought, the soundtrack of the ancient classic *Rocky Horror Picture Show*, and stepped up to her easel.

When the session came to an end, Lindsay and Carmen begged to see the sketch, but Lily quickly whipped a sheet over the canvas. "Can't risk jinxing the magic," she told them. They both winked at her as if they knew exactly what she meant. Which was possible, Lily decided and sent them off to change back into street clothes.

She was cleaning her brushes, still dressed in costume but minus the hat, when she heard a laugh behind her. Turning, she found Daniel leaning in the doorway.

"I see you're already dressed for tonight's formalities," he said.

She looked down at herself, "If the shoe fits . . . "

Then he was across the floor and kissing her, arms grappling, brushes and rags dropping unheeded at their feet.

"Christ's Apostles, I've missed you." His teeth nipped her ear and his mouth fed on hers until she was too weak to stand. She'd completely forgotten Carmen and Lindsay until she heard them giggling. Breathless, struggling to retain some dignity, she introduced Daniel. Each girl gave him a shy but inquisitive smile. Daniel plucked up one of Lily's paint smeared rags and stuffed it inside his closed fist. When he opened his hand, a pair of multi-colored butterflies flew out to land on each child's shoulder.

Carmen and Lindsay dispensed with shyness and closed around him. As Lily tidied her workspace, Daniel entertained them by changing mundane articles off her table, a paint smock into a bright feather boa around Lindsay's neck, and a piece of quartz into a tiny crystal dragon Carmen discovered in her pocket. Of course the girls had seen magic shows and couldn't tell real magic from fake. Or so Lily hoped as she left the three in order to change out of her fool's costume. By the time Mrs. Wilson picked up her daughters, they were well and truly charmed by Daniel. Go figure, Lily sighed, well and truly smitten herself. She curled happily at his side as he drove them home in his ancient truck.

*

That night Lily perched nervously on the edge of her couch waiting for Daniel's knock. This was it. Their first date. Her heart refused to beat normally. It raced and died and raced again. She guzzled a glass of wine, eyes closing as the heady rush of alcohol loosened her bones. She gargled, again, and reminded herself to breathe in and out.

He was just Daniel, for Christ's sake. Her own Daniel, best friend, companion through thick and thin, the man who set her on fire with just a look . . . oh, why couldn't she stop shaking? For two years he'd been no different than any other guy in her life. Then she drinks a love potion, her world spins topsy-turvy, and all of a sudden she discovers he's gorgeous, lit up with this shiny omnipotence she tumbles headlong into.

Deep steady breaths, she told herself, throwing off her coat and running to check her appearance in the mirror for the umpteenth time.

Ruby from downstairs had insisted on doing Lily's face and hair. Standing in the newlyweds' kitchen in her slinky blue dress, Lily felt suddenly self-conscious and afraid, as if time had shifted along a major fault line and she'd missed making the jump.

"This dress is perfect, Lil." Ruby sighed. "Hugs your curves nicely, makes your eyes all mysterious and dreamy." Ruby, who was studying cosmetology, brushed Lily's hair until it shone before sweeping the blond curls up off her neck. She pinned them loosely with a series of delicate, jeweled clasps leaving a few wispy strands trailing down her back. The girl powdered Lily's nose and applied eye shadow, liner and mascara with the subtlety of a true artist. When Lily was finally allowed a look at herself in the mirror, she couldn't believe her eyes. Ruby's magic had turned a whey-faced, drifty Lily into a beautiful, alluring woman. In spite of her enormous eyes broadcasting panic like a satellite signal. Brian flung her a kiss like some Italian lothario.

"Can you grant me the confidence to go with all this glamour, oh fairy godmother?" Lily asked with a nervous laugh. Ruby, pushing her out their door, said all the right words of reassurance. But climbing the stairs back to her apartment Lily knew her beauty tonight was as unreal as the apparitions stalking her.

Now she sat on her couch, butterflies playing capture the flag in her belly. She contemplated another quick glass of wine, rejected the idea, and, grabbing up her coat, jerked open the door to find Daniel standing there.

They stared at each other.

He looked incredible, his thick hair combed back with unruly curls already springing loose around the open collar of a brandy colored shirt that hugged his chest and shoulders. He wore dark trousers and a navy wool coat. And sneakers.

His stunned gaze took in her dress, a clingy sheath that accented her breasts and tiny waist, the silk stockings, the dainty shoes, before swinging back to her face. Looking at her, he could barely breathe. "Gods and Saints, Lily, you're . . . you're so beautiful!"

"I'm really nervous," Lily said and launched herself at him. He pulled her into a hungry kiss that felt like coming home. Her panic faded. He was still just Daniel. With a sigh, she let him take her deeper with his mouth playing on hers, trapping, torturing. His hands slid down her back, roughly cupped her bottom to lift her against him. A whimper rose in her throat, fire whipped to life in her belly. She parted her lips for him and strained closer.

*

Daniel knew if he didn't slam on the brakes, and now, they'd end up on the floor tearing their dress-up clothes off each other. With a ragged sigh, he let his arms fall away. Stepping back, he saw the dazed, needy look in Lily's eyes. Before he could grab her again, he snatched her hand and dragged her quickly down the stairs and out the front door.

After walking a few blocks he cooled down, slowed down, and could look at her again without wanting to strip her naked. She darted a quick glance at him. He suddenly realized she thought he was angry. He stopped, pulled her into a more gentle kiss. Lily raised on tiptoe to meet him, lips wet and eager.

"Let's skip this damn opening," she whispered against his mouth. He gasped as her magic plunged into him, hot and alive with lust.

He laughed shakily. "Guess you're not nervous anymore."

She blushed so bright he could see patches on her cheeks in the dark.

"You do know you just zapped me with magic, Lily."

"Did I? Did it . . . hurt?" She pulled away.

"Not even a little." He tucked her possessively under his arm. "Your magic can't hurt me anymore, Lil. We're integrated, remember?"

"Lords, yes, I remember," she said shortly. "It's why I'd rather shag you silly right now than go to this bloody opening."

"Well, the feeling's mutual so stop looking at me with your eyes all big and sexy."

"Then stop looking at me as if you want to—"

His kiss was sudden and searing and unrepentant. Her legs gave out and he caught her against him with a frustrated groan.

"Yeah." She grinned. "As if you want to do that."

"Later." Daniel determinedly set her on her feet, tucked her hand in his and jammed them both in his jacket pocket. "That and a lot more."

"I'm hating this opening more and more. You know, don't you, the second we walk in the gallery that Megan girl will have her hands all over you. And Gradyn will take me off to parade around like a prize fighter."

"You'll be toasted with champagne. By really rich, influential clients."

"Who I'll never remember later. Names will run into faces and . . . why are we going again?"

"Lily, you are an amazing artist. Gradyn is ecstatic over the paintings you brought him."

Lily glanced at him. "Have you seen them?"

"I saw one. It made my nose bleed."

She slugged him.

"Seriously." He laughed. "The, well, the heat in that painting, when the paint was still wet . . . Gradyn took one look at it and said you wanted me bad and not in a rated 'G' way."

"Like, duh!"

"You painted us into it."

"Yes." Lily slipped away to dance around him. "A paradigm. You and me. Loving each other up."

"I'll take it." Daniel caught her, lifted her to kiss her laughing mouth.

"I don't think you're taking me seriously, Daniel." Lily buried her hands in his no longer tidy hair. "I'm proposing marriage, kids, a house in the country."

"I know. And I'm saying hallelujah."

She went still in his arms. "That's not a yes."

"It is!" he cried. "It's a resounding yes. No, don't start with the—" Daniel felt her wild magic stroke his skin, saw it as golden stars in her eyes before her mouth hit his. She pulled him under with her lips and tongue and the press of her body.

After a long time she let him go, saw *his* eyes unfocused and dumbstruck for a change. "If you keep distracting me this way, Daniel," she said in a perfect mime of Madame Bagasha, "we won't make it to this opening, which will then never end and we'll never consummate—"

He spun around to drag her back towards the Lennox. "We need to drive. It's faster."

Laughing, Lily ran to keep up. "I like fast."

Night dropped a shutter of darkness over Little Belfast, the old houses, last century's apartment and office buildings. The solar street lamps cast deep, elongated shadows across yards piled thick with leaves. A cold wind blew off the lake smelling of muck and fish. It swept the leaves into crackling little dervishes around Daniel and Lily's racing feet. There were few people about. The night lay quiet except for the far off sounds of expressway traffic, the snarl of an alley cat, a mother calling her kids home.

It took awhile for Daniel's old truck to warm up. And while warming Lily up, he realized kissing her was like drinking in springtime, full of promise, provocative, unexpected and ever fresh. He drove downtown with her arms around his waist and her head on his chest, half drunk at the feel of her against him.

Parking was not a problem this late in the day. When Daniel turned off the ignition, Lily stayed wrapped around him, suddenly too nervous to move. He held her quietly until at last she sat up with a huff of breath and slid across the seat to climb out of the truck. They held hands crossing the street, hers cold and trembling in his. She stopped abruptly at the sharp edge of light cast through the windows of the Gallery. Her pulse throbbed beneath Daniel's palm. Standing in the shadows beyond the light were Rodney and Look-Alike.

"Damn them," Lily shivered. "Can't they leave me alone for just one night?"

"They won't come in," Daniel said. "They never do."

"Except in the magic shop. Do you suppose they're attracted to the magic in my paintings? I mean, that's what they are, technically speaking."

"No," Daniel said. "I think they're attracted by emotion, Lily. You loving me."

Lily looked at him in surprise.

"You painted them with love, didn't you? All your paintings are full of love and light and passion."

She shivered. "Not Rodney."

"Yes, even Rodney. I can sense their longing, Lily. It matches yours, bittersweet and lonely. Desperate."

She threw her arms around him. "Say you forgive me, Daniel. For not wanting you when obviously you were all I wanted."

"I forgive you, my darling girl." Daniel kissed her lightly. "When will you forgive yourself?"

"Are you saying . . . ?"

"All I sense in them is longing and hungry, unexpressed need."

Lily's face lit up. "Then when we finally have sex they'll disappear?"

He laughed. "We can only try, can't we?"

"Half an hour, max," Lily said sternly. "After that, rescue me. Tell Gradyn I have meningitis or something."

Still laughing, Daniel buried himself inside another of her kisses before letting her go.

Lily stepped into the light to peer through the window. "Look, a crowd already. There's Ellen. Whoa, she's actually talking to Gradyn! I thought they hated each other."

"Like the sun and the moon." Daniel nudged her through the door and they were inside the gallery and beyond escape.

*

Megan was there to take their coats. Then she took Daniel. It seemed she'd made it her personal mission to introduce him to everyone while leading him possessively by the hand. He sent a despairing look at Lily. She tried to kill the rise of jealousy, but had no time before the claustrophobic swarm of strangers overwhelmed her. Then Gradyn was beside her. Draping his arm around her shoulders, he thrust a glass of wine into her hand and planted a lusty kiss on her cheek. He grinned a taunt at Daniel across the room.

Spencer Gallery glowed with goodwill and beauty. Gorgeous bouquets of ivory-colored flowers filled the air with subtle scent. The lighting was both bright and mellow, pulling warm colors from the wood, the frames, pedestals, and display cases. There were catered trays of shrimp and crispy stuffed pastries. Waiters stood ready to refresh goblets with champagne, wine and other spirits. Everyone smiled, relaxing. The room filled with boisterous conversation. Gradyn, arm draped possessively around Lily, introduced her to one group of people after the next until her head felt ready to pop with too many names and facial features. She longed for a moment to just breathe and settled for drinking instead. After an endless amount of circling the room, they ended up in front of her oil painting, *Paradigm*.

"Oh, Gradyn, the frame . . . it's perfect." Lily was delighted with the baroque style of molding he'd chosen for the frame and how it added a grandiosity to the already stark drama of the work.

"I've had four offers for this tonight, Lil." His voice dropped to a whisper. "All above thirty thousand."

She turned, angry at him for mocking her, and saw he was serious. "It's a masterpiece, Lily. I'd buy it myself if I didn't know you painted it for Daniel. It's shocking and beautiful, tormented and poignant all at the same time. And brilliant, truly."

"Thank you," she said with her first genuine smile of the evening. They stood together looking up at the paradigm figure with her perfect angel face, womanly yet naïve and childlike, her eyes rapturous yet tortured. One luminous arm stretched up from a naked shoulder and bare breast while swirling cloth fell away in dark, brooding folds. Rising above and dominating the figure were two large, powerful wings, feathers angry and clasping . . . a threat or perhaps redemption.

"Tell me it's not a self-portrait, Lily." She heard compassion in Gradyn's voice.

"It isn't, not really. Why, has someone asked?"

"No. But no one here knows you, except Ellen and Nila. And Daniel, who already knows what this painting is about."

"Yes. He's the only one who does. Though Nila probably understands. More than she'll ever reveal, anyway."

Gradyn's glance shot across the room to where Nila stood, a Nila unlike any they'd seen before. Slim and chic, her unbraided hair fell in shining auburn waves past her waist. She wore a dress of saffron silk slit up one side to expose a long, perfectly shaped leg.

"I've never seen her reveal so much, actually," he growled and downed his champagne in one gulp.

Gradyn wasn't the only man in the room who couldn't keep his eyes off Nila, though he was the only one who mattered, Lily knew. Catching her attention, Nila grinned and was, for a moment, recognizable as the prankish, urchin witch. Who stayed close by Daniel's side, Lily noticed.

"She scares the hell out of me," Gradyn muttered and seemed shocked at Lily's burst of laughter.

"Really? She said the same about you." Lily tucked her arm in his and pulled his head down for a peck on the cheek. "Thank you, Gradyn. For all this. And," she grinned, "for thinking I might be this dark and tormented soul. But then a hint of madness in an artist never hurt sales, did it?"

Chapter Twenty-five

Megan, arm stuck like crazy glue to Daniel's, very pointedly kept him away from Lily and her work. When at last he managed to shrug her off, he and Nila slipped through the crowd to join Ellen standing in front of Lily's largest painting. An abstract landscape, it was overpowering in scope. An almost threatening darkness in the background broke open under grand, incandescent sweeps of light.

"Good Lord," Daniel said, stunned by such darkness dissolving into mercurial pools of golden luminosity.

Ellen laughed. "And to think she was nervous about showing these, the darling."

"This one is . . . breathtaking," Nila whispered.

Daniel's fingers itched to trace shapes that seemed to pulse with primordial life. Planets swirled in nebulas of color . . . no, not planets, eggs. He stepped back and the eggs became pebbles on a river bottom wavering in brilliant rippling water.

"Shocking to the senses, huh? Kind of like her," Ellen said.

"Where does this come from inside her?" he murmured in soft wonder.

Ellen leaned close. "You should know. Been there yet?"

Daniel's face reddened and Ellen strolled away with a smile.

Beside him, Nila let out the breath she'd been holding. "I have this compulsion to just dive in," she murmured. "Is that the pull of her magic, Daniel?"

"I'm afraid so. Thank the Gods Madame Bagasha can't see these. The Cohort would freak."

"Are all her paintings this . . . this demanding?" Nila asked.

"All the ones here tonight." Daniel led Nila to *Paradigm,* heard her shocked gasp, saw her eyes fill with tears.

"But this, this manic intensity, it isn't Lily," Nila insisted.

"It is sometimes," Daniel said.

"This is the painting that burned you?"

"Yes. It's her declaration," he spoke carefully. Her unconditional offering of herself to him, her binding of him to her, though he didn't say so out loud. He hated the fact that this intimate display hung here for all to see. The vulnerable figure trapped on canvas with her tormented yet hopeful face, revealed too much emotional honesty and tore too brutally at his heart.

"And then afterwards your magics mingled and recreated themselves," Nila mused. "Amazing." Then she asked, "Do you really love her, Daniel? Because she is going to take everything you are."

"Love isn't a big enough word for what I feel, Nila. And she already has all that I am. She's had it for a long time."

"The Cohort could, well, temper her power if that would—"

"Never!" Daniel turned suddenly hostile eyes on his cousin. "Her power can't hurt me, Nila. It's part of my magic now. As mine is part of hers. You must promise not to involve the Cohort. And convince Madame to leave us be."

"Is that wise? Or even responsible?" Nila ventured. "I saw those creepy apparitions outside."

"Just back the hell off, Nila," Daniel snapped, a kind of agony on his face. He leaned to whisper. "It's the sexual energy in the paint, can't you feel it? That's why the paintings are so mesmerizing. It's what draws Rodney and company. When we finally—"

"You mean you two haven't had sex yet?" Nila blurted out and Daniel walked away from her, too angry for words. Glancing at his watch, he found they'd been at the opening for over an hour. It was past time for a kidnapping. But scanning the gallery, he saw no sign of Lily.

*

As the showroom floor filled with more and more people, drink flowed and conversations grew louder. Lily met a couple of the other featured artists in the show, a potter, and a mixed media sculptor who seemed as startled by the crowd and the attention as she was. Somewhere in there, Lily escaped to the ladies room and locked herself in a stall.

Ellen found her there and cajoled her out to splash cold water on her pale face.

"Are you crying?" Ellen tore off a paper towel and passed it to her. "Why, Lily? This is your night!"

"I sold every painting," Lily scrubbed at the mascara bleeding down her cheeks.

Ellen's mouth fell open. "Wow! They are truly magnificent, you know. You should be very proud."

Lily turned on Ellen. "You don't understand. I painted these after I took the potion!"

"So?"

"I've never painted anything so . . . so multi-dimensional before. Not without magic. I don't just pick up a brush and paint like this. What if I can't do it again? What if the potion fades?"

"Lily, get a grip. Here, sit." Ellen lifted her onto the counter as if she were a child and tucked more tissue into her hands. "Deep breaths, Lily."

"I never used to cry," she sniffed angrily.

"That a girl, get mad. A little anger works wonders for a crying jag. See? You're already drying up."

Lily blew her nose, eyeing her boss. "I saw you talking to Gradyn. Flirting with Gradyn. Shamelessly."

"And I saw you drop Daniel's hand as you stepped through the door. Who attacked first?"

"He did. Then I did."

"Well then, all is right with the world." Ellen held up her hand as Lily's eyes began blurring with tears again. "You will paint like this. Again and again and again. The power is inside you, Lil, not in a bloody potion."

"The cosmic landscape was supposed to be yours, Ellen. Gradyn put a huge price on it so it wouldn't sell and someone bought it anyway."

"Good for him. After all, he's in the business to make money. What'd it sell for?"

"Twenty-two thousand dollars," Lily cried mournfully.

Ellen stared at her. "Gods and Saints! Lily, you're rich! Not only that, Gradyn will spread the word like wildfire that your paintings sold out. Which will make everyone in town ravenous to own a Lily Barnett original." She rubbed her hands together in greedy delight. "We can *so* take our clients to the cleaners! No wait, what am I thinking? You'll quit! Damn, lost the painting and lost the artist! Not a good night for me, let's get sloshed!"

Laughing, Lily jumped off the counter and turned to the mirror to reapply lipstick. "You're ridiculous."

"Aren't we a pair."

"Thank the Powers. And Ellen, thank you."

"Anytime. Want me to sneak Daniel in here for a quickie?"

"No. And stop teasing or you'll jinx it." Lily took a last look at herself in the mirror. The girl staring back with nervous eyes was a long way from glamorous now, with her puffy face and wane skin. She certainly didn't look as if she'd just leaped into fortune and fame. She was so out of her league here in this beautiful salon, meeting people with more money than sense. But then . . . so what?

These people might buy her best paintings but they couldn't buy her passion. Ellen was right. She would always paint with feeling and zest and magic. *Paradigm* would live on Daniel's wall and she'd paint something new for Ellen, a masterpiece that lived and breathed because she created it for someone she loved.

Ellen held the door open for her, a strange smile on her face. "Follow me, Lil. I've got something to show you."

Lily followed her across the floor towards a short wall beside the sales counter. Hanging, one above the other, were four mid-sized drawings all the same size, matted and set in long, narrow frames.

"G.I.L.?" Lily stared in astonishment at the signature on four original inks of the cartoon strip *Lost and Found.* They were done larger than they appeared in newsprint and vid-strips, of course. Hand drawn, the strips were broken into G.I.L.'s typical four frame format. Lily found them more appealing and stylized in their original form. She liked the quick, strong strokes that defined character and humor as clearly as any portrait she'd ever done.

"They must be part of the show." Ellen turned to take in the people crowding the showroom floor. "Which means G.I.L. is here somewhere, right? I so want to meet this guy."

"I don't," Lily said forcibly. But Ellen was already gone, weaving through the crowd to find Gradyn.

Lily turned her attention back to the strips. Only one was familiar. Two others made her laugh out loud. And one opened a melancholy ache inside her. The computer nerd character with his big glasses sat slumped in front of his computer. A balloon above his head said: "The course of true love never did run smooth." A quote from William Shakespeare's *A Midsummer Night's Dream*!

Delighted, Lily leaned closer. An answering balloon out of the computer read: "What wound did ever heal but by degrees?"

In the second frame the nerd argued, "The private wound is deepest." To which the computer responded, "Praising what is lost, makes the remembrance more dear."

The third frame showed the nerd resting his chin despondently in his hand. "When sorrows come, they come not in single spies, but in battalions." And the computer answered, "Love sought is good, but given unsought is better."

In the final frame, the guy was striding away upright and determined, a baseball cap on his shaggy head. The light is turned off in the room behind him where the computer sat in the dark, thinking, *"Love all, trust few, do wrong to none."*

Lily stood stunned, moved, a hand pressed to her heart. Each quote was from one Shakespeare play or another. How whimsical and wonderful and endearing! She loved it, the computer geek pouring his heart out to his hard drive. And a computer that offered hope, wisdom, and possibilities.

Lily suddenly wanted it hanging on her wall at home, an original drawing of a famous syndicated cartoon strip. And she could probably afford it, having sold all her paintings! So yeah, she might have railed a bit against the cartoonist G.I.L. But this particular vignette revealed more heart and pathos than she'd have ever guessed the writer possessed. Lily wondered if the computer nerd might be something of a self portrait. Turning, she scanned the thinning crowd, wondering if one of these glittering personages could indeed be the illusive, enigmatic G.I.L.

She saw Nila standing with Gradyn, their hands oh so casually brushing, his head bent close over hers. Nila's face looked flushed with pleasure . . . and a few more complicated emotions. Then Lily found Daniel standing beside Megan in a crowd of four attractive women who were all talking vivaciously. He looked relaxed and interested in their conversation but his gaze wandered the room.

And suddenly she couldn't breathe. In that moment there was no one else in the room but him, with dark curls falling over his forehead and his beautiful eyes casually vacant behind his glasses. She wanted him touching her, now. As if he heard her, Daniel lifted his head and met her gaze. A grin split his face. She felt his rush of love and pride in her and then he excused himself from the group. Lily was already halfway across the floor. When they met his fingers grasped hers, and locked tight around them. At his touch, she breathed again. A crackle of heat melded their palms together and he pulled her towards the door, snatching their coats from the rack on the way.

*

Once outside and free of the gallery, he paused long enough to help her into her coat, then hauled her across the street to his waiting truck. His fingers shook as he unlocked the door. Hands on her bottom, he heaved her into the seat and clambered up behind her. Ramming home the key and gunning the engine several times, he whipped the truck into a U-turn. Rodney and Look-Alike swayed like empty barrels in the back.

Daniel drove like a mad fiend through the near empty streets. The ancient engine, cold and sluggish, died twice. Muttering vague obscenities, Daniel restarted it but refused to let the truck sit and warm up properly. On the seat beside him, Lily laughed at his impatience while her hands tugged his shirt tails loose.

He hooked an arm around her neck to pull her into a hungry kiss, one eye on the road. The cab steamed with breathless laughter and frenzied excitement. In the street out front of the Lennox, Daniel spun wildly into a parking spot, two wheels on the curb. The clutch popped, the engine died with a jerk. Then he turned to take her mouth in a devouring kiss while she fumbled open his shirt. He grabbed her breasts, thumbs stroking hard over her nipples until, with a quivering cry, she hiked up her dress and straddled him, the steering wheel digging into her back.

*

"Christ, Lil, not here," Daniel choked and wrenched open the door. They half fell out to run hand and hand across the lawn. Lily lost a shoe and with a growl, Daniel picked up the shoe and at the same time tossed her over his shoulder like a sack of grain. He took the stairs two at a time as if she weighed no more than a bag of feathers. When he lowered her to the floor in front of his door, she slammed him against the wall, pulling him into kisses that set his head spinning.

Fighting for breath against her mouth, he fumbled his key into the lock. Then they were staggering backwards into his apartment. He dragged off her coat while she tore away his jacket and then his shirt. Fierce, unrelenting, Lily forced him across the room until the couch hit him in the back of the knees and he sat. A delirious laugh bubbled in her throat as she leaped astride his lap, heard his strangled gasp, and felt him hard and ready between her legs. Her fingers fumbled open his belt, his hands slipped under her dress, gliding up her thighs to pull her deeper against him. At the same time he leaned forward to cover her breast with his hot mouth, clamping his teeth down on her erect nipple through the silky fabric.

"Gods!" Lily cried as her blood burst into flames. Time and space melted into roaring need. She lifted her arms, and Daniel dragged the dress over her head. His breath was ragged, his eyes burned black as he looked down at her while he skimmed trembling hands over her petite breasts and tiny waist. He paused when he saw the lacy, thigh-high stockings, shockingly erotic in contrast with her girlish cotton bra and panties. Embarrassed by his perusal, Lily pressed her face to his bare chest and felt his arms fold around her.

"I can't seem to slow down," Daniel panted into her hair, "and I want to."

"No." Lily sank her teeth into his throat and thrust deeper in his lap.

"Jesus . . . " he groaned and took her mouth again in an open, driving kiss with teeth and tongue. He stripped away her bra in one quick move and flipped her under him, skimming his hands over her skin while his lips tasted her neck, her shoulders, her breasts. All Lily could do was hold on and try to breathe.

Her tongue flicked over his skin, tasting the heady flare of his magic. His fingers burned fire down her spine and her power rose to wrap him in steamy swirls of green that lit the dusky room. She wanted penetration and their two magics locked together, wanted her senses swimming with him, wanted the silky glide of his skin damp and yielding under hers.

She *needed* them exploring each other with a kinetic intensity more arousing than just the ache for physical release. So she caressed, fingertips softly stirring, gently igniting. His magic poured like quicksilver through her nerves aquiver under this most intimate of touches.

For Lily only Daniel existed, the male scent of his skin, the aggressive press of his body wanting hers, his magic ardent in the blood racing under her skin. She drank him in and just when she felt too full to hold one more sensation, Daniel's magic opened and drew her inside his consciousness. She tumbled into the sea of his emotions: excitement, love, exhilaration, and sexual hunger. There was no telling where she ended and he began. This time she reveled in the disorienting power of knowing him so thoroughly.

He kissed her thighs where lace stocking met tender skin, curving his hands up the backs of her legs to clasp her bottom. She couldn't stop shaking, and tried to close her knees. But he moved between them to brush his lips over her belly.

He stopped, suddenly. "Fuck." His whisper was harsh.

"Yes, please," she sighed.

He lifted his head to look at her. "Tell me you have condoms, Lil."

She blinked, tried to climb out of the sensual haze enough to focus. "I . . . I don't."

His breath gusting in a ragged sigh, he pressed a last kiss on her stomach and sat up to reach for his pants. Lily clasped her arms around his neck and rose with him.

"We can't, Lily."

"That is not the impression I'm getting." Her tongue slicked over his bottom lip. "You know that I know you haven't had sex since we both got tested last spring."

"I know, but—"

"And you know I've been celibate . . . "

"Yes, but . . . " He was laughing.

"What you don't know is I got an IUD back when—"

Daniel sprang to his feet, holding her slung about his hips. In half a dozen strides, he had her on his bed, fingers stripping away her panties. Off came the sexy stockings, off came his glasses and boxers, and at last they lay naked together, breathless at the sweet agony of skin against skin. Lily wanted his mouth on hers but Daniel had other plans, sweeping hands and lips over her shoulders, her belly, her ribs, his mouth suckling her breasts until she cried out.

Grabbing his hand, she thrust it between her legs and heard an exultant sound in his throat. He took her then, all wet and ready and so tight when he shoved into her, he felt the torturous tug of his orgasm coming too fast. He forced himself to stop, gasping against her neck for control. He felt like a teenager, it had been so damn long . . . for both of them. He plunged deeper in short, gentle thrusts that had her whimpering and curling her legs around his waist. Then he was driving harder. Her head fell back, and she came suddenly in a blaze of fire and violent magic.

The psychic backlash zapped his nerves, hot and dangerously exciting. He felt her go limp. Closing his hands around her wrists, he stretched her arms above her head. She squirmed under the vigorous plunge of his body. He kissed her face, tasted tears, and seeking her mouth, found it open and seeking his. She rocked her hips to meet his pounding rhythm, rejoicing at how perfectly he filled her.

Magic soared around them in crystalline harmonics that danced on their skin, rising and diving in arias of pleasure pulling him ever deeper into her and clenched her ever tighter around him. Locked together, they ascended breathless and fierce to climax together inside cascading light and throbbing, relentless magic.

Chapter Twenty-six

They lay unable to move for a long time, Daniel sprawled between her legs, Lily gasping into his damp curls, their hands locked together. As she slowly surfaced, she wondered if she'd ever be able to exist outside his bed again, even for a moment. Love had stitched her so tightly to him she knew she'd die if she couldn't breathe the same air he breathed.

Daniel turned his face into her shoulder and opened his eyes. His lashes brushed her skin and, shivering at their silky touch, she swept her arms around his back.

"I never knew!" She drew him in for a long kiss. "I've ever only had sex. Never this. Never this all consuming taking and giving. In all my life I've never made love before, Daniel. Have you?"

"Not like this." Chest heaving for air, he rolled onto his back. She rolled with him to splay loose-limbed on top, her face inches above his. She'd never been in his bedroom but could look no further than his contented smile and the warm dark of his half closed eyes brimming with emotions too heavy for words.

*

There were parts of his body Daniel couldn't feel, let alone move. Never had he been so ripped apart, his psyche stripped bare and scattered before being knitted back into one being again, whole and complete. It no longer frightened him, this absolute exposure, such naked vulnerability. Lily's joy rushed him in tidal waves. She pressed her body tighter to his and he discovered something could move after all.

"Wait, Lil—" he gasped when she reached to take him firmly in hand.

Grinning, her eyes never leaving his face, she sat up and drove herself down over him. He arched off the bed at the suddenness of it and she rocked forward to brush her hair, her breasts, her lips against the soft hair on his chest. His body shuddered, his hands curled around her. God, he wanted deeper inside her . . . but she held him pinned between her knees, her teeth biting his chin, her heated eyes warning of further exquisite tortures.

She lifted off him to roll his nipple between her teeth before plunging down on him again. And again. She took him with joyous command, with her dancing fingers, her driving hips and her pounding heart, transporting his body to places he never knew existed. His hands clung to her tiny waist and when her thumbs began a slow, circling massage on his belly, he bit his lip to keep from crying out.

A storm of color swirled up as she drew his magic out. It shot around them like streaks of blue lightning. He felt the pull of her where she clutched him deep and where his heart hammered and his bones melted into hers. Her magic breathed across his thighs, his ribs, and chest until he was gulping for air . . . and his sanity. Every nerve screamed for respite.

She splayed across his chest to sooth him with her tongue. It seemed physically impossible for him to orgasm so soon and yet he felt the sweet wrenching rise as Lily drove forcefully onto him. He heard her cry, watched her spine arc and her head fall back, felt her knees clamp tight around his ribs as together they exploded in release and fell clinging to each other like victims of a cataclysmic storm.

They slept then, at peace, their fierce magic satiated for the moment. Often during the night, one would half wake to reach for the other. They made sleepy, murmuring love in the early hours of dawn and Daniel slept again.

*

Not Lily. She lay in his arms and knew absolute happiness for the first time in her life. It felt like gravity, more solid than any force in the universe.

As daylight strengthened she saw Daniel's bedroom grow in detail. The room was small, barely large enough to hold the double bed, a tall, antiquated dresser and a beat-up trunk from his childhood, probably still full of boyhood treasures. The walls showed a variety of framed artwork. One painting was a soft oil of a stream babbling its way between mossy rocks and ferns before bursting into an effervescent pool. She knew this painting well, though she hadn't known Daniel when she painted it or when he bought it.

There were other works too, a lovely, airy watercolor of mountains, an etching of flying birds and a pen and ink line drawing of a gawky, teenage Nila. Lily rose on her elbows to see, in a row across one wall, a series of inked and colored graphic novel heroes and villains. Obviously originals, some had been rendered in an ornate, art nouveau style, while others were more typical of the modern genre, boldly dynamic with exaggerated musculature and distorted heroic proportions.

Lily slipped out of bed to check the signatures and was impressed to discover all had been drawn by Daniel. His pen technique was beautiful, fluid and natural. He could have been a very good artist, she realized and wondered why he'd settled for staying a simple colorist who filled in the work of others. She recognized the hero Hellketcher from the graphic novel series he'd helped write and illustrate a few years before. Something about the way he captured expression and character struck her as familiar but she couldn't place where she'd seen it before.

Out of bed and away from Daniel's arms, she found the room cold. Goosebumps rose on her skin. She snatched up the nearest piece of clothing, one of Daniel's T-shirts and slipped it on, pressing it to her face to breathe in the scent of him. It hung loose to her knees as she moved along the wall, pulled by one drawing after another. Behind her, Daniel sighed and rolled onto his stomach.

She looked back at him, her eyes softening as they traced the naked curve of his shoulder blade folding into his long spine sliding down to narrow hips. So filled with love was she, she almost turned away from the hallway where more of his work beckoned. But curiosity killed the cat . . .

Daniel's office was private, she understood that. She'd only been invited in half a dozen times and only when it was neatly organized. Lily leaned in through the doorway to see it messily disorganized this morning. He'd obviously been at work on a project. Loose sketches lay in untidy stacks on his work table and crammed in beside his computer on the desk. Lily reached to turn on his work lamp. Some of the papers were covered in random concept doodles. Others showed full workups, detailed portrait studies.

A large corkboard held rough renderings pinned in overlapping chaos. Lily found herself wondering when he found time to draw so much. Between building maintenance on the Lennox, seeing to tenant needs, and his freelance jobs as a colorist, when did he manage to sketch the Formans' golden retriever lying asleep or leaping in play with the twins? Lily was amazed and plucked up a study of a man and woman walking together, eating in a booth at the local diner, talking on a street corner. In another sketch she recognized the McCready sisters and gasped at how he'd managed to capture their primary characteristics-the erect, protective Eleanor and stodgy, rumpled Ruth-in just a few simple strokes.

Scanning the board, she saw the corner of a sheet of paper with a doodle of her fishbowl and, plucking out the pin, took it in her hand. The page was filled with small flash illustrations of herself, glancing over her shoulder at the top of the stairs, digging for her keys with a hang-dog expression, laughing, scowling, concentrating. He'd captured her easily, her quicksilver energy seemed alive in every pencil stroke. Flipping through other drawings stuck to the board, she found all of them, Lonnie Ranchero, the Forman twins, the newlyweds Ruby and Brian, Mr. Newman across the hall, even Gradyn Spencer.

Her eyes moved back to the drawing on his work table and looking closer, she caught her breath. It was a girl wearing a baggy shirt similar to her paint smock. The girl even had her long, large eyes and pointed chin. Breadsticks, celery stalks, and a candy cane stuck up from a knot of curls at the back of her head. Almost against her will Lily leaned closer and saw the drawing was not of her at all, but the leggy, neurotic girl in the comic strip *Lost and Found*. The one Ellen called "Lesser-Lil."

She stumbled back, confused. How could a character from a comic strip be here, in Daniel's office? On his drawing table? Unless . . . oh, Gods and Saints! He couldn't be . . .

Lily glanced wild eyed at the mass of drawings again, saw sketches of the *Lost and Found* computer nerd with his crooked glasses. In a blinding revelation, she recognized Daniel. And there were drawings of the on-again, off-again couple, slightly resembling Brian and Ruby from downstairs. And the loner techno geek looking too much like Gradyn Spencer for comfort. Still clutching the sketch of Lesser-Lil in fingers gone numb, Lily felt her legs go weak and she crumpled to the floor.

Daniel was G.I.L.? No! Impossible! Lily's vision blurred into surreal, disorienting snippets of memories, past conversations, subjects nimbly avoided. She threw the sketch away from her. Closing her eyes against the damning proof, curled against the wall, she began to cry. Daniel, her beloved Daniel, had spied on her. Had spied on them all! Studied them like specimens, dissecting and analyzing . . . and then turned them into public caricatures. What kind of man did this, used his friends in so callous and mercenary a fashion? And how could she have loved him so unreservedly without seeing this side of his character?

"Lily . . . "

Her paralyzed mind didn't register him crouched beside her wearing only jeans. Not until he touched her. She jerked then, flinging her arms out in an instinctive defense as she scrambled to her feet.

Daniel's face was bleak. "Jesus . . . Lily, I'm sorry you found out this way. I've tried to tell you a dozen times—"

"I don't want to hear!" She covered her ears and shrank away, sobbing brokenly.

"Let me explain."

He grabbed her as she tried to dart past him. At the feel of his hands on her she fought him, kicking and clawing until he let her go. Lily ran then, pausing only long enough to snatch her spare key from the hook beside his door before racing out of his apartment. Terrified he was seconds behind her. She fumbled the key into her lock, fell through the open door, and kicked it violently shut behind her. A hysterical scream filled her throat. She choked it down. His scent still filled her senses and she furiously tore his shirt from her body. Diving into her bed, she pulled the blankets over her head and cried until exhausted sleep finally claimed her.

*

Daniel stood in the door of his office for a long time, head bowed, shaking fingers gripping the frame for support. He couldn't move, didn't dare follow Lily. She hated him now. He'd seen her disgust in the one venomous glance she'd thrown him when she jumped to her feet. He'd felt it in her furious kicks when he grabbed her. For so long he had lived in dread of this moment . . . the revelation of his biggest secret. The naked truth had gone so much worse than he'd ever imagined, seeing the betrayed pain in her eyes, the loathing on her face. She believed he'd taken advantage of her, of everyone. But it wasn't like that. If only he could explain.

He couldn't remember a time when he didn't draw comic strips, little illustrations of events happening around him. "Boxing in life," his mother used to tease. And she'd been right. The boxed vignettes had helped him come to terms, through humor, irony, and objective images, with the frightening emotions his Reader's gifts revealed about people. By looking for clues in lines of body language, character, and expression, he could maintain a distance and still *see* the nuances of personality. And eventually he grew to understand human emotions rather than fear them.

He'd started writing *Lost and Found* three years ago, not because he found the people in his life interesting subjects, but because he wanted to *know* them with his heart and not through his Gift. What he discovered astonished him. He found courage where he least expected it, fortitude in the seemingly weak and perseverance in the fanciful. In writing the comic strip, he uncovered the deepest strengths, love, and integrity in his friends, family and neighbors.

Then Lily catapulted into his deliberate, boxed-in world. Never had he met anyone like her, so strange, so mercurial and elusive. He'd found it impossible to understand her and grew obsessed, he admitted it. So he recreated Lily as a character in *Lost and Found*. Getting under the surface of who she was brought him riches beyond his wildest imagination. Each revelation about her became more precious and exciting than the last. And with each new insight, he found it harder and harder *not* to write more of her into the series.

Oh God, would she ever forgive him?

When he could finally breathe again, Daniel showered and dressed. He listened for Lily next door, longing with every cell in his body to go to her. But only silence met him. When he stretched out his senses, he slammed hard and cold against a barrier that tasted so much of her essence it nearly brought him to tears. He didn't know what to do, how to get to her . . . and so he did nothing.

*

Lily felt pain everywhere, as if all her bones had been broken and reset crooked. She woke slowly to the ringing of the phone and lay shivering under a mountain of blankets. The answering machine clicked on. She could hear Ellen's voice reminding her she had an appointment with clients in less than an hour. Lily could not have cared less. All that was once alive in her felt dead. Daniel's betrayal cut too deeply and with a harsh despair made more wicked because of his tender and absolute loving only hours before. Why didn't he tell her? And how could she fall so much in love with a stranger?

Oh, wouldn't Ellen be delighted when she found out? How illustrious she'd feel that she personally knew the creator of the famous strip! In that moment Lily despised her almost as much as she did Daniel. Will I always be the biggest fool on the planet, she wondered? Always the idiot, the perpetual joke who now had to get out of bed and shower away Daniel's precious kisses, his fingerprints on her skin, his scent in her hair? As the hot water beat down on her head, Lily cried like an abandoned orphan.

*

Moving around her apartment like a silent ghost, she dressed quickly before slipping out the door to hasten down the stairs. She could not imagine facing Daniel ever again. Not three blocks from the Lennox, she felt them at her shoulder, Rodney and Look-Alike. They pressed closer this morning, like an icy shroud eager to settle. She turned to face them, saw their colorless eyes brimming with pain and sorrowing love.

"I'm sorry, guys. For you, for me. This is what I do . . . I fuck up. I'd hoped you'd peacefully fade away once Daniel and I finally . . ." She swallowed hard. "But since you're still here, I've somehow missed the magic punch line to this macabre joke." She cracked a mirthless laugh. "And believe it or not, I'm glad of your company today."

"Well that's a start, at least," a voice said from out of the blue. Lily wasn't even surprised by Madame Bagasha standing on the walk in front of the magic shop.

Lily didn't stop. "I'm already late for work."

"I know." Madame fell into step beside her.

"I won't even ask how you know." Lily felt a flare of anger. "There's nothing you or magic can do for me now, Madame."

"You've never spoken a truer word, child."

Her cryptic remark stopped Lily in her tracks. Madame gave her a quizzical look, and Lily, surrendering, followed the tiny witch up the steps and through the purple door. The shop smelled different today, like bittersweet memories lost under dust. Even the crystals looked dull and lifeless. It pained Lily that, in this shop filled with beauty, her eyes could no longer see and her heart no longer feel its wondrous grace.

Only Rodney and Look-Alike seemed to expand like balloons filling with air. They looked as vivid and fresh as the moment they first stepped off the canvas. For a breath of time, the sorrow faded from their faces. Their eyes closed, their nostrils flared as if they suddenly possessed the biology to smell, to taste, to feel. In the next second they deflated back to gray sadness.

Madame watched them, too. "They long to leave and can't find the way, Lily."

"And just when I need them most. How typically male."

Madame laughed and wound a path through the cluttered store back to the kitchen where she poured Lily a cup of tea and forced her to a sit long enough to drink it. "You can feel sorry for yourself, girl, or you can do what needs to be done."

"I know." Lily breathed the reviving scent of ginger rising from her cup. "I must take responsibility. For them. For my feelings. And for the fact that Daniel was afraid to tell me who he truly is. Which says more about me than it does about him, doesn't it? Oh, yes, I'm perfectly aware of why he couldn't tell me." After a long silence, she said, "I imagine writing the comic strip keeps him connected to those around him."

"See? You are more astute than you think, Lily." Madame sat

down across from her.

"What's that saying?" Lily sighed. "It's no good fooling yourself about love. You can't fall into it without dirtying your hands . . . or something like that."

Madame laughed. "Yes. And then there's this one. 'There is a smile of love and there is a smile of deceit, and there is a smile of smiles in which these two smiles meet.'"

"On another day I might appreciate that one," Lily murmured and stood to go. At the door she thanked Madame for the tea. And the obscure advice. With firmer resolve, she set out for Faces in Time.

Chapter Twenty-seven

"What do you mean. Daniel is G.I.L.?" Ellen stared at Lily like she'd sprouted the six arms of Shiva. "That's impossible!"

Lily shrugged but had no energy to argue the point. Or rather the smoking gun, Lily thought humorlessly. She'd managed to get through their meeting with the new clients. Ellen had done most of the talking to the young married couple, wife six months pregnant and radiant, husband proud and radiant. They'd signed the contract for an oil portrait despite more than a few inquiring glances in Lily's mute direction.

Now the two women sat in Ellen's office. Lily watched as compassion slowly replaced astonishment on her boss's face. "So you feel he betrayed your trust?"

"Yes! By not having the balls to tell me. And by spying on me."

"But, Lily, all artists take from real life, especially writers. They create an amalgam of characters from different people they've met, cared for, lived with day to day. I imagine if Daniel had known you when he wrote graphic novels you'd have been featured as the greatest diminutive super-heroine of all time. The poor guy's smitten, for pity's sake!"

Lily dug her fingers into her hot, tired eyes. "Pity's sake? Last night I finally felt honest-to-God love, Ellen. Love with a capital *L*. I lived inside it, felt it fill all the holes in my soul. But how can a man who won't share himself truly love anyone?"

"Are you pissed that you don't know him well enough or that he might know you too well?"

"I'm pissed that he didn't trust me enough to tell me he was G.I.L! He could have, anytime. Last night, even. He saw me looking at the framed originals at the opening."

"The guy was about to get laid. You can't blame him for—"

"I can and I do!"

"He knew you'd react in just this way, Lily. That your anger would rev you up beyond reason and he'd never get a chance to explain. And did you let him explain? No."

"I was humiliated! He's been drawing me, drawing all of us, like he's some . . ."

"Like he's some kind of peeping psycho, Lily?"

"No! I understand why he draws, Ellen. I don't understand why he didn't tell me!"

"You understand that as well, Lil. You're just looking for a reason to be angry. Both you and Daniel have lived as outsiders your entire lives, always keeping people at arm's length. Now you're both tangled in love and vulnerable. Fear of losing someone you finally let yourself care about makes a person desperate. Surely you can forgive—"

"I can't!" Lily wailed and drummed her forehead on Ellen's desk. "I wish I could. My heart feels like stone. And there's no light in this tunnel, no escape, no painting my way into some distracting vision. My broken heart is bleeding all the colors from my brain."

"I'm sorry, Lily. Maybe you just need time to cool."

"I can't stay at my apartment. I can't see him, it'll just kill me!"

"Then stay with me for a few days. And try to paint, Lily. Work always clears that stubborn, jumbled-up head of yours. I'll go by your place and pack you some clothes."

*

Ellen locked Lily's apartment door, a duffel bag slung over her shoulder, and turned to find Daniel standing awkwardly against the hall railing, hands deep in his jeans pockets, his hair rumpled and tragically boyish. She flashed him a smile.

"Did you feed the fish?" he asked.

"She won't stay away that long, Daniel."

"I know." He shrugged, looking at the floor.

"What do you mean, you . . . know?"

"Lily never told you what I am?" He asked, surprised. "I'm a Reader, Ellen. A kind of overqualified psychic."

Ellen snorted. "Really, Daniel—"

"I know Lily feels betrayed. She's hurt almost as much as she is angry. She can't work and is at the studio right now with two scary looking men, one of whom looks like me. You're playing at supportive when you're really just pissed off and impatient with her for not behaving rationally. Or professionally."

Ellen's cheeks paled.

"I have a powerful magic, Ellen. So does she. A lot of sometimes frightening magic. Because of it, she and I have been telepathically linked pretty much twenty-four-seven since Friday night." Then he heard what he'd said, and gave her a sharp glance. "Please don't tell her I can sense her. She thinks the link is broken, and she's already so bloody mad at me."

"So you're still spying on her?"

Daniel was startled. He raked his fingers through his hair and said miserably, "I can't let go of her!"

"Then don't. You are both supreme idiots, overcomplicating a thing that's pretty damn basic. Do you want her?"

"Very much."

"Then all you need to know is if she still wants you." Ellen hefted the bag higher on her shoulder. "You and I both understand Lily well enough to know that she gets off punishing herself. Not consciously, of course. But self-deprecation is her default, her automatic go-to place."

Daniel nodded. "She feels safe there."

"Does she?" Ellen looked impressed. "Then my advice is go yank her free. She is hurt, Daniel, and very confused. You're the one person who can, with a simple apology, make her world right. And I'd do it sooner rather than later because when I left she was getting pretty chummy with those two hotties."

"They don't usually come into a building."

"You know these guys?"

"Yes. I told you her magic was frightening. The men aren't real, actually. And they aren't human. What they are, quite literally, are portraits she painted that came to life through her magic. Like manifestations, apparitions. Ghosts."

Ellen put a hand on the wall to steady herself.

Daniel continued. "Everyday these manifestations get bolder and emanate more emotion. Even Madame Bagasha doesn't know how to de-spell them."

"Madame Bagasha? Oh, Christ," Ellen exploded. "Is this about the love potion?"

Daniel cast her a wry glance. "You and Lily should talk more." Ducking inside his apartment, he grabbed a coat and pulled it on.

Ellen pushed away from the wall. "Yeah, well you're not one to cast stones, big guy. Tell me, what does G.I.L. stand for?"

"Guy In Limbo."

"Seriously?" Ellen smirked. "More like Guy Lovestruck, Lascivious, and Ludicrous! And you deserve it, using Lily in your strip—"

"It's not Lily! It never was. All the characters are fictional, for Christ's sake! It's just that when I draw them they sometimes take on recognizable features. Do you see yourself in the strip?"

Ellen looked startled. "Am I in it?"

"No! That's the point. No one person is in it, not even Lily."

"But I see a lot of Lily in that character, I always have."

"And I'm damned for it. But don't you see other people in that character as well?"

"My sister, sometimes. Even me, occasionally."

"I rest my bloody case!" Daniel reached to take the duffel bag from Ellen's shoulder. After a brief hesitation, she let him have it.

"Are these guy-ghost things with Lily dangerous?" she asked, following him down the stairs.

"I don't know. They've always kept their distance before. Do you want a ride back to the studio?" He slammed through the front doors of the Lennox, practically running.

"No." Ellen tossed him a set of keys and smiled. "It seems my job here is done. Best of luck, Daniel. Oh and FYI? I'm a huge fan of G.I.L. But Lily is not. She thinks he picks on artists and nerds . . . go figure! She is, however, crazy about Daniel Harris."

*

The downstairs restaurant, Taste of Thyme, had a *Closed* sign in the window. As Daniel fit Ellen's key into the side door leading upstairs to Faces in Time, his stomach growled at the rich smell of marinating meat coming from the kitchen. He took the narrow stairs two at a time. The second floor, a great rambling maze of hallways and studios reminded him of his old middle school, with echoing, hardwood floors, the smell of dust and varnish and aging wood. His footsteps echoed in a silence he found unsettling.

He'd felt Lily's magic five blocks away, stirring powerfully enough to raise the hair on his arms. Now he glided quickly past Ellen's dark office, his heart pounding, afraid for her. Before he rounded the corner to Lily's studio, he sensed the presence of Nila and his Gran.

Damn it to hell! Nila had ignored his request to keep the Cohort out of their lives. With Lily's uncertain state of mind and her unpredictable power, anything could happen. And none of it good. He stopped when he saw Nila and Gran standing, on guard and obviously terrified, in the hallway outside Lily's open studio door. Panicked, he shot a querying call through the link to Lily and felt her gushing relief at his presence. Her engorged magic leaped in elated greeting. Gran lifted her arms in defense and Daniel shoved past Nila to step into the studio.

"You have no business here, Daniel," Gran said, her voice razor sharp. You have betrayed my trust by not informing me or the Cohort that Lily possessed magic so volatile."

"Nila fulfilled that obligation very nicely."

"As she should have!" Gran snapped.

"Did she bother telling you that Lily's magic has taken on properties of mine? Lily sensed you both coming long before you arrived. Yet she stayed because she is not afraid. Not of what her power can do, nor of what yours can, Grandmother Gilmore. You must sense by now her magic will never, ever be shackled again. Or worked by a coven or the Cohort. It is a magic uniquely her own."

He pushed the door open further and saw Lily standing on the far side of the room near the large windows. She was flanked, closely, by the two ghoulish apparitions. Her face was pale, her arms dangled weak at her side, and her legs trembled. Daniel guessed she hadn't eaten anything since the day before. A smile flitted across her face at his thoughts. Then her mouth tightened, and he saw the determined focus in her eyes.

Daniel suddenly realized what Lily was attempting to do. "Have you asked her why she's conjuring so much power, Gran? Nila?"

"If she's trying to dispel these creepy things, she'll need our help," Nila blurted out.

Daniel laughed. "Will she? Why, because you helped create them through the love potion, Nila?"

"Yes."

"No." Lily spoke in a restrained, quiet voice. "The manifestations are and always were completely mine. There is no spell you or Madame or Gran will ever find that can vanish them. Only I have the words and the power to make them disappear. I've always had the power. I only just realized it today."

"Madame Bagasha has been advising you?" Gran asked.

"Yes, but not in the way you're thinking." Lily turned a beaming grin on Daniel. "She advised me in the ways of the heart. And the simple truth of mine."

"So you've forgiven me?" he asked.

"Like I had a choice," she answered.

He felt the warm brush of her phantom kiss on his lips and stepped forward to go to her but she held up a hand. He stopped.

She turned her attention back to the two women. "And now, Nila, Mrs. Gilmore, if you think it your responsibility to stay, then please stand back. Let me do what I do best."

Through the link, Daniel felt her absolute, passionate surrender to the love they shared. A love that would weather worse storms than the exposure of one embarrassing, surprising, somewhat disturbing but altogether minor, secret. Then he felt nothing as she severed the link.

The magic in the room suddenly spiked with power. Overhead, the lights brightened momentarily and then went out. A soft luminescence grew inside the room, drifting like a green mist to eddy across the floor. Gran stepped back before it could touch her. Lily laughed and pushed away from the windows to stand, feet slightly spread, head high. Ribbons of color, violent reds, rich purples, and radiant yellows snaked around her arms raised as if in supplication. Her hair glittered gold on her shoulders and her skin burned the pale blue of death. But her eyes blazed the rich blue of strength and resolution as the first apparition stepped close to her.

An irrational rush of jealousy nearly launched Daniel across the room. Lily's unspoken command echoed in his head . . . *Wait!* His shoulders twitched but he stopped, poised and ready. He didn't trust these . . . these *things*. And the triumphant look the Rodney apparition shot him out of eyes suddenly alive and glowing confirmed he had reason to be wary. The ghostly flesh no longer looked gray but gleamed with color, warm yellows, soft oranges, and reds.

And the thing that looked like him towered over Lily as fresh and dramatic and naked as the night it had stepped off the canvas. The hand that reached out to touch her face was textured with brush strokes.

Daniel heard Lily's quick intake of breath and gave an involuntary jerk. She seemed under an enchantment, oblivious to all but the man-figure stepping close to press its body against her.

*

Lily felt the apparition's weight as solid and real. The ghostly features were so like Daniel's she started crying. It drew a finger down her cheek to lay against her lips. She shuddered at the icy touch but stood firm.

"Yes," she said in a voice almost rejoicing, rising on tiptoe until their lips met. "I am yours as you are mine," she breathed against its mouth. "And I love you as a lonely piece of my heart. Come home, come back to me."

The spectral being kissed her then, a long press of inhuman lips against hers. Everything in Daniel screamed to tear the thing off her but somehow he stayed still. Lily's arms gathered the naked man close and held it. Colors began to spin away from their two bodies in ragged strings that whirled and danced. Daniel felt Lily's magic spike, searing his newly healed senses. Gran fell to her knees, and Nila dropped to wrap a protective arm around her. Neither woman took their eyes off the tableau before them.

Above the pounding of her heart, Lily heard the keening cry of the apparition. She clasped her arms tighter around it until, with an explosive sigh, it melted into her. One moment the apparition stood solid against her, the next it was gone. An ache swelled in her chest. She felt her ribs expand to the point of cracking as she absorbed all of the manifestation's bitter loneliness and longing. She recognized its emotions as the echo of her own on that terrible night she'd painted the nude and tears fell thicker down her cheeks.

"Lily!" She heard Daniel's cry as she swayed unsteadily for a moment.

"Not yet," she told him. After drawing a couple deep breaths, she reached out to Rodney. He stepped close, and she folded him close to her breast, cupping the head in her hand and pressing the face to her shoulder as if he were a frightened child.

"I am yours as you are mine." Her voice rang out a second time. "I love you as a lonely piece of my heart. Come home, come back to me." Once more color shredded away from the figure like rags; jade greens, yellow ochres, Prussian blues. Rodney bent to kiss her, then sank as quietly as midnight snow into her.

Lily lifted a trembling hand to wipe her face. She looked at Daniel. "I'm so sorry . . . " Her gasp painful, she collapsed unconscious to the floor.

*

Daniel was at her side in seconds, heart in his throat. He lifted her, ice cold and loose limbed, onto his lap. Pressing a finger to her throat, he felt her pulse, faint but steady. He buried his face in her hair and pulled her closer to the warmth of his body. He could feel her magic, volatile and stormy, whipping about the room. Cautiously, he began to siphon the hot magic through him and into her. Little by little Lily's pale skin began to warm.

He'd forgotten Gran and Nila and started in surprise at the sound of Nila helping the older woman to her feet. Quick anger tightened his mouth, but eased when he saw the awe and respect on their strained faces.

"I've never seen such courage in the face of so much Rogue magic," Gran said, clinging to Nila's arm. Daniel knew that was as much of an apology as Lily would ever get.

Nila bowed her head to him. "I'll never forgive myself for doubting her. Or you."

Daniel's mouth twisted. "Yes you will, you always do. In a few hours, you both will have talked yourself into disbelieving most of what you just saw. As you should."

Nila felt the brush of a forgetting spell, highly illegal, in her mind and knew he spoke the truth.

Gran opened her mouth to chastise him, then snapped it closed. With a faint gleam of humor in her eyes, she said, "Perhaps Lily and I can learn to be friends."

"I doubt it." Daniel barked a laugh. "But the effort will make for interesting fireworks."

"She's okay, isn't she?" Nila nodded at Lily's head tucked under Daniel's chin. "Do you need Madame?"

Daniel shot her a heated look too obvious to misinterpret.

She blushed. "Oh! Right, then. I'll see Gran home." Nila ushered the other woman from the studio and closed the door behind them without a backward glance.

Daniel cradled Lily against him and waited. His legs cramped, he ignored the pain. Outside, the sky faded to a rose sunset and then into night. Traffic sounds picked up as the day ended and, after awhile, quieted. The ancient radiator ticked on, ticked off and still he held her, pressing murmuring kisses on her temple, her cold cheeks, her closed eyelids. Reading her, he found her consciousness far away as if she were traveling through deep sleep. He left her there, afraid to tug her back too soon.

God knows she looked like death. Exhaustion, fear, pain, the day's sorrows, all showed in the hollows of her cheeks and purple smudges under her eyes.

He could hardly fathom the kind of power she'd worked in order to unbind, release, and absorb the two apparitions. Hints of residual magic still stirred the air, occasionally flicking his skin. What audacity she had, he marveled. What heart and force of will. She'd accepted her own weaknesses, faced them, embraced them and loved them. He bent to kiss her lips and felt them stir beneath his.

"Lily," he whispered. "I'm sorry, too. I never meant to keep you out."

Her eyelids fluttered but didn't open. Her mouth barely moved. "Old habits . . ."

"Yes." His voice caught.

*

Lily was so tired. Every bone in her body felt like a brittle icicle. At the same time, her heart brimmed full to the point of bursting. The other shoe had dropped and it hadn't destroyed her. It had hurt, yes. But happiness came with a price, always. Today, at last realizing her own guilt kept the two manifestations manacled to her, she'd found the strength to take responsibility for them. Despite her fear of failure, of pain, of loss, and in spite of her impetuous, flaky temperament. She, and her powers, had swung full circle. Her feral magic no longer frightened her. She would drive it, not let it drive her. Life would still try to buck her off, but she'd just have to take a firmer grip on the reins . . . with Daniel's help, of course.

Forcing her eyes open she found his face close above her, a little worse for wear but achingly dear and home to her wild heart. She wondered, with a dreamy sense of distortion, why she'd been so angry at him. So he created a syndicated comic strip and used life and real people as a template. How could she blame him when she did the same thing, if not quite so literally?

She lifted arms still weak and touched his face, looked deep in his warm, brown eyes. "Thank you for waiting for me to grow up, Daniel."

He kissed her with a grin. "Think we can survive each other?"

Lily tightened her arms around his neck. "You know what The Bard says: 'To fear the worst oft cures the worst.'"

He lifted her from the cold floor and carried her to the portrait set, laying her on the thick velveteen throws. She pulled him down with her, pressing her body full against him, kissing his face, his chin, his mouth.

"Lily, don't you think—"

"No." She peeled the jacket from his shoulders with a determined force. A wanton smile set his blood boiling as she lifted her arms for him to strip off her sweater. Her skin heated under his hands and her pulse leaped eagerly against his mouth. Wanting them skin to skin, Lily fumbled with his shirt buttons until, beyond patience, he dragged it over his head. His fingers made short work of her bra and then her breasts were bare and against his chest. She sighed, stretched against the artfully arranged, and soon to be savagely disarranged, velveteen folds.

Daniel's mouth hot on hers left her gasping and gripping his hair. She tore frantically at the buttons of his jeans, but he wanted her naked first. He dragged off her skirt, her panties. His knees pried her legs wide, and she pressed close as his hands played over her skin. Her magic roared in a frenzied draft around them. The lights blinked on then quickly off.

Brain dissolving beneath the feverish drive of his body, Lily knew she must use the residual magic now before rational thought vanished. But Daniel was already working it. Murmuring words of love against her belly, he warped her power into soft currents of flowing color. Pulling back, he looked at her and caught his breath. Her skin pulsed with color just as the crystals had in her geode, her every curve, every shadow painted in flickering light. He bent to taste a golden breast. The night she'd painted *Paradigm*, her apartment had filled with unruly passion. He'd walked into it open and rejoicing. Now she lay beneath him, eyes alive with the same radiant invitation. Her fingers traced his lips and he realized she was Reading him.

Lily shrugged, shameless. "I am yours as you are mine, Daniel."

Grinning, he bit her neck. She laughed and stuck her hand down his pants.

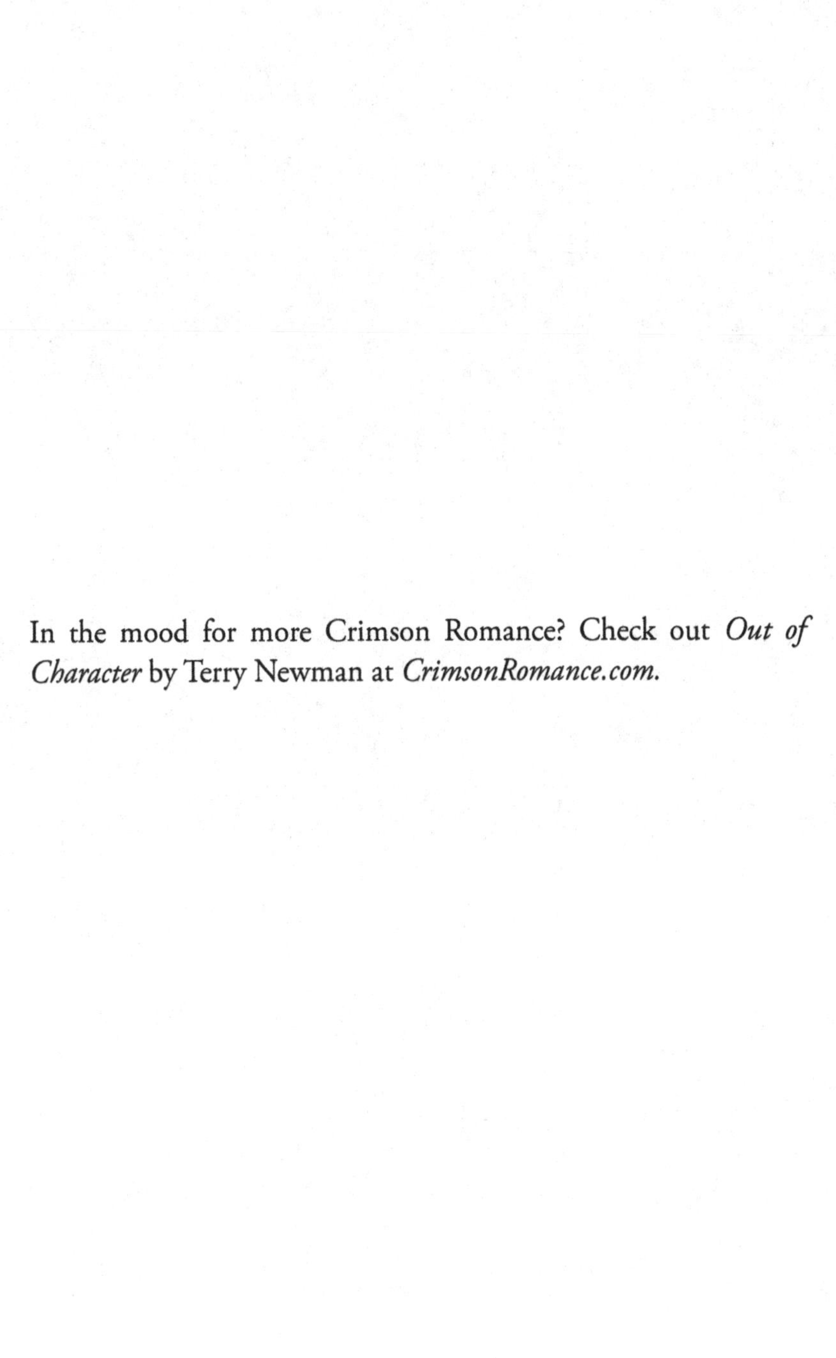

In the mood for more Crimson Romance? Check out *Out of Character* by Terry Newman at *CrimsonRomance.com*.

www.ingramcontent.com/pod-product-compliance
Lightning Source LLC
Chambersburg PA
CBHW010634100726
47900CB00011B/2828